NO INNOCENCE IN EDEN

The air smelled of a sweet perfume. The throng of women chanted a foreboding message into the night.

His body tensed as he watched her slit his upper arm and catch his warm blood in her silver cup. Her caressing hands were all over him as the chanting grew louder. And he could not resist the mesmerizing power she held over his senses even in the midst of the quivering terror he felt.

He had come to Eden, Vermont, to solve a mystery, but wound up caught in the grasp of a horrible curse. Her body pressed against his as he closed his eyes to try to escape the insanity that had become all too real.

CULT

Edward J. Frail

AN ONYX BOOK

ONYX
Published by the Penguin Group
Penguin Books USA Inc., 375 Hudson Street, New York, New York 10014,
U.S.A. Penguin Books Ltd, 27 Wrights Lane, London W8 5TZ, England
Penguin Books Australia Ltd, Ringwood, Victoria, Australia
Penguin Books Canada Ltd, 2801 John Street, Markham,
Ontario, Canada L3R 1B4
Penguin Books (N.Z.) Ltd, 182–190 Wairau Road, Auckland 10, New Zealand

Penguin Books Ltd, Registered Offices:
Harmondsworth, Middlesex, England

First published by Onyx, an imprint of Penguin Books USA Inc.

First Printing, April, 1990
10 9 8 7 6 5 4 3 2 1

REGISTERED TRADEMARK—MARCA REGISTRADA

Printed in the United States of America

PUBLISHER'S NOTE
This is a work of fiction. Names, characters, places, and incidents either are
the product of the author's imagination or are used fictitiously, and any
resemblance to actual persons, living or dead, events, or locales is entirely
coincidental.

BOOKS ARE AVAILABLE AT QUANTITY DISCOUNTS WHEN USED TO PROMOTE PRODUCTS
OR SERVICES. FOR INFORMATION PLEASE WRITE TO PREMIUM MARKETING DIVISION,
PENGUIN BOOKS USA INC., 375 HUDSON STREET, NEW YORK, NEW YORK 10014.

To Vicki and Gary Aldrich. Thanks for opening the door to success.

Prologue

April, 1984

A KALEIDOSCOPE of changing colors danced before
Lieutenant Colonel Sam Canfield's eyes. His body
ached from the plane crash, but he managed to
struggle to his knees. There was a thin layer of snow
on the ground, not unusual for April at the foot of
the Rockies. The jagged cut across his brow throbbed.
The last thing he remembered was watching six Air
Force Academy cadets drop from his plane and drift
through the air like puffs of clouds on a summer
day.

Suddenly, the colors before his eyes faded and a
picture of a young boy and his dog appeared. The
vision had haunted him since November 12, 1965. It
had happened on Highway 13 north of Bau Bang,
South Vietnam. Troop A, 1st Squadron, 4th Cavalry
had called for air support. Sam Canfield had responded and raked the wooded area north of the
fire base with 20-mm cannon fire from his plane. He
had swooped over Highway 13 and had strafed a
column of Vietnamese peasants fleeing Bau Bang.
Everyone had run for cover, except a young boy
clutching his dog. The boy was no more than eight
or nine years old. He looked up at Sam Canfield and
their eyes met for a brief second before Canfield
released his tight grip on the trigger. It was too late.

The boy and dog were hit from a burst of 20-mm cannon fire.

"Colonel, sir." A tall lanky man in tattered military fatigues knelt over Sam Canfield. It was Lieutenant Phil Jenkins, Sam Canfield's copilot. Blood stained a white bandage tied around his arm. He pushed a long queue of dark hair off his forehead and pulled back his shoulders before he spoke again.

"Colonel, sir." His tone was louder. Phil Jenkins held Sam Canfield in high esteem. The colonel's heroics as a pilot in Vietnam were legendary in the academy. Jenkins had been in the fifth grade when the Vietnam War had ended. He was jealous of the opportunity Sam Canfield had been given to serve his country.

Colonel Canfield ran his hand up Jenkins' arm and touched his face. "Jenkins?"

"Yes, sir." The young lieutenant knelt at attention in the snow.

"You O.K.?"

"Yes, sir."

"Is it day or night?"

Jenkins studied the large gash across Sam Canfield's forehead. "It's Wednesday night, sir. You've been unconscious for a good part of a day."

A rescue was improbable. Their mission had been a secret: the concocted plan of Superintendent Grimes to discipline six insubordinate second-class cadets by ordering them to jump into the wilds of Wyoming on a survival exercise. Secrecy was imperative because no commanding officer was to accompany the cadets; on the ground they would be left to fend for themselves. Grimes thought the exercise would toughen them up. Sam Canfield had volunteered for the assignment to fly the cadets to the drop zone.

Lieutenant Jenkins had retrieved a flashlight, medical kit, and a compass from the plane's debris. Although his wounded arm hurt, Sam Canfield's well-being was all he cared about. Men like Colonel Canfield had fought and had died for America. Now, it was Jenkins' turn to repay the debt; he would bring home a wounded American hero.

The path across the clearing led to a road that cut through a thick forest of tall trees guarded on each side by rugged mountains dressed in a blanket of wet snow. Dusk had arrived, a fact lost in Sam Canfield's world. He didn't see the colorful dots dancing recklessly before his eyes anymore. He saw what his other senses told him—the hard dirt floor of the forest cushioned by a thin layer of last year's leaves, the rustling of naked tree limbs from a stiff evening breeze. Sam Canfield's cheeks told him it was going to be a cold night.

The smell was faint at first, but pungent enough to attract the colonel's attention. He pulled away from Jenkins and turned his head like an antenna to find the source of the stench.

"What is it, sir?"

"Don't you smell it?"

Jenkins shrugged his shoulders. "Smell what, sir?"

"An odor like kerosene or old tires burning. It's coming from over there."

Sam Canfield's finger pointed in the direction of a black forest. Dusk had given way to evening. The thought that Sam Canfield was suffering from shock entered Jenkins' mind at the same time he smelled the putrid odor.

"Do you see any car tracks, Jenkins?"

The young lieutenant swept his flashlight up and down the well-traveled road with rounded rocks pushing up through the packed dirt.

"I don't see any tracks, but the road we're on is well used. It could be a logging road."

"Did you see a trail cutting into the woods?"

"Yes. Back a way."

"Let's take it."

"Yes, sir."

"Use your flashlight, sparingly."

"Yes, sir."

Sam Canfield doubted his own caution. Perhaps his blindness triggered suspicions about a world unseen. He told Phil Jenkins it was possible that campers were waiting at the end of the narrow trail with a truck to take him to a hospital where doctors would diagnose his blindness as temporary. As they hiked through the woods, Sam Canfield's thoughts flashed back to Vietnam. The smell reminded him of napalm dropped over areas suspected of hiding Vietcong infiltrators. Again, his memory flashed the picture of the boy clutching his dog.

Phil Jenkins didn't share Sam Canfield's hope of a rescue. Instead, an unexplainable fear gripped the young lieutenant as he guided Sam Canfield deeper into the Wyoming woods. He was sure the pungent odor was an ominous sign of an unseen danger lying ahead in ambush. But he kept his fears locked up within his pounding heart and said nothing to his superior officer.

Branches swiped the men's faces as the trail narrowed and the starless sky disappeared behind a roof of thick treetops. Suddenly, the sound of a drum invaded the silence of the forest. Jenkins tightened his grip on Canfield's hand. His heart pounded louder and beads of perspiration surfaced on his brow. The drum sounded again and Jenkins pulled Canfield to his knees.

"Can you see anything?" Canfield asked.

"It's weird sir, but there's a light coming out of an old quarry about a hundred yards ahead." Jenkins' mouth turned cottony dry.

Sam Canfield heard chanting like monks praying in an abbey. The odor he smelled was coming from burning torches lighting up the forest. He stood up and tugged the young lieutenant forward.

Phil Jenkins tightened his sweaty grip on Canfield's hand as he watched billows of black smoke rise from the lighted quarry. A smoky light cut through the naked trees. As he searched the thick brush for an unseen enemy, he drew his side arm from its leather holster. His head swiveled like a periscope, his eyes alert for any movement, his gun cocked and ready. Suddenly he stopped dead in his tracks.

"Sir," he whispered. His voice quivered; he struggled to keep his composure. "The cadets' clothes and parachutes are stacked in a pile on the rim of the quarry just ahead."

The chanting stopped and silence fell over the woods. Jenkins and Canfield arrived at the edge of the quarry just as a figure in a rainbow cloak climbed a rock pulpit. The six cadets lay naked and tied parallel to one another on a stone altar. They were gagged. Four guards wearing black robes with floppy hoods surrounded the cadets. One of them held a sword with two lions' heads carved into an ivory handle. The inside rim of the pit was lined with three other guards holding lighted torches.

Slowly the robed figure raised his head and stared up into the empty night. Phil Jenkins froze at the sight; he struggled to control his fear. He told himself that he was a trained officer in the United States Air Force and that his admiration for Sam Canfield demanded a soldier's bravery.

The man in the rainbow cloak raised his hand. "The sign foretold by Baal has been fulfilled. The sound of wings has been heard over the land and our enemy has descended like locusts upon our land divided by rivers. Listen, everyone who lives on earth: a time is coming when Baal will rise from the land of Mot, and the Soldiers of the Sword, a tall and smooth-skinned people, will be feared all over the world. The revenge of Lamech must soon begin. May the headless bodies of our enemies be left to the birds and wild animals as told by the prophet Isaiah."

Two of the guards walked over to the far corner of the quarry and removed a black cloth that had been placed over a large wicker cage. Suddenly the deafening sounds of five screeching hawks echoed loudly off the quarry's stone walls. One of the guards reached for a metal pole on the ground and carefully threaded it through a ring at the top of the cage until his partner could safely grab it on the other side. They then lifted the cage and proceeded back across the quarry toward the six waiting cadets. The hawks fluttered angrily about inside. A third guard, holding an ivory-handled sword high in the air, awaited their arrival at the stone altar.

The six cadets struggled in vain to free themselves from the terrible nightmare unfolding around them. The cadet nearest the robed figure arched his back as the guards slowly lowered the wicker cage toward him. The hawks took dead aim at their evening meal through wide openings at the bottom of the cage. Tears streamed down the young man's face. The other cadets torqued their bodies to catch a glimpse of their comrade's fate. Finally the cage came to rest upon the cadet's muscular chest. He closed his eyes and clenched his fists in fear. In seconds, blood and sinew flew everywhere as the ravenous hawks tore away at the cadet with their razor-sharp beaks and talons.

The guard with the ivory-handled sword bowed to the robed figure, then raised the sword and severed the head of the young cadet. The others struggled hysterically, emitting muffled screams against their gags.

"What's happening?" Canfield whispered.

Jenkins hurried Canfield away from the open quarry

and began hiding him under some leaves beside a hollow log. "I've got to rescue our men, sir. It's some crazy ritual," the young lieutenant sputtered. "They killed one, sir."

Sam Canfield grabbed the lieutenant by the arm and tried to calm him.

"Don't go down there, son. Go back to the logging road and find some help. I'll be all right here."

Phil Jenkins ignored the advice of his superior. His thoughts focused on his captured comrades in the quarry. He saw himself among them and felt the horror of waiting his turn to die. He heard the wishes of his comrades for a quick death by the executioner's swift sword.

The young lieutenant stood up and scattered some branches over Sam Canfield's concealed body. He felt a wave of confidence surface through his fears. He wasn't going to allow his comrades to die; somehow he was going to free them. He felt he had no choice; it was his duty. Tears crested over his eyelids. Out of respect he saluted Lieutenant Colonel Sam Canfield, then turned and edged his way back to the quarry.

1

Fort Ann, New York

January, 1986

THERE WERE few signs of life visible along Route 149 from Lake George to Fort Ann on a cold Sunday morning. The homes seen through the naked trees were hidden behind walls of snow and cut firewood. Icicles hung like steel bars in front of frosted windows wrapped in clear plastic. Barns, bleached from sun and rain, shielded barnyard animals from winter's biting wind. The animals stood frozen in place, spewing how steam over their thick, heavy coats. At Sue's Breakfast Nook, the road climbed sharply. Atop, the landscape broadened for miles, and silos, like silver rockets, dotted the land on each side of the road. In the distance, camelback mountains beckoned the weekend skiers, who regularly traveled the roller-coaster road to Fort Ann, then north to Vermont, where snow-covered slopes lay in abundance.

Matt Senacal's spirits were as lifeless as the road he traveled when he entered Fort Ann. Lieutenant Robert Schiff's early-morning phone call had altered his dreamy plan of a late breakfast of yesterday's bagels.

"Get your ass up to Fort Ann. There's been an execution."

A traffic light dangled over Fort Ann's only intersection. Earlier, Lieutenant Schiff had directed Senacal to take a left at the traffic light, then another left onto Charles Street past Saint Christopher's Church.

Senacal waited for the light to turn green. Nothing seemed unusual in the village. Red brick storefronts lined the sidewalks in sleepy disrepair. He reached for a beef-jerky stick on the dashboard of his car. It had been seventeen days since Kimberly, his sixteen-year-old daughter, had persuaded him to quit smoking. She was one of only a few people in the world he cared about. If she wanted him alive at sixty, he figured it was worth the effort. He saw a convenience store on the corner to his right. He pulled off the road, parked next to a white van, and entered the store. Lieutenant Schiff could wait a few minutes longer for his senior investigator to arrive on the murder scene.

"Tea, please, Gracie. To go." Senacal smiled and waited for the cashier's attention. She was watching the activity in the parking lot. Senacal looked down and noticed some white specks on the right sleeve of his gray nylon jacket. He recalled brushing up against the white van in the parking lot. He tried to remove them, but succeeded only in grinding the chalky substance deeper into the sleeve. He called his bad luck shit and looked up. The cashier pointed to pots of steaming coffee and water that sat on a wobbly card table near the frozen-food section. She returned her attention to a young woman outside.

"Did you ever see such beautiful jewelry? She's dressed like a hippie, but what a beautiful necklace." As the cashier spoke, the woman entered the white van. Senacal looked up from his tea and caught a glimpse of the woman's legs as she entered the van. She wore tan calf-length boots with red leather tassels at the top. The van, caked with winter dirt, left the parking lot and headed north on Route 4.

"How much do I owe you?" Senacal rummaged through his pockets for some loose change.

"Your sneakers make a hell of a noise over my clean floor. Must drive your wife nuts."

Matt Senacal's handsome face was camouflaged behind a sloppy appearance that made mothers nervous and children cautious. Not many strangers had the courage to verbally admonish Matt Senacal. Those who did he liked. As he stirred his tea, he looked down at his blue sneakers and said, "Fortunately, she's planning a divorce."

"I'm sorry," Gracie said.

"Don't be. I'm going to have a helluva party when it's final. You're invited, so long as you don't nag me." He playfully waved a finger at her.

She looked at his uncovered head and smiled. "You must get cold on days like this."

Matt Senacal was bald, except for a few strands of thin hair that stood up on the top of his head like cornstalks after harvest and a ridge of black curly hair that circled his head above his ears. He smiled, patted his precious head, and stared at the name tag on her sweater.

"Thanks, Gracie. I love you too."

The rancid odor of burning flesh filled Senacal's lungs as he passed Saint Christopher's Church. It came upon him with the suddenness of a summer storm. His tea lost its tangy appeal. He noticed some parishoners, covering their faces with handkerchiefs, leaving mass. At first, he thought the odor had come from the burning of garbage, an unsanitary but common practice in rural places like Fort Ann. But it hadn't. His heart beat a little faster. The odor triggered memories of Vietnam, a buried chapter of his life that rarely surfaced. This morning was one of those exceptions.

As directed, he entered Charles Street. It was a small street, only a few hundred feet long before it met perpendicularly with Catherine Street. Police blockades were stuck into snowbanks in front of a large house on the left side of the street. It was an old Victorian home, mustard in color, with a rainbow slate roof. A yellow plastic tape, randomly looped around trees, circled the house like a corral. Fort Ann's fire house, a small white brick building, stood across the street from the mustard house. The firehouse was framed in Christmas lights and a large wreath hung on each of the three bay doors. Senacal parked behind a police car where an officer lay slumped over the steering wheel. The officer's partner was busy stringing up yellow tape to block traffic entering Charles Street.

Senacal quickly scanned the roof of the mustard house for the source of the human stench. He observed three chimneys. Two red brick chimneys jutted up through the slate roof and a gray cinder block one ran up the left outside of the house in the rear. No smoke emerged from the red chimneys. A steady flow of white smoke drifted toward Saint Christopher's Church from the gray chimney.

Lieutenant Schiff, flanked by two members of the state police, marched directly toward Senacal's car. He scratched his beard and stared at Senacal in silence. Schiff had the weekend off, but had been immediately notified of the Fort Ann murder. That was standard procedure according to the state-police manual. Being clean shaven on duty was standard police procedure, too. Lieutenant Schiff lived by the book. He claimed its rules were bricks on the yellow road to a troop commander major position. Since the lieutenant had forgotten to shave before reporting on duty, Senacal knew the Fort Ann murder was somehow different.

Schiff's eyes bulged as he spoke. "There's a fucking weirdo out there, Senacal. I've never seen anything like it in seventeen years."

Senacal raised his hand. "Don't say any more. Let me conduct my own investigation."

Matt Senacal had joined the New York State Police thirteen years ago after four inglorious months of study at Lehman College in the Bronx. Senacal claimed his high arrest record over the years as a senior investigator was due in part to what he had learned at Lehman in Philosophy 101. He flunked the course, but had loved listening to Professor Leavitt. A saying, covered with glass and framed in black wood, hung over the professor's green chalkboard. The words later became Senacal's investigative creed. "Inductive reasoning, from the particular to the universal, is often free of ignorant premises. Use it, it's fodder for the brain."

He opened the trunk of his car and retrieved a small tape recorder from a fishing tackle box. He wrote, "Fort Ann" on a tape and shoved it into the recorder. He walked down the street to where the yellow tape sealed it off. He observed the street in silence, then spoke into his recorder.

"Three cars and one truck are pointed toward the victim's house. A station wagon with rusted-out fenders is the only vehicle facing away from the victim's house. The fourth house on the left has three cannons on the front lawn. The third house on the right with the small red porch has a large snowblower in the driveway."

He motioned over the officer guarding the intersection of Charles and Catherine streets. "Were you two the first members to arrive?" Senacal pointed to the officer still slumped over the steering wheel.

"Yes, sir."

"What's wrong with your partner? Why isn't he assisting you?"

"He got sick, sir. He puked after he saw the body all . . ."

Senacal raised his hand for the officer to stop.

"Talk to the owner of that snowblower over there." Senacal pointed to the small house with the red porch. "Just ask him how long it's been sitting there. That's all I want to know. Next, feel the hoods of the three cars and the truck parked on the street. If they're warm or the frost is off the windshield, then bring the owner to me. Don't question them. Let me do that. Last, tell the owner of the rusted station wagon that I definitely want to talk to him."

Senacal turned off his recorder and asked. "Who called in the murder?"

The officer pointed up Charles Street to a man with a dog holding on to a metal pole supporting a blue New York State historical marker that read, "Old Well-used in Fort site. Built before Revolutionary War by Queen Anne of England."

"Did you question him?" Senacal studied the old man with the dog.

"No, sir. Lieutenant Schiff instructed us to wait for you. He said you were the best in G Troop."

Senacal patted the officer on the back. "He's full of shit. I'm the best in the whole goddamn state of New York."

A black miniature poodle barked and clawed up clumps of ice and frozen dirt as Matt Senacal approached. The dog's owner remained still. He was tall, thin, and elderly. He wore red-and-black-plaid pants filled with crusted hills of last week's menu. The pants hung from his waist like a flag on a windless day. Blue moonboots exaggerated his height by three inches. A kelly-green sweater encircled his body from his hips to his chin. It fitted him like a life jacket, and was just as thick. Stitched into the sweater, across the back, was a picture of a white-and-black cow. A Boston Red Sox baseball cap sat on his head. Senacal figured the old man hadn't been home since Halloween.

"Excuse me. I'm Inspector Senacal of the state police. I'd like to ask you some questions about the murder. I'd also like to record your answers if you don't mind."

The old man just stared at the mustard house across the street. His dog continued to bark. Senacal snapped his fingers in front of the man's eyes. "Sir, I'd like to ask you some questions. What's your name?"

The old man's head jerked like he had awoke suddenly from a deep sleep. "The name's Graham Twitchell." His voice was low and craggy. "This here is Patton." He pulled slightly on the leash and the dog stopped barking. "Use to call her Jenny when she was a pup. She's a good fighter, so we changed it to Patton. Hell of a general was George."

"May I tape our conversation?"

"Hell, yes! I watch all the gangbuster shows on television. My wife there . . ." He pointed to a woman behind the yellow tape wearing a green sweater with the head of a black-and-white cow over her heart. "She watches all them goddamn 'who screwed who shows' on the black-and-white upstairs. Once she asked to watch one of her shows on the colored set in the living room, but I said no. I'm not going to take her shit when it comes to television." Patton barked his approval.

"Sir, the machine is recording. Is that O.K. with you?"

The old man shrugged his shoulders. "I already told you it was all right."

"O.K. Tell me how you discovered the murder."

Twitchell cleared his throat and pointed toward St. Christopher's steeple. "Me, Patton, and Nel live by the high school, about a mile past the church. If it ain't too cold, like this morning, we . . ." He looked at Patton. "Well, we take a walk down here, then

7

loop home like horses around a racetrack, but slower."
The old man paused and smiled.

Senacal motioned for Twitchell to continue his story.

"This morning, we got about halfway down Catherine Street and it stunk. Worse than now. Horrible smell like burning fingernails in an ashtray." Twitchell looked down at Patton.

"She likes to shit here in the morning around the Old Fort." Senacal moved his feet to check his tracks.
"Then she plays with Laddy, that's Curt Newell's dog." Twitchell pointed to the mustard house. "Curt usually leaves Laddy out early, or if Curt doesn't, then Evelyn does or young Ken. This morning was different. Patton never left my side. The smell was awful. We got in front of the house and Patton finally ran up the driveway crying like a baby. I walked after her and saw Laddy's head split open with an ax."

"What time was it when you arrived here in front of Newell's home?"

"Between seven and five-past."

"Why so sure? Did you check your watch?"

"Nope. Don't need one since I retired from Edwards and Reed down in Schuylerville some six years ago. They're a paper mill, you know." A twinkle sparked in Graham Twitchell's eye. "You'll understand when you retire, son. I leave the house at six-thirty every morning for my walk and I'm back home in an hour or so. The Old Fort is the halfway point. That's why I trained Patton to shit here in the morning, so I can rest."

Senacal laughed. The old man was a relic of rural America. Senacal had never known either of his grandfathers. The coal mines of Wilkes-Barre and the sweatshops of Manhattan had laid an early claim to their lives. He wondered if either of them had been like Graham Twitchell.

The old man touched Senacal's shoulder. "I may

be an old fool, but I'm not a dumb one. I wear this damn cow coat because Nel over there cries like hell if I don't. She made it for me this Christmas. Last Christmas, she made me a brown one with a big deer with antlers. The damn antlers were bigger than the buck. She's making a cow sweater for Patton too. Says we'll look nice, all three of us, when we go out. Are you married?"

"Sometimes."

"Sometimes is bad enough." Twitchell turned and stared at the mustard house for a few seconds, then looked at Senacal. "I went into Normandy three days after the invasion. I saw a lot of twisted, mutilated, and burned bodies stacked like cords of wood. That's O.K.; it was a war. A lot of bad things happen in war. You get the one who done this." He pointed to the mustard house. "You get him real soon, 'cause his type will do it again. You been inside yet?"

"No, I haven't."

"You'll see. I'll keep my ears open. The eyes aren't too good, but the ears are fine. Can Patton and me go?"

"Yes. Give your address and phone number to the police officer."

Twitchell walked toward his waiting wife. Senacal yelled after him.

"Where did you make the phone call from?"

"Over at Henry Hemple's. Woke him up, though. He's only a rookie retiree. Give him a few more months with his wife all day, and he'll be out here with me in the morning."

Shadows of leafless tree limbs danced ominously across the front and side of the mustard house. The white lawn was a highway well traveled. The bootprints in the snow were small and the discarded gum wrappers on the road in front of the house suggested to Senacal that Curt Newell's house doubled as a school-bus stop. A picnic table blanketed by snow stood its winter vigil on the lawn near the driveway to the left. A large screened-in porch stretched across the front and halfway down the driveway side of the house. It was cluttered with remnants of seasons past: wicker furniture covered with plastic, a hoe, two rakes, a garden hose, a Rototiller, a lawn mower, and a rusted charcoal grill. The snow on the driveway was packed down like cement. Three aluminum garbage cans lined the driveway. Senacal stood in front of the house and listened to his earlier recordings. He wrote "Mustard House" on a new tape and put it into his recorder. He walked up the front steps of the mustard house.

"So far, I have a murder or multiple murders. The body or bodies are probably cut up and burning in something connected to the gray chimney. There's snow on the front steps of the house, but no footprints are visible. No pawprints from Laddy either. Family and guests must use the back door off the driveway. The murderer probably did too."

He opened the front door and gagged.

The stench of burning flesh attacked him in waves of hot air. His mouth dried up instantly. The floor shook from the furnace rumbling in the cellar. He heard a sizzling, popping sound coming from the rear of the house. He gagged again; his jaws tightened. He ran out the house and vomited over the porch railing.

He immediately charged back inside the house. With a handkerchief over his face, he searched for the thermostat. The smell was awful. He held his breath for as long as he could. He pressed his nostrils tight, forbidding any air to enter and register its stench. He saw the thermostat on the wall below the upstairs staircase. A stack of clean towels lay on the steps. He set the tip of his pen into the teeth of the plastic, circular control and pushed down, counterclockwise. The furnace shifted gears and the floor stopped vibrating.

He sat on the front steps for some air. Lieutenant Schiff came running across the snow-covered lawn just as an unfamiliar voice sounded from Senacal's left.

"Smells bad, like burned chicken at the church bazaar."

A short man with a low center of gravity approached along the shrub line. He wore a nylon parka, fireman's boots, and blue-and-red wool mittens. A yellow knit hat adorned his head.

Senacal barked, "Who the hell are you?"

"Sheriff Clune of Washington County. What's cooking in there? Got a fire?"

Senacal looked at Schiff. "Get this county mounty out of here. I'm sick enough as it is."

"This is my county." The sheriff threw his shoulders back and stared at Senacal. "I have jurisdiction here. In fact, your police cars are blocking the firehouse. That's a violation."

"Do you know where you can shove your goddamn firehouse, Mr. Sheriff Clune of Washington County?"

Lieutenant Schiff ordered Senacal to be quiet, then escorted Sheriff Clune back to the firehouse. Senacal yelled after them. "I want a transfer, Schiff. I've got to get the hell out of this loony wilderness and back to Long Island before I crack up!"

Senacal felt cold; the seat of his pants was wet from the snow on the front steps. He told himself to be patient and concentrate on the investigation. He thought of how pleasurable a cigarette would taste at this time, especially that first, long drag and slow exhale. He felt for a jerky stick, but he had none. He hoped someday Kimberly's children would appreciate the effort their grandfather made to stay alive.

As he shook his head, he mumbled, "A sheriff with blue-and-red mittens! Oh, my God! Get your shit together, asshole, and get back in there." Senacal had nicknames for everybody, but asshole was special. He found no one but himself worthy of its honor.

The house was cooler, but the odor was still strong. He entered the den and clicked on his recorder.

"Den is to the right through the front door. The room is immaculate. No empty glasses, no dirty dishes, no TV. That's unusual." He walked to his right along the wall. "Red light of a stereo is still on." He pushed the eject button with his pen and the plastic door of the stereo opened. "Tape is of a group called Demons Beware." He pulled the electric cord from the wall. He moved around some other tapes with his pen. "All the tapes are of country singers."

He checked a glass door that led from the den to the front porch. It was locked. He walked over to a picture hanging on the wall near a gray metal desk. "A picture in the den is of a thin man with a mop of black, curly hair and a feather mustache. Hudson Lanes can be seen in the background. Number 299 is written on the bottom of the picture. Name of Curt is written on the shirt."

The gray metal desk was messy, not like the rest of the den. He opened the top drawer with his pen and spread out a folded wad of cash. He talked into his recorder. "Forty-two dollars in cash in the top drawer." He sifted some papers around with his pen. "Electric utility bill, Cable TV bill, car coupon book, date issued 09/04/85." An empty envelope slid out of a hunting magazine. "There's an envelope with no letter addressed to Security Officer Curt Newell, Comstock Prison, Whitehall, New York. The return address reads: Rita Arroyo, 2065 Haviland

Avenue, Bronx, New York. There's also a New York State tax form . . . bank statements . . . card entitled 'Twelve steps of A.A.' "

The odor of burning flesh from the back dining room reminded Senacal of his grisly search for clues.

He entered the kitchen from the den. "Spotless like the den minus Curt Newell's desk." He smelled gas. The window over the sink was locked. He opened it and the cold morning air rushed in. He took a few deep breaths and walked over to the washer and dryer on the back wall of the kitchen. He opened the dryer door with his pen. "Dryer is empty. Filter trap is free of lint. Mrs. Newell must sleep with her vacuum cleaner. Probably fights like hell with Curt about his messy desk and front porch." He lifted the washer door. "Holy shit!" He paused to catch his breath. "A large tablecloth is soaked through with blood." He moved the heavy material around in the tub. "Some clumps of flesh and hair are stuck to it."

He dropped to his knees and inspected the green indoor-outdoor carpet around the washing machine for bloody footprints. Nothing. He crawled on his hands and knees to the dining-room entrance. Still nothing. Not even a drop of blood was visible. He sat down on the floor and talked into his recorder.

"Why aren't there any bloodstains? The tablecloth must have been dripping with blood." He looked under the kitchen table. "Not a crumb anywhere. The floor is spotless." He rose to his feet and headed into the dining room.

He immediately forgot the rancid odor. The bloated body of a beheaded young boy lay sizzling on a large gas barbecue grill. Had he not been naked, his sex would have been indiscernible. A large knife with an ivory handle protruded from his chest. Senacal's jaws tightened; he was going to vomit again. He approached the dead boy. The smell returned to his senses and added to the horror before him. The victim's body undulated like the ocean surf from the hot juices boiling up inside him trying to escape. His rib and chest area resembled a dried-up riverbed with large cracks crisscrossing back and forth. His abdomen was brown, the skin had peeled back in layers allowing water and blood to ooze through a thin membrane and run down his side onto the hot coals. Senacal ran to his right and gagged over the dining-room table, which had been put up on its side against the maple breakfront. He couldn't vomit; his stomach was empty. He returned to the body and inserted his pen into the small handle of the gas tank and shut off the gas. He flinched from the hot juices hitting his face. The grill popped.

"The body of a young boy, probably Ken Newell, lay on a gas grill in front of a small wood stove. His head is severed neatly. No ragged edges. The boy was probably playing his tape on the stereo in the den when the murderer arrived. The knife handle is unique. Looks like ivory . . . very old with two lions' heads carved into it. It's two or three inches wide and about eighteen inches long. It could pass for a small sword. Boy is naked."

An altar of cut firewood stood next to the gas grill. It was carefully built, each piece on top of the other like Lincoln logs. Senacal knelt down and examined the boy's hands.

"Boy's hands are filled with splinters, probably carried the firewood in from outside. Why?" Senacal stood up and continued his investigation.

"The dining-room table is placed on end against the maple breakfront on the kitchen side of the room." He looked for the chairs. He remembered seeing them in the living room when he was looking for the thermostat. He would check them out later. The back wall of the dining room was covered with blood, especially the section over the television. Senacal checked his recorder to be sure there was enough tape left.

"The wall behind the television is covered with blood and even the ceiling is machine-gunned with red droplets. The television is unplugged. The murderer must have needed the outlet for his power saw and used the television as a chopping block to saw off the victim's head."

He stumbled over the dog's chain on the back porch. Snowboots stood erect on an old rug to the right of the door. His eyes scanned the snow between a cord of wood stacked along the back fence and the porch. He was looking for a particular print in the snow. He found it, the bare footprint of the victim. The boy had been made to carry in the wood for his sacrificial altar. He flicked on his recorder.

"There's an ax embedded in Laddy's head. Looks like a boy-scout type. Probably picked up by the killer from the nearby cardboard box of kindling wood for the wood stove. Wheelprints in the snow are visible on the porch from the gas grill being dragged inside the house. It was probably a last-minute substitute for the wooden altar."

Senacal examined the living room. "The murderer must have moved the chairs in here before the killing. The living-room carpet is immaculate. No blood anywhere. Probably raised the thermostat at the same time." He turned to leave when his eye caught something written on the living-room mirror. He studied the writing, then recorded it.

"A reference to the Book of Genesis in the Bible is written in blood on the living-room mirror. It reads: 'Gen. 22:6–10. 67 left.' "

Senacal walked out the front door and down the steps of the mustard house.

"Stop!" Lieutenant Schiff raised his hand. "What did you find? Was it Ken Newell? Were his parents around last night?"

"They went bowling, sir. I don't think they came home. The son was alone."

"Why are you so sure?"

"Because there was a clean stack of towels on the stairway. Mrs. Newell certainly would have brought them upstairs on her way to bed if she had been home. She's a fanatic house cleaner, as was the murderer."

"Who told you? Her parakeet?" Lieutenant Schiff bit his bottom lip; his eyes bulged.

"No, sir. She would never have allowed a bird in her house. In fact, their dog, Laddy, was always chained up on the back porch."

"Here." A uniformed officer handed Senacal a hot Styrofoam cup of tea and a jerky stick. "That fat lady with the cow over her tit gave them to me for you." The officer pointed toward the crowd as he spoke.

Senacal waved a thank-you to Nel and Graham Twitchell. The tea washed away the taste of death from his mouth.

Senacal instructed Lieutenant Schiff to have the police lab carefully check the kitchen carpet for evidence. He also explained how the head of the victim had been severed by some type of power saw and that the tablecloth was probably used to carry the head to the murderer's car. He had no answer to Schiff's question as to why the murderer had taken the time to bring the tablecloth back into the house and place it in the washing machine. He told Schiff he was sure more than one person had been involved in the death of Ken Newell. Someone had to prepare the dining room for the human sacrifice while another murderer probably stayed with the boy as he carried in the wood.

At his car, Senacal lifted the radio receiver. "Two-six-seventy-eight to South Glens Falls."

While he waited for a reply, a familiar voice yelled from the crowd. "Did you puke your guts up?" It was Graham Twitchell. Senacal motioned for a police officer to bring the old man over to him.

"This is Zone Two headquarters," said a muffled voice over the car radio.

"This is Senior Investigator Senacal calling from Fort Ann. Listen carefully. Send a team to Hudson Bowling Lanes in Fort Edward. It's right on Route Four. Ask the owner if he remembers seeing Curt and Evelyn Newell last night. They're probably in a Saturday-night bowling league. The owner should know Curt because he's a hell of a bowler. If their car is not in the parking lot, search along Route Four for it.

"Second, I want to know about a Rita Arroyo, 2065 Haviland Avenue, Bronx, New York. Her husband or boyfriend is serving time in Comstock up the road from here in Whitehall. Curt Newell is a maximum-security guard there. If you can, find out Newell's relationship with her.

"Third, have a team check a few record shops in the area. Ask if there's a fan club in the capital district for a rock group named Demons Beware. They're into satanic type music, I think. In fact, find out if any groups like Demons Beware have fan clubs in the area. If so, I want the name of the president of the club."

Senacal smelled the odor of Ken Newell's charred body on his jacket sleeve as he replaced the phone on the dashboard. He removed the jacket and threw it into his trunk. A trooper handed him a gray, thigh-length, standard-issue police coat.

Graham Twitchell remarked, "The jacket makes you look fat." The old man pulled on his Red Sox baseball cap and winked.

Senacal retorted, "You look like the Jolly Green Giant yourself." It felt good for Senacal to laugh. "Listen, I hope you—"

Twitchell stopped him. "Nope. I didn't say a word

17

about the murder to anyone. Told Nel that the dead guy was a salesman and that he tripped into the fireplace while selling Evelyn a new scrub brush."

Senacal looked over at Nel Twitchell; she waved at him with a big smile stretched across her cherub face. He shook his head in disbelief, then turned to Twitchell. "Find me a priest or rabbi around here. Tell him to bring a Bible."

"Am I deputized?"

"Yes." Senacal gently pushed him on his way.

The officer to whom Senacal had earlier given orders approached. His name tag read, Lutz, Kenneth. "Sir, the man who owned the snowblower on Catherine Street said he leaves it on the side of the driveway all winter. The guy said it's not much good keeping a snowblower in the shed behind the house, if you have to shovel snow to get it out."

Senacal agreed with the man's reasoning. Earlier, he had thought robbery may have been a motive for the murder. The forty-two dollars in Curt Newell's desk drawer ruled that theory obsolete.

Senacal followed Lutz into a dirty room in the back of the firehouse. A wooden desk stood in front of the only window in the room. The desk was grimy like the window and cluttered with empty soda bottles, filled ashtrays, and neglected stacks of papers and envelopes covered with dust. Rings of coffee stains were everywhere a wooden surface could be found. A few pieces of fossilized crust lay beside a discarded pizza box in the corner. The gray walls were covered with pictures of firemen standing proudly in front of burned homes and barns.

"Inspector, this man was up and around early this morning. His car hood was warm and his name is Bill Hulka." Lutz turned to leave the room; Senacal called after him.

"See if the owner of that home on Catherine Street

with the cannons on the front lawn is the town historian. I want to question her or him, or whomever."

"Yes, sir."

"How's your partner doing?" Senacal asked. Officer Lutz nodded O.K.

"Have him go for the town historian. You stick around and assist me."

Officer Lutz left the room and a man in his early fifties sat down on a metal folding chair. He wore a sharkskin gray suit with a white shirt and a black tie.

Senacal looked at the man and said, "You're dressed like the mayor or the church organist, which one are you?"

"Neither." His lips barely moved.

"You're Bill Hulka?"

"Yes."

"Mr. Hulka, do you mind if I tape our conversation?"

"No."

Senacal clicked on his tape recorder. "What time did you get up this morning?"

"Four-forty-five."

"Is that a normal time for you to get up?"

"Yes." The man remained motionless in his seat.

"Feel free to talk, Mr. Hulka. I don't bite."

"Yes, I know."

There was a slight pause. "Well, talk! Why do you get up so early in the morning?"

"I take my nitro pill at that time every morning. I like to shower and shave and dress nicely beforehand, so in case . . . I get the big one." He weakly snapped his fingers and managed a quick smile across his thin lips. "I want to look good when I go. That's how my father went. They just picked him up and put him in his coffin. That made a wonderful impression on me."

Bill Hulka's stupidity only made Senacal's body

crave more desperately for nicotine. He reached inside his pant's pocket for the jerky stick Twitchell had given him. He struggled to maintain his patience.

"Was there anything unusual this morning, before or after you took your pill?"

"Shannon, our dog, barked about four-thirty."

"Is it unusual for Shannon to bark so early?"

"Yes."

"Does she ever bark?"

"Yes."

Senacal flipped his jerky stick into the air. "Will you speak, for Christ's sake. Your goddamn dog barks more than you talk."

Bill Hulka hurried a quick answer. "She barks at strange sounds like when teenagers walk in front of the house carrying those big radios that look like suitcases."

At least Shannon's barking was helpful, thought Senacal. It substantiated his belief that Ken Newell's murder had taken place just before dawn. If the boy had been killed earlier on Sunday morning, the body would have dried up from the heat of the gas grill. Senacal was also beginning to think that Curt and Evelyn Newell had never returned home from bowling last night.

"Inspector?" said Ken Lutz, entering the room. "This is John Yarter. He owns the rusted station wagon. You wanted to speak to him?"

The young man was tall with collar length hair and a blond handlebar mustache. He shifted weight from foot to foot and his eyes danced around the room. He wore a red-and-white high school jacket.

"Mr. Hulka, would you excuse us," Senacal said.

Hulka walked mechanically from the room.

Yarter began the conversation. "I don't know anything. I didn't see anything."

"Who said you did?"

"Somebody said Curt Newell was killed or his son, or somebody."

"Do you know Curt?"

"Yes. We work at Comstock. We ride up together sometimes."

"Do you mind if I tape our conversation? I'm sure you know about Miranda and all that."

Yarter agreed to the taping.

"Is Newell liked by the inmates? Does he get along?"

"Real well. He's a good guy."

"Who's Rita Arroyo?"

Yarter's eyes searched the room for a place to hide.

Senacal turned off his recorder. "I know the game," he said. "You get a little ass from the inmate's girlfriend or wife and then turn your head when she sneaks her old man his drugs. I don't give a shit about that. Is Newell screwing her?"

Yarter nodded yes.

"Are you?"

"No. She's Newell's."

"Does her old man know?"

"Of course. How else is he guaranteed his drugs?"

"Is she up this weekend?"

"No. Her old man was released last month."

"What time did you come by Newell's house last night after screwing around?"

Yarter paused, rubbed his hands together, and played with his gold wedding ring. He said nothing. He looked twice at the open door.

Senacal continued his questioning. "The way your car is facing on the street, you had to pass Newell's house some time last night. What time was it?"

"Three, three-thirty in the morning."

"Why the hell are you whispering? You don't want your wife to know you were screwing around last night?"

"That's pretty stupid," Yarter replied. "Do you want your wife to know?"

"When I come home late, I ring the doorbell three or four times and beat my chest like Tarzan. You're young. You'll be doing the same thing in a few years before your divorce." Senacal clicked on his recorder. "Does Newell drive a truck or a car?"

"A truck."

"Was it in his driveway last night?"

"No."

"Were there any lights on in the house when you went by?"

"Yes. In the den. It was a low light. Could have been a candle."

"Describe Ken Newell."

"Quiet."

"Is he into hard-rock music?"

"I don't think so. Curt likes western music. Has a WCAM station sticker on his pickup. He and Ken are close. They go camping together a lot."

"And Evelyn? Real bitch type, right? Loves television I bet?"

"She even has it on while they eat supper. Super bitch too. Everything has to be just right with her."

"Keeps a hell of a clean house, doesn't she?"

"You have to take your shoes off when you go into the house."

There was a slight pause, then Yarter asked, "How come you know the Newells so well?"

Senacal munched on a jerky stick in front of the firehouse and stared at the mustard house. Lieutenant Schiff was busy with a television crew that had arrived from Albany. Murders don't happen often in Fort Ann. There was a morbid excitement in the air as the crowd stood their somber vigil behind the yellow tape. The emergency squad had left with Ken Newell's charred body. Senacal hoped the boy hadn't suffered long. His own son, Joachim, was not much younger.

He replayed the horrible execution over and over in his mind as he continued staring at the house for answers. Why had the murderer been so neat? What kind of person would saw off another human being's head and then have the presence of mind to place a bloody tablecloth in the washing machine? That fact disturbed him. Why weren't there any footprints in the kitchen? The murderer's shoes must have been soaked with blood. Evelyn Newell was neat. Could she have done it? What about Arroyo? Would he come up from the Bronx to kill the son of a guy screwing his wife? Gen. 22:6–10 plagued him. What did it mean? Why hadn't Ken Newell screamed or run for his life? What did "67 left" mean? Why had the thermostat been raised so high?

"Inspector?"

Senacal turned around.

Officer Lutz was standing next to an elderly woman wearing a gray curly wig and heavy blue eye shadow. She was short with fat wobbly legs that looked ready to collapse at any time. Her smile was warm and her perfume strong. Her hands glittered with rings and bracelets. A young freckled-face girl, about eleven or twelve years old, stood next to the woman holding her hand.

"You wanted to speak to the village historian?" Officer Lutz pointed in the direction of the white house with the cannons on the front lawn. "This is Dorothy Hanlon and her granddaughter, Myra."

The woman told her granddaughter to stay put. She approached Senacal cautiously over the ice and snow. She grabbed his arm and pulled it tightly to her side, then spoke out of the corner of her mouth.

"Did he kill the bitch?" Her head danced around the street in search of unwanted listeners.

"Excuse me?"

"Did he kill the bitch?" She looked up at Senacal with warm, blue, doelike eyes. "He'd of done us all a favor if he had. Mind you, now, I don't think murder is right, but nobody likes Evelyn Newell. Bossy all the time. Telling everybody what to do at the church bazaars and village functions. Curt could have done better. Wished he had married my Allyson. She married a bum from Albany."

There was a pause in her tale.

Senacal asked, "Mrs. Hanlon, I'd like—"

"Call me, Dot. Some folks call me Dolly because I sing the 'Hello Dolly' every night at closing. You've got nice teeth, but your breath is awful. What did you have for breakfast? Horseradish?"

"Thanks. I love you too. Are you the village historian?"

"Hell, no. I own a bar over in Lake George. Why the hell would you think that?"

"The cannons on your front lawn. I thought you might know something about Fort Ann's myths, legends, or past murders. You know, things like that."

Dorothy Hanlon called for her granddaughter to come forward. She patted the young girl on the head and motioned Senacal to one side. She pulled on his sleeve and whispered while her eyes darted back and forth between her granddaughter and Senacal.

"The little shit's a genius. She needs a good spanking once in a while, but she's a good kid. I take her on weekends while my Allyson runs the bar. Allyson's divorced and spends Saturday and Sunday nights with her boyfriend. I don't want Myra around while her mother's spooning. I'm telling you, it ain't easy raising a granddaughter these days."

"Are you telling me that your granddaughter is the village historian?"

Dot Hanlon smiled proudly at her granddaughter. "Didn't I just say that?"

Senacal hesitated about questioning the young girl. The rights of minors were strictly outlined in the state-police manual. Consent forms had to be filled out, parents had to be present, and a homey atmosphere had to be guaranteed for questioning. He turned Dot Hanlon around and walked toward the standing girl.

"Myra, I'm Inspector Senacal with the state police. I would like to ask you some questions about the history of Fort Ann."

"Aren't you going to give me my Miranda rights? Of course, any information I do give would be invalidated in court because of the infringement of my rights under the Huntley decision." She stood proud as a peacock.

Dot grabbed Senacal's arm and whispered. "See what I mean. She gets a little too smart for her own good sometimes. If you want to smack her, be my guest."

Senacal patted Dot's arm and shook his head. "Myra, does the expression 'sixty-seven left' have any significance in Fort Ann history?"

"In relationship to what? Could you be more specific?"

"Murders . . . cults . . . prophecies, things like that?"

The young girl thought for a second. "There are three popular legends in Fort Ann history: the legend of Furnace Hollow up in South Bay, the Hogstown Cabin deaths, and the mystery of Jack's Cave. But the numerical expression 'sixty-seven left' is not directly attributable to any of them."

Senacal asked for a brief history of each legend.

"The Furnace Hollow legend involved a pirate's treasure from colonial times."

"Any murders, perhaps even burnings, connected with the legend?"

"None that I'm aware of. The Hogstown Cabin legend has some grisly details."

Senacal nodded for her to go on.

"Hogstown is a section of Fort Ann a little west of here. In the 1820s, as legend records, a family was found slaughtered in a cabin. Thereafter, anyone who stayed in the cabin was scared away by strange sounds at night. Years later, another family moved in and they were found all butchered up one morning. The townsfolk burned the building down."

"Was a large knife with two lions' heads carved into an ivory handle, ever connected to the murders or any murder in Fort Ann for that matter?"

"No."

Dot pulled Senacal's arm. "Do you know Graham Twitchell? He's waving at us."

Senacal turned and saw Twitchell walking down Charles Street with a beautiful young woman.

"The man's a pervert," whispered Dot. She looked at her granddaughter before she continued whispering. "He'll grab an ass as sure as there's shit in Shanghai. Of course, I heard Nel has had her own bedroom for years, but still!"

Senacal squeezed her arm and returned his attention to Myra. "What about Jack's Cave?"

"That one is rather silly," replied the young historian.

"Try me." Senacal's infectious smile was contagious; the young girl blushed.

"O.K., if you insist. Legend has it that a young girl was often seen running barefoot through the woods. When chased, she'd disappear into thin air behind a tree or bush or whatever. She was finally chased into Jack's Cave one day up in the mountains and was never seen again. Some believed she killed the family who spent the night in the haunted cabin in Hogstown. Lumberjacks were the ones who told the story for years and they were probably drunk

26

most of the time. They even claimed that the girl had never left any footprints in the snow."

Senacal took a deep breath and glanced over at the police carrying out Evelyn Newell's kitchen carpet.

Graham Twitchell spoke up. "No priest, but I brought you a nun." He looked at Dot Hanlon. "Howdy, Dot. You look fine this morning, like most."

"Anything warm in a skirt looks good to a pervert." She grabbed her granddaughter's hand and turned toward Senacal. "Anything else?"

"No." Senacal's attention had remained riveted on the mustard house.

"You look like you've seen a ghost, Inspector," said Dot Hanlon as she steadied her legs for the trip home. "Drop into Hanlon's Bar if you're ever up the lake near Bolton Landing. We'll soak down a pitcher or two."

Senacal managed a weak smile and said good-bye.

The nun was young and beautiful. Her blond hair glistened like gold in the morning sun. It was pulled back tightly alongside her smooth face. Her eyes were green and surrounded by long black lashes. She stood tall and cradled a Bible against her chest.

"I bet you're wondering how I found such a beautiful nun in a place like Fort Ann, New York?" said Twitchell.

"After today I'll believe anything," Senacal said. He looked at the nun. "What's your name?"

"Sister Angelica." Her voice purred like a kitten.

Senacal gave Twitchell a suspicious look.

The old man raised his arms. "It's true; it's her name. Trust me. She's really a nun too."

Senacal explained the lettering from the Newell's living-room mirror.

Sister Angelica's face remained stoic as she spoke. "That's a reference to the Book of Genesis, chapter 22, verses six through ten, but I don't know what 'sixty-seven left' means."

"Could you look up the passage and read it to me, please?"

Quickly, her long fingers searched through the Bible for the Book of Genesis. She looked up at Senacal. He nodded for her to begin.

"Abraham made Issac carry the wood for the sacrifice and he himself carried the knife and live coals for starting the fire. As they walked along together. Issac spoke up. 'Father!'

"Abraham answered, 'Yes, my son?'

"Issac asked, 'I see that you have the coals and the wood, but where is the lamb for the sacrifice?'

"Abraham answered, 'God himself will provide one.' And the two of them walked together.

"When they came to the place which God had told him about, Abraham built an altar and arranged wood on it. He tied up his son and placed him on the altar, on top of the wood. Then he picked up the knife to kill him."

Senacal and Twitchell stared at each other in front of the firehouse until Twitchell broke the silence. "He'll kill again, Senacal. You can bet your last dollar on it, he will."

2

Mount Horeb, Wisconsin

January, 1986

THE THOUGHT of sharing a sleeping bag with Nina
Sadler had excited Harry Gilcrest about camping out
under a cold January sky in Blue Mound State Park.
Nina Sadler was a kook in flea-market pick-overs. In
one semester at the University of Wisconsin, Nina
had eroded Harry's morals faster than it had taken
his parents and the finest Catholic prep schools in
Michigan a lifetime to forge. Harry knew she wasn't
the type of girl he'd settle down with in Pontiac,
Michigan. Like oil and water, Nina Sadler and the
Whitestone Country Club just wouldn't mix. She
affectionately called him Horse, due to the size of his
penis. No girl in Pontiac, Michigan, had ever called
him that. But she was perfect for this time in his life.
He had fun with her and she could make him do
anything, even chase her up a mountain on a cold
night.

"Nina," Harry Gilcrest yelled from under the observation tower on Blue Mound, southern Wisconsin's highest elevation. Only silence answered his
call. Earlier, Nina had run up the mountain ahead of
him. "We'll play hide-and-seek," had been her child-
ish words in flight. Harry was a worrier; he had
stayed behind for a few minutes to make sure the
car and camping equipment had been secured. Also,

he had left a note on his tent telling Geoffrey Ovington and Patrick Sherwood to join Nina and him at the top of Blue Mound when they arrived with their dates after a late-afternoon class.

"Nina!" Still no answer to his call. He scanned the vicinity around the tower with his flashlight. Everything was peaceful. A white blanket of snow had securely wrapped the earth in a tranquil sleep. A few picnic tables stood as lonely sentinels around the tower. He climbed the stairs to the top of the observation tower and put a quarter into the steel binoculars anchored to the wooden floor.

His attention focused in on Madison, located on an isthmus formed by two lakes. The State Capitol Building, a facsimile of the United States Capitol in Washington, D.C., but seven inches shorter, shone brightly from floodlights at its base. The dome looked like a Christmas bulb suspended over the city. The red-and-white car lights moving around the city streets and adjoining highways reminded Harry of an army of ants about their nightly chores. He wondered if Geoffrey, Patrick, and their dates were in one of the cars.

His attention was drawn to Mount Horeb, a small community just a few miles east of Blue Mound on Route 151. He was amused at the sight of the twisted trail of parallel lights along the streets of the tiny Wisconsin community.

"Harry Gilcrest, you have entered the sacred burial ground of the Winnebago Indians. You must be punished by Anath, goddess of sex and war."

Harry jumped at the sound of Nina's voice and bumped his head on the steel binoculars. He looked down and saw Nina standing on a picnic table. He shouted, "Oh, fair maiden of the Blue Mound, I'm your prisoner. Please, be merciful." He raced down the stairs of the observation tower as fast as he could. He liked Nina's games because they all ended in sex. Harry had more sex in three months with Nina than he had thought he could in a lifetime.

Nina ran to the far end of the mountaintop. She jumped up on another picnic table and spoke in the manner of a high priestess shouting incantations. "Follow me, Harold Gilcrest. Follow me. Only I may save you."

She waited until he was near, then she knifed her way through the thick brush and down the mountain, with Harry in clumsy pursuit. She turned and urged him on. "Harry Gilcrest, you must find me in the night or you will be killed by the spirits buried in this sacred ground."

He tried catching her, but she was too fast. He brushed off the snow on a tree stump and sat down. He waited for the sound of her voice, which would signal for the game to continue. Everything was perfectly still. The sky was barely visible through a thick umbrella of tall pines. He waited, only his breathing was audible. Finally, he chanted, "Oh, dear maiden of the Winnebago and sister of the goddess Anath, come and get me. I desire sex greatly."

He laughed. Then he stopped laughing. He waited. The ominous silence in the woods became deafening. He was sure she was nearby. He walked about out of nervousness and stumbled over a buried log in the snow. A branch grazed his face. He scanned the thick woods with his flashlight, but Nina was not to be found.

He looked at his watch and mumbled, "Eight-thirty! It won't be light for another ten hours. What if those guys don't come? Thank God I left them a note." Thoughts of death entered his mind. He remembered reading that freezing to death was painless, actually peaceful, like falling asleep. A few clumps of snow fell around him. He looked up and saw the shadowy figure of a woman falling on him. He screamed, "Help!"

It was Nina. She sat on his chest and pinned his arms to the cold ground. She stared at him with cold, piercing eyes as if she were in a trance.

Harry spoke up. "You're carrying this game a little too far. Get off me!"

Suddenly, her mood changed and a smile appeared on her face. She stood up and said, "Come. I will reward you with warmth."

She spread out a blanket under the observation tower and took Harry by the hand. "I'm sorry, if I worried you." She smiled innocently. Her tone was apologetic, her mood playful.

"You're forgiven. But you had me guessing there for a while. It was like you were hypnotized or something."

"It was fun watching you stumble around like that." She puffed up her cheeks in mimicry of his weight and clumsiness. "You know, there's a legend that a treasure is buried on Blue Mound. Also, a fort was built here in the 1840s, and when the Indians attacked, the settlers would run up here for protection. It didn't do them any good. Their blood soaked deep into this mountaintop. Isn't that exciting?"

She unzippered her jacket and slowly unbuttoned her flannel shirt. She stared at Harry with the eyes of a mystic. He sensed her mood slipping into another of her multiple personalities. Her flannel shirt parted like a curtain, revealing the smooth lines of her soft breasts. Nina never wore a bra.

Harry's eyes bulged. "What are you doing? You'll catch pneumonia."

"I want to make love with you in the snow." Her shirt slid off her shoulders.

Nervously, Harry looked around to be sure they were alone.

She kissed him on the neck, then on his cheek. She unbuttoned his shirt, ran her hands across his back, whispered, "I want you, Horse."

He touched her naked back; her body was on fire in the cold. He looked at her and said, "What if Geoffrey and Patrick come up in the middle of us going at it? Shit, I don't know. I'm not the outdoor type. I like sheets and blankets and showers and heat. My ass is going to freeze."

She laughed and unbuckled his pants. "I'll keep you warm. Touch my breasts, Horse." She wrapped him in a blanket and pulled him deep inside her. "You feel so good, Horse. Hold me, Horse. Hold me."

A sense of fear settled over Harry Gilcrest as Nina Sadler's fiery passion swelled under him in the Wisconsin night. She thrashed about on the blanket, oblivious to the cold and snow. There was no tenderness in her lovemaking. She seemed obsessed like an animal in heat. Her fingernails dug deep into his back. Between gasped-for air, she repeated the same words over and over again. "Praise Anath, goddess of war and sex . . ."

Back down the mountain, Harry found a note pinned to his tent. "Went to Scudder's Caverns in Mount Horeb. Join us."

Harry greeted the note with suspicion. Geoffrey's and Patrick's behavior was always predictable; they wouldn't just take off in the night. Harry sensed something was wrong. The note wasn't signed either. He looked inside the tent for their camping equipment. Nothing. The area was unchanged from when he had left it to join Nina on the top of Blue Mound. Harry wondered why they hadn't dropped off their gear before going to Scudder's Caverns.

Nina was already in the car. Her eyes were filled with excitement. She yelled to Harry, "Come on. It's just a few miles from here." She jumped up and down on the seat and clapped her hands like a child about to be treated to ice cream. Harry paused to write another note to his friends, just in case.

"Hurry up, Horse. I want to play in the cave."

In Mount Horeb, a large arrow sign read, SCUDDER'S CAVERNS AHEAD. Reluctantly, Harry turned left on the snow-packed road and followed the arrow. His head swirled with unanswered questions. Why would those guys go exploring caves at night? They're political-science majors. Maybe they got stoned or something? Maybe their dates wanted to visit the caverns?

Nina rubbed the inside of his thigh and said, "Spelunkers make great lovers, Horse. Did you know that? Did you ever have it in a cave, Horse? It's terrific."

Harry failed to appreciate her suggestions.

The parking lot was empty. Nina jumped out of the car and ran to the back of Timothy Scudder's old house.

In 1828, Timothy Scudder had "struck it rich" mining lead in the Blue Mound area of Wisconsin. After a short period of time, he opened a smelting furnace and a small community developed around his lead mining business. In 1922 a cave was discovered behind the house, and tourists flocked to explore the underground cavern. Each year, by Thanksgiving, Scudder's Caverns settled into its winter sleep. There were no visitors in the winter or busloads of children on a school holiday. There was no life at Scudder's Caverns in the middle of January on a cold night.

The path behind Timothy Scudder's house led Harry to a red building, where Nina was waiting for him. A nearby sign read, ENTRANCE—SCUDDER'S CAVERNS.

The inside of the building was brightly lit. Nina opened the front door and ran toward the elevator that descended into the cave below.

"Who unlocked the front door?" Harry mumbled.

Nina stood inside the elevator and beckoned Harry to enter. He reluctantly accepted her invitation, and the steel doors slid closed. The overhead motor kicked into gear and Nina and Harry descended into the earth. He heard his heart pound inside his chest. He felt trapped inside a coffin about to be buried alive. He saw scribbled on the elevator wall the words, "Cave of Macpelah." The doors opened and Nina screamed for joy.

Harry stared into the open mouth of a giant dinosaur. Large rock teeth hung from the cave's ceiling over slimy brown rocks. The mounds varied in size. Some looked like huge eyeteeth jutting up from the jaws of the earth. Others reminded Harry of frozen ice cream perched precariously on the tip of a sugar cone.

"Horse," Nina yelled from his right.

At the mention of his nickname, Harry knew what meaning Nina had interpreted from the rock formations. He found her amid a small clump of stalagmites stroking and kissing one that resembled a giant penis.

The cave was alive from white lights carefully hidden behind a few stalagmites. Harry circled his mouth with his hands and yelled, "Geoffrey . . . Patrick." The echo was louder than he had anticipated. Nina laughed and ran along a path of red arrows to the back of the cave. It was warm in the womb of the earth; he unzippered his jacket and followed Nina deeper into the cavern.

The red arrows led to a narrow passageway dimly lit by night-lights recessed into the rock. As he walked alone, Harry hoped that Ovington and Sherwood were playing a joke on him. Maybe even Nina was in on the scam. Suddenly he found himself on a concrete bridge that spanned a green lagoon. Underwater lights glistened off hundreds of coins that had been tossed into the water for luck. The sound of dripping water was hypnotic. He heard a splash and looked down. Nina swam out naked from beneath the bridge.

Nina Sadler had a magnificent body, her legs shapely and her breasts full, with large nipples. She wrapped her legs around a stalagmite protruding through the water and, with a suggestive smile on her face, kissed and caressed the pointed stone.

For a moment his fears left him. Visions of Eve swimming in a pool of innocence filled his head. He thought Nina appeared more gentle and feminine than she had earlier under the observation tower atop Blue Mound. She licked her lips with the tip of her tongue and motioned for him to join her. Her long black hair stuck to her shoulders.

The faces of his friends flashed before his eyes. He asked, "Where do you think Geoffrey and Patrick are hiding?"

"I don't know. Maybe they left. Who cares?" She turned and floated on her back. She looked so inviting. "Are you coming in, Horse? I'm going crazy in here without you." She spread a handful of coins across her navel.

He ached to join her, but the whereabouts of his friends worried him. He told Nina he'd be back after he had investigated the rest of the cave.

She giggled like a little girl as she swam in the cool water.

The concrete bridge over the lagoon led Harry to a rock tunnel: a room of terror waited on the other side. Red, purple, and orange floodlights illuminated a ceiling covered with icicles of stone. There was no clear path through the room. Stalagmites of every shape jutted up from the ground. Some were thin like pencils, others resembled large chess pieces ready to attack. Everything was colored in different shades of red and purple. The ceiling bowed toward the walls, making it impossible for Harry to stand up straight, except in the middle of the room. At any moment he thought the walls of the room would move in and crush him to death.

He ran into a large bell-shaped room with a ceiling that had been sculptured by water millions of years ago. An organ, covered with clear plastic, stood on a concrete platform next to a stone stage. The lighting in the room was soft and pleasing. Cafeteria tables had been stacked against the wall near a stainless-steel lunch counter. To his right was a stairway leading up to a catwalk, with a protective railing, that circled the top of the entire room. It was like being in a stone church. His eyes focused on something hanging from the railing above the stone stage.

He squinted at a collection of indistinguishable objects bound together by a rope. His mouth went dry and fatigue gripped his body. The whole evening began to take its emotional toll on his nerves. Harry continued his march toward the stage. Suddenly he saw himself behind a line of red car lights circling the capitol building in Madison. He shook his head to dispel the dream. His heart beat faster. The rope was green. Harry looked up and examined the swaying collage with the eye of an art critic.

He raised his sweaty hands to his mouth and gasped at the sight of four hands tied together by a wire to four legs that had been cut off from the knees down. He recognized Ovington's brown boots.

He stood below the stage unaware that droplets of blood bounced off his head from above. Only his eyes moved. On the stage floor, a biblical inscription, written in blood, read, "2 Sam. 4:12. 65 left."

His body trembled as he hopped up on the stone stage and discovered his friends' beheaded bodies in the rear of the stage. A sword, with two lions' heads carved into an ivory handle, protruded from each man's chest. He felt sick. He thought he was going to faint. He jumped off the stage and ran back to the green lagoon yelling, "Nina! Nina!"

3

Saratoga Springs, New York

March, 1986

SITTING AT a table in Bergman's Bar and Restaurant on Phila Street in Saratoga Springs, Matt Senacal scribbled some notes across the back of an FBI envelope while he waited for a beer and his favorite sandwich of Velveeta cheese on rye with strawberry jam. Since his wife, Donna, had thrown him out of the house in February, Bergman's had become Senacal's favorite watering hole, an oasis to rest and sip a few beers in anonymous comfort. His meeting earlier in the day with the FBI had been frustrating, but he felt relaxed now as he munched on a beef-jerky stick. He liked the Phila Street area of Saratoga; there was a touch of Greenwich Village along its network of dusty bookstores, antique shops, and brownstone restaurants. It was nice having a little bit of New York City so near; it soothed his transition from the Big Apple.

Two years earlier, to appease his wife by accepting the advice of her psychiatrist that a change of scenery might salvage their crumbling marriage, Senacal had asked for a transfer from Lake Success on Long Island to South Glens Falls in Warren County. He had adapted with little difficulty to the slower pace of life in upstate New York, except for his policework. He had been bored until the Fort Ann execution of

Ken Newell. Yet, he had discovered Saratoga Springs quaint and its inhabitants pleasant. His fourteen-year-old son, Joachim, enjoyed romping on his trail bike through the woods behind their Wilton home, and Kimberly, his daughter of sixteen, had found a new boyfriend and was immediately content with the change in her life. Her Long Island boyfriend had worn an earring, her Saratoga boyfriend wore a blue high-school football jacket. Senacal had approved of her change of taste.

To Donna McClusky Senacal, Saratoga Springs was too cold in the winter and the snowbanks at the bottom of the driveway too high. There were not enough shopping malls and she missed her Sunday visit to her mother's grave at St. Raymond's Cemetery in the Bronx. Worst of all, the hatred she had felt for her husband hadn't lessened with the move upstate as her psychiatrist had promised. Donna's permanent state of unhappiness had begun the day her umbilical cord was cut. Thereafter, she had searched her whole life for a route back to the warm waters of the womb. Senacal had observed the problem for the first time after their honeymoon in Aruba. Donna had thrown her arms around her mother at Kennedy Airport and had cried of loneliness.

Matt Senacal had somehow survived nineteen years of marriage by ignoring it. It had been Donna who had initiated the divorce proceedings by asking him to leave the house. He hadn't been much of a husband and only an average father. He loved his work; he was married to the New York State Police.

Senacal studied his notes on the back of the FBI envelope.

1) Curt Newell's truck—found at Hudson Lanes.

2) Curt and Evelyn Newell found in the woods off Route 4 near Whitehall. Heads cut off!

3) Ricky Arroyo had returned to Puerto Rico before the murders.

4) Footprints in the back of the house—inconclusive.

5) No bloodstains on the kitchen carpet.

6) Ken Newell belonged to no rock-'n'-roll fan clubs.

Senacal had investigated the Fort Ann murders for three straight weeks in January before Lieutenant Schiff had him reassigned to a robbery investigation in Clifton Park near Albany. Senacal hadn't complained; his Fort Ann investigation had uncovered no major leads or suspects. He also knew the FBI had taken over the case. It was their practice in such bizarre murder cases. Yet the memory of Ken Newell's charred body sizzling on a gas grill had been his constant companion since January. Its memories followed him everywhere, even in his dreams. It was the most heinous murder he had ever seen. All previous murders he had investigated had been crimes of passion, committed at home by lovers or distraught spouses who, in a moment of uncontrollable rage, had reached for a convenient weapon—a gun, a knife, or a blunt object—to strike at their temporary enemy.

Liz Ruth, Bergman's only waitress and a friend of Senacal's, plopped his sandwich on the table and said, "The cook wants to know how long your pet rat's liked strawberry jam."

He took a swig of beer and slid his arm around her waist. "You look sexy in waitress white, Ruthy. I sign my divorce papers tonight at seven o'clock. What do you say you help me celebrate my new freedom?"

"Freedom! When were you ever married?" She told him to leave a big tip, then left to serve another table.

Senacal removed the worn letter from inside the FBI envelope. He would try one more time to understand the FBI's reasoning behind Ken Newell's execution. He flattened the letter out next to his plate.

Like a starving shark, he lunged at his cheese-and-jelly sandwich while his eyes remained fixed on the letter.

Federal Bureau of Investigation
9th Street and Pennsylvania Ave.
Washington, D.C. 20535
March 12, 1986

Superintendent John McNeal
New York State Police
State Campus, Bldg. 22
Albany, New York 12226

Dear Superintendent McNeal:

The Federal Bureau of Investigation, in conjunction with the President's National Security Council, have carefully studied the evidence of thirteen killings recently committed in New York, Wisconsin, Maine, Kentucky, Vermont, and South Carolina. It is the opinion of the President of the United States and the Federal Bureau of Investigation that, judging by the locations selected, methods employed in execution, and the evidence left behind by the assassins, terrorism has become a reality within America's borders.

"Violence for effect," a brief but accurate definition of terrorism, will not be realized in America. There will be no sanctuary for terrorism here. The slaughter of innocent American citizens by those who perpetrate terrorism on American soil will not be tolerated. Presently, known Libyan and Palestinian political sympathizers and suspected terrorists are under round-the-clock surveillance. The President of the United States has pledged his full and undivided support to eradicate any terrorist installations in America. The major news bureaus have cooperated fully by denying media coverage of these acts.

It is imperative that our special agent Robert Hawkins meet Lieutenant Robert Schiff and Chief Investigator Matthew Senacal of Zone 2, G Troop, of the New York State Police. A direct dialogue with your investigating officers of the Fort Ann, New York, murders might prove to be mutually beneficial. Security clearance has been granted both your men, thus the enclosed descriptions of the thirteen executions may be studied prior to the scheduled 10:00 A.M. meeting on March 20, 1986, at Troop G Headquarters in Loudonville, New York.

Sincerely,
Joseph K. Porter
Director, the Federal Bureau of Investigation

Senacal shook his head and put the letter aside, then retrieved the report of the thirteen executions from the inside pocket of his jacket. Rereading the letter hadn't helped. He still couldn't accept the FBI's theory that Middle East politics had played a role in Ken Newell's execution. Would a terrorist take the time to put a bloody tablecloth into Evelyn Newell's washing machine? His objections to the terrorist theory had fallen on deaf ears at the Loudonville meeting. Senacal held the lengthy report in his hands and took a deep breath. He was convinced the FBI was wrong. He was sure that somewhere in the report lay the key to unlock the killer's warped mind.

Federal Bureau of Investigation
Status Report on Biblical Murders:
For use by approved personnel only:
No duplications:

Fort Ann, New York—January 4, 1986
The body of Kenneth Newell, age fifteen, was found dead sizzling on a gas grill in the

43

Newell's dining room. A small sword with two lions' heads carved into an ivory hilt protruded from the boy's chest. Later that day, the decapitated bodies of his parents, Curt and Evelyn Newell, were found alongside Route 4, north of Fort Ann near Kelsey Pond. The biblical reference below was written in blood on the living-room mirror: "Gen. 22: 6–10." The lengthy biblical quote recounts the sacrifice of Issac on a wooden altar by his father, Abraham.

"67 left" was written at the end of the biblical reference. Significance unknown.

Mount Horeb, Wisconsin—January 20, 1986

The decapitated and dismembered bodies of Geoffrey Ovington and Patrick Sherwood were found in an underground cave near Mount Horeb, Wisconsin, by a friend, Harold Gilcrest. A small sword with two lions' heads carved into an ivory hilt protruded from each man's chest. Mr. Gilcrest suffered a nervous breakdown shortly after the executions and has been unavailable for comment. The three men were college students at the University of Wisconsin in nearby Madison. A message written on the elevator wall read: "Cave of Macpelah." The biblical reference below was written in blood on the cave floor: "2 Sam. 4: 12"—"David gave the order, and his soldiers killed Rechab and Baanah and cut off their hands and feet, which they hung up near the pool in Hebron. They took Ishbosheth's head and buried it in Abner's tomb there in Hebron."

"65 left" was written at the end of the biblical quote. The number is two less than the number left at the Fort Ann, New York, execution site.

Bethel, Maine—February 3, 1986

The bodies of Richard Winslow and Curt

Toomey were found in the lobby of the Livington Museum, 28 Cooper Street, Bethel, Maine. Each man apparently killed the other by sword before they were decapitated by their killer. They were tied by wire to separate chairs so as to remain upright in a sitting position. Each man held the handle of the sword thrust into the other's chest. The swords were old, with two lions' heads carved into an ivory hilt. Both men were seen earlier in the evening dining together at the Snake River Inn and Country Club. Mr. Winslow was an instructor of chemistry at the Madden Academy and Mr. Toomey was a forest ranger with the White Mountain National Forest Service. The biblical reference below was written in blood on the museum wall.

"Leviticus 20: 13"—"If a man has sexual relations with another man, they have done a disgusting thing, and both shall be put to death. They are responsible for their own deaths."

"63 left"—was written at the end of the biblical quote. The number is two less than the number left at the Mount Horeb, Wisconsin, execution site.

Fort Knox, Kentucky—February 17, 1986

The charred remains of two decapitated soldiers were found sitting in General Patton's jeep that is permanently on display at the Patton Museum in Fort Knox, Kentucky. A small sword with two lions' heads carved into an ivory handle protruded from each soldier's chest. Both soldiers were tank trainees at the United States Army Armor School at Fort Knox. They were torched by an army flamethrower that was afterward left outside the United States Gold Depository in Fort Knox. The biblical reference below was written in blood on the jeep's window.

Edward J. Frail

"Leviticus 10: 1–3"—"Nadab and Abidhu, sons of Aaron, were set afire by God for presenting an unholy sacrifice. All who serve me must respect my holiness."

"61 left" was written at the end of the biblical quote. The number is two less than the number left at the Bethel, Maine, execution site.

Barnard, Vermont—March 1, 1986

Lillian and Jill Fowler were found decapitated and mauled by a panther's claw on the gravesite of Elizabeth Dolton in the Barnard Cemetery. Both mother and daughter were killed after finishing work at the Browner Glass Shop in nearby Quechee, Vermont. They were decapitated by a chain saw, and traces of bar oil and blood were splattered over their leather pants and jackets. A small sword with two lions' heads carved into an ivory handle protruded from each woman's chest. The panther's paw used in the killings had been stolen from the State Historical Society Museum in Montpelier, Vermont. The biblical reference below was written in blood on the gravestone of Elizabeth Dolton.

"Deuteronomy 22: 5"—"Women are not to wear men's clothing, and men not to wear women's clothings."

"59 left" was written at the end of the biblical quote. The number is two less than the number left at the Fort Knox, Kentucky, execution site.

Rock Hill, South Carolina—March 11, 1986

The dead bodies of Helen Grossbeck and Joseph Zerilli were found hanging by their feet from the 340-foot tower at the Washington Amusement Park on the North Carolina–South

Carolina border. They were apparently abducted by the killers from an inexpensive motel near the Washington Amusement Park. Both were beheaded by a chain saw and a small sword with two lions' heads carved into an ivory hilt protruded from each of the victims' chests. Helen Grossbeck was married with two children. She lived in nearby Tirzah, South Carolina. The biblical reference below was written in blood on a yellow piece of paper and tied to Zerilli's penis by piano wire.

"Deuteronomy 22: 22"—"If a man is caught having intercourse with another man's wife, both are to be put to death."

"57 left" was written at the end of the biblical quote. The number is two less than the number left at the Barnard, Vermont, execution site.

SUMMARY

After careful analysis of the facts in the case, it is the opinion of this agent and his investigative team that a Middle East terrorist group was responsible for the deaths of the thirteen innocent Americans named above. It has been widely recognized by this agency that terrorism would someday infiltrate our national borders. Unfortunately this day has arrived. Below are the conclusions reached by this agent that give credence to the terrorist theory.

(A) The locations of the executions have direct namesakes in biblical and Middle East history. For example: (1) Bethel, Maine, and Bethlehem, birthplace of Christ. (2) Mount Horeb, Wisconsin, and Mount Horeb in the Sinai, where God appeared to Moses. (3) Fort Ann, New York, and Ann the mother of Mary who gave birth to Christ. (4) The word "Macpelah" written on the elevator wall in Mount Horeb, Wisconsin, is the burial site of Abraham, father of the Jewish nation. (5) Helen Grossbeck, victim of the Rock Hill, South Carolina, murders, lived in Tirzah, South Carolina, and Tirzah was an ancient city in Palestine.

(B) The methods of execution in all thirteen deaths are recreations of ancient Hebrew and Philistine conflicts recorded in the Old Testament. The terrorists even left behind in blood the biblical citation from which they copied their murders.

(C) The Fort Knox executions of two American soldiers clearly illustrates the presence of terrorist activities in America. American military installations and embassies have always been a primary target of terrorists groups in the Middle East.

Sincerely,
Robert Hawkins, Special Agent, FBI

Senacal jammed the report back inside his jacket pocket. He still wasn't satisfied with the FBI's terrorist theory. There were too many questions left unanswered. The numbers followed by the word "left" bothered him. At the Loudonville meeting the FBI had admitted that they had not yet solved the meaning of the expressions "67 left" or "65 left" and so on. The Barnard, Vermont, murders disturbed him too. Why would a terrorist steal a panther's claw from a museum and maul his decapitated victims?

Suddenly, Liz Ruth shoved Senacal's change into her apron pocket and said, "Thanks for the tip, lover boy. If you're getting divorced at seven o'clock, you better move your ass. You're late."

Senacal's soon-to-be-former living room smelled like a church on Easter Sunday. Next to the fireplace, green and red votive candles flickered on a mahogany table before a five-foot statue of the Blessed Virgin crushing the head of Satan with her heel. The statue was Senacal's favorite coatrack; he thought Mary looked good wearing a New York Yankee baseball cap. A framed picture of Donna's mother took center stage on the fireplace mantel. A red cardboard heart of Jesus, wrapped in barbed wire, dangled in the middle of the living room from red crepe paper that swooped across the ceiling from each corner of the room. In front of the fireplace, a velvet confessional kneeler faced the invited guests.

Senacal sat alone on a kitchen chair opposite the Blessed Virgin. Joachim and Kimberly sat on the floor because the room was filled with Donna's friends. They had been invited to participate in the divorce ceremony, or second baptism, as Donna preferred to call it. Everybody was dressed in his Sunday best, except Senacal. He wore red sneakers, blue corduroy pants, and a tan ski jacket.

Donna was attired in a white chiffon dress with a matching veil pinned to her hair by two white pins. Her stockings were white, as were her shoes. She sat in the middle of the sofa flanked by ex-priest Frank Lattimore and Doctor Jules Harrison, her psychiatrist. She was the perfect picture of innocence, like a virgin about to be tossed to the hungry lions of Rome. Bill Johnson, Donna's lawyer, sat near the kitchen tapping his briefcase and checking his watch. Senacal had never met Frank Lattimore, but he had heard Donna speak of him when she and the ex-priest had been outpatients at the Nassau General Mental Health Clinic on Long Island. Lattimore had left the priesthood shortly after the Senacals had moved to Saratoga Springs.

Frank Lattimore was a handsome man in his forties with a tanned, chiseled face. His brown hair was speckled with gray and cut very short. He wore a single-breasted houndstooth sports coat with matching shirt, tie, pocket square, and belt. An expensive rectangular watch, with Roman numerals on the case, was strapped to his left wrist by a gold band. He wore a pair of French calfskin black shoes. Senacal concluded that the silver sports car parked in the driveway belonged to the yuppie ex-priest. He felt compassion for Lattimore. If his stay with Donna was permanent, he was inviting a fate worse than hell itself.

Donna rose from the sofa, blessed herself, and prayed before the statue of the Virgin Mary. Kimberly sighed and buried her face in her hands. After genuflecting before the Virgin, Donna walked to the fireplace mantel, lit a small white candle, and placed it in front of her mother's picture. She turned and knelt down on the velvet kneeler.

"Mother," said Donna with clenched hands, "I'm so happy tonight. I only wish you were here with me as you were at my birth. Yet, you are here spiritually, and that's what counts."

Kimberly inched her way down the hallway toward her room.

"Tonight I'm purging Matthew from my soul. I'm cleansing his sinfulness, his vileness, his indifference, and his insensitivity from me forever."

Senacal crossed his right leg and wiggled his foot up and down. Donna despised his red sneakers more than she hated him as a husband. She knew he wore them to annoy her. She stood up and faced her guests. She told herself not to allow her husband to anger her—not tonight, anyhow. She smiled at Frank Lattimore, then turned to Doctor Harrison.

"I have asked my psychiatrist, Doctor Harrison, to attend my divorce-baptism in order to give some psychological guidelines to the children that God deemed I bear and raise with little help from their biological father." She turned and glared at Senacal.

He rolled his eyes. "Where the hell are the divorce papers? I can't stand looking at you in your first-communion dress."

Donna ignored her husband and motioned for her psychiatrist to speak.

Doctor Harrison, a short, robust man with tiny feet, inched his buttocks to the end of the sofa. He steadied the papers on his lap and was about to speak when Donna plopped down next to him. He lost his balance and toppled backward, his papers falling to the floor. He regrouped and moved forward again while his audience patiently waited.

"I think you need an anchor, Doc," quipped Senacal.

Frank Lattimore sublimated a smile with a phony cough.

Donna patted Doctor Harrison on the back and encouraged him to speak.

"Donna has asked me to attend the divorce ceremony tonight so as to help everyone make the transition to a new life smoother. I'm here to calm the troubled waters of her mind, if I may be so poetic."

Only Donna smiled.

"Donna is a remarkable woman. She has come a long way since we met a year and a half ago. At that time, she was an emotionally battered woman who had been brutalized by the insensitivities of her environment. She had been victimized by the cruelties of those most dear to her. She—"

Senacal had heard enough. "Is he shacking up here with you?" He pointed at Frank Lattimore as he stared at his wife.

"God, you're crass and inhuman." Donna crossed her arms against her chest. "Frank and I have a wonderful relationship."

"I don't care about your sex life; I just want to know if he's living here."

Joachim spoke up. "He took over the two rooms

in the basement, Dad. One's his study with these old maps and skulls and bones around. It's real neat."

Kimberly yelled from her room, "Why can't I have my boyfriend sleep over? She has hers!"

"What's good for the goose is good for the gosling," said Senacal as he wiggled his foot faster.

Donna screamed, "Our relationship is spiritual. We both hate sex."

Joachim asked, "What's a gosling?"

Johnson spoke for the first time. "Is the ceremony over? Can we begin with the legalities of the divorce?"

Slowly, Donna rose to her feet. Her body shook noticeably. Doctor Harrison reached inside his jacket pocket for her pills. She pointed at Senacal. Her voice quivered. "I hate you. I really, really hate you. You are despicable. You are Satan in the flesh. You are hell on earth. You are beyond God's forgiveness."

Senacal beamed a proud smile. He unwrapped a stick of gum and put it into his mouth. Donna sat down and swallowed her pills without water. She hated the sound of gum chewing as much as the sight of her husband's red sneakers.

Senacal looked at Bill Johnson. "Where do I sign?"

"May I say something?" Frank Lattimore paused and rubbed his hands back and forth in a priestly manner. "I may be the cause of this fiasco, simply by being here tonight. I had told Donna I thought her ceremony would be a bit theatrical, but I supported her nonetheless." Lattimore and Donna exchanged quick smiles.

The ex-priest looked at Senacal and said, "I imagine it's difficult for you to accept my living in your home?"

"It's O.K. I was hardly ever here."

Donna's body shook from her husband's remark.

"Let me say something about my decision to leave the priesthood. It was made independently of my spiritual relationship with Donna. I entered the seminary at the tender age of sixteen and followed a very cloistered existence for a number of years. I threw my life into my biblical studies. I attended Catholic University in Washington, D.C., the British School of Archaeology in Iraq, and the Oriental Institute at the University of Chicago, plus a number of summers at Notre Dame University, Fordham University, and so on. Though I became proficient in the fields of biblical history and archaeology, I sublimated my human feelings as a man. I was unhappy and afraid to come to grips with the realities of my celibate life. I—"

"Cave of Macpelah?" asked Senacal. He moved to the edge of his seat and tossed his gum into the fireplace. The look on his face was intense, like a boxer waiting in his corner for the bell to sound.

"Excuse me?" Lattimore queried.

"What is the Cave of Macpelah? Is it important in biblical history?"

"I don't know if it's important or not, but it's the burial cave of Abraham and his wife, Sarah. Genesis makes reference to Abraham purchasing it from Ephron the Hittite for four hundred shekels of silver."

Senacal hadn't questioned a Bible expert since speaking to Sister Angelica on the morning of Ken Newell's murder. Maybe the ex-priest could help him unlock the mysteries of the biblical murders, he thought. It was worth a try.] He continued with his testing of Frank Lattimore's biblical knowledge. "Does a two-foot sword with two lions' heads carved into an ivory hilt ring a bell? Anything significant in biblical history about such a weapon?"

Donna looked at her husband. "Matthew, I never knew you read the Bible! Perhaps there is hope for your immortal soul." Senacal didn't hear her; his attention remained fixed on the ex-priest.

Lattimore asked, "Straight blade or scimitar?"

"Straight."

"Inlaid ivory hilts have been traced back to the tenth century B.C. The lion had particular symbolism in Babylonia. The famous Ishtar Gate of Babylon was adorned with glazed-tile lions through which ran Procession Street to the famous hanging gardens of Nebuchadnezzar and the Temple of Anath. My guess would be that the sword may have had some ceremonial significance."

Senacal's heart beat a little faster; he asked, "Are there any combinations of numbers in the Bible that are preceded by the word 'left?' Maybe, something like '65 left' or '57 left.' "

"Numbers are an interesting aspect of biblical history. The numbers seven, twelve, and forty are popular. Jesus had twelve apostles and there were twelve tribes of Abraham. Jesus fasted forty days and forty nights and He ascended into heaven forty days after His resurrection. But to specifically answer your question about a combination of numbers preceding the word 'left,' I can't. Is it a riddle you're trying to solve? Maybe if you gave me more information, I could help."

Senacal looked at Donna and said, "I'm sorry for tonight. It was dumb. Now, you know why I call myself asshole." She nodded in agreement. He turned to Doctor Harrison. "I think we should have a little rap session before the divorce, Doc. I've got some things I want to say to Donna and the kids. I think we should talk, don't you? The whole family should. How do you say it, Donna?" He snapped his fingers to rush her memory.

"Purge. To purge ourselves. A catharsis."

"Right. We've got to open up our feelings to one another." He motioned Joachim over and put his arm around his son. "Sit! We're going to purge." He yelled, "Tommy's here, Kimberly." Senacal winked at Donna; she blushed.

Kimberly rushed into the living room looking for her boyfriend.

"Come here." Senacal put his arm around his daughter and squeezed her. "Listen, I'm sorry. I tricked you. Sit down. We all have to talk about our feelings. The good psychiatrist here is going to help us purge."

"Daddy!"

Senacal kissed his daughter and said, "Come on, baby. Do it for the old man. I quit smoking for you, didn't I? Don't I go to all your basketball games and watch you shake your buns as a cheerleader? Don't I?"

"You're giving me a guilt trip, Daddy."

"I know." His smile was infectious.

Kimberly sat down on her father's vacated chair.

His forcefulness went unchallenged. With arms flailing and fingers pointing, he directed everybody to a seat. Like a maestro, he stood ready for the curtain to rise and the drama to begin.

"Now, Frank and I are going downstairs to talk about death. Is that O.K. with you, Donna?"

Her head bounced up and down on command. She felt good; her divorce ceremony was going smoothly, though she had hardly expected her husband to play such a vital role in its success.

Finally, Bill Johnson spoke up. "What about me? I've got to wait around here while all you nuts purge yourselves? Come on! Can't you just sign the divorce papers and get on with your miserableness without me?"

Senacal patted him on the back. "Go for a walk. The dogs in the neighborhood are friendly; it's the owners who bite."

Frank Lattimore's cellar study was a museum of ancient artifacts, a mosaic of stone and clay from a time buried in sand. A large colorful map of the Exodus and the Conquest of Canaan covered one entire wall. It was bright and alive with red arrows showing the path of Moses from Egypt, through Marah, Elim, and Mount Horeb in the Sinai, to Canaan on the shores of the Mediterranean. Names like Moab, Edom, and Basham were marked as battlegrounds in Hebrew wars against her enemies.

The room was neat, everything in its proper place and dusted. A glass case of ancient figurines adorned the wall over the desk. Metal shelves flanked each side of the desk holding clay pottery and broken pieces of Assyrian art. The twentieth-century anachronisms—like his electric typewriter, his overhead projector, and a small copying machine—were carefully positioned so as not to disturb the B.C. atmosphere of the room.

"Where are my Grateful Dead posters?" asked Senacal as he stood in the middle of his former den—or penalty box, as he called it, when Donna chased him out of their bedroom for unhusbandlike conduct.

"Kimberly has them. Your children are fond of you."

"Does that surprise you?"

"Quite the contrary."

Senacal walked over to the glass case of figurines over the desk. "What the hell are these little statues? They're all feeling themselves up. One guy's holding his dick. Another's feeling up someone's tits. I'll bet Joachim's down here all the time. What are they? Horny gingerbread cookies?"

Lattimore shook his head in disbelief. "They're teraphims. The people in biblical times used them as good-luck charms. Sometimes women wore them in hopes of becoming pregnant. Some were used in cult practices, like the lewd depictions of Anath."

"You mentioned Anath upstairs. Who was she? Some kind of happy hooker of Jerusalem?"

Lattimore laughed; he had never met anyone as

frank as Matt Senacal. "You could say that. She was the goddess of sex and war to many pagan people." Lattimore paused a second as he watched Senacal continue his inspection around the room.

"You're not at all what I expected. In fact, I'm envious of you."

Senacal tossed the FBI report of the biblical murders on Lattimore's desk. "Envious of me?" He eyed the ex-priest's wardrobe. "Your sports jacket costs more than my whole wardrobe."

Lattimore smiled, picked up the report, and browsed through it for a few seconds.

Senacal sat down on the edge of the desk and asked, "Where did you get your money?"

Lattimore looked up from his reading. "That's not important. My father earned it and I spend it. I wish I had your confidence with people."

"You're still confusing me. I hardly think I'm a person to envy. I'm bald, potbellied, broke, and a cop. That's not what you'd call jealous material."

"But you know who you are. You're yourself. When you walk into a room your body language says, 'Here's Matt Senacal, take me or leave me.'" Lattimore stood up and paced the floor as he spoke. "I've spent all my life acting out parts written for me. 'The son of a bank president is supposed to act this way, Frank. A seminarian is supposed to act this way, Francis. A priest is supposed to act this way, Father Lattimore.'"

Senacal realized that Lattimore, like Donna, was taunted by the deep-seated guilt that feeling human was sinful. He knew Donna was incurable; her only hope was a direct miracle from God. But Senacal sensed there was hope for Lattimore because he was willing and open to talk freely of his feelings. Senacal decided to try to help the ex-priest.

"Have you ever been laid?"

"Excuse me?" Lattimore's cheeks turned bright red.

"Laid. Screwed. Sex. Whatever you call it in the priesthood. Are you a virgin?"

The yuppie priest sat down on a rocker next to his desk. His eyes darted around the room looking for a place to hide. He rubbed his palms in thought, a priestly habit hard to break. After a few seconds of contemplation, he looked at Senacal and said, "Yes."

"No big deal. You've just got to get laid, then you'll be O.K. You'll never get anything from Donna. She's never seen me naked, not that my body is anything to write home about. I'll help you. I know a gal who'd love to screw a wealthy, good-looking, sensitive, forty-five-year-old virgin. In fact, you're in demand. There aren't many with your qualifications looking to get screwed. The fact that you're an ex-priest will make the package even more attractive. But you've got to do me a favor."

Lattimore retrieved a black bottle from his desk drawer. He looked at Senacal and said, "I think a drink is in order to celebrate the end of my virginity."

Senacal squinted at the bottle. "What is it?"

"It's a fine cognac, produced and bottled in France. Would you like a snifter full?"

"You got any beer down here?"

Lattimore went into an adjoining bedroom and returned with a brown bottle of beer. He gave it to Senacal. "It's an import, brewed in Holland and only ninety-six calories."

"You're a pisser for a yuppie priest. I like you. I'm going to call you Virg, for virgin." Senacal picked up the FBI report. "Now, finish reading this and see what you think."

Lattimore sipped his cognac and carefully read the first page of the report. He looked up at Senacal. "I don't know anything about murder."

Senacal moved forward on the edge of his chair. He cupped his beer between his hands and looked hard into Lattimore's eyes. "I'm not asking you to visit the morgue, Virg. There's a weirdo out there who's chopping up people with a sword while reading his Bible. I think the bastard wants to be caught because he leaves behind biblical clues at every murder scene. Now there's some key to unlocking the mystery in this report. I can't find it. Maybe you can. You and this weirdo have one thing in common: you both love the Bible."

"Are you calling me a weirdo?"

"We're all a little weird now and then. But you're O.K., Virg. You'll be even better after a night with Ruthy."

"Who's Ruthy?"

"She's a waitress at Bergman's. A night with her, and you'll need a chisel to take the smile off your face."

Lattimore's cognac circled the rim of his snifter in an endless chase nowhere as he read the murder report. Like the approach of dusk, imperceptibly, his face changed. Furrows grew deeper across his brow with every turning page. His eyes narrowed, his breathing became more irregular. At times he grit his teeth in disgust. Finally, he placed the document down, poured himself another drink, and said, "Have you seen any of these murders?"

"I investigated the Fort Ann murder of Ken Newell."

"How could you?"

"By puking three times on an empty stomach. Now, do you see anything in there connecting the murders?"

Lattimore thumbed through the report one more time as he gathered his thoughts. "The FBI's terrorist theory seems very logical. Their biblical facts and conclusions are impressive too. The Fort Knox murders would certainly give credence to a terrorist theory. But . . ." Lattimore paused as his face twisted in thought.

Senacal touched Lattimore's arm and smiled. "The numbers, right?—'sixty-seven left' and 'sixty-five left' and so on. It bugs you that the FBI skipped right over it. Doesn't it? You know what I think?" Senacal didn't wait for an answer. "I think there's a real sicko out there who gets his jollies playing God, and I want his ass. You study that FBI report and call me when you've got something. Meanwhile I'll work on your coming-out party with Ruthy."

Frank Lattimore grabbed the steel neck of his overhead projector and turned his car into Marion Avenue in Saratoga Springs. His portable movie screen rolled off the back seat of his car, but he didn't hear it crash to the car floor. His thoughts were on his upcoming date with Liz Ruth, Senacal's waitress friend from Bergman's. Sexually speaking, the ex-priest felt woefully inadequate to have a relationship with a woman. It was embarrassing to be a middle-aged virgin. Yet, Senacal was right: he was overdue; his curiosity about sex was killing him. As a priest, he had heard the sin of adultery confessed more than any other broken commandment. And as sorrowful as his parishoners had been for committing it, they kept going back for more. Frank Lattimore just wanted to be like everybody else. He liked Donna Senacal, but he didn't lust for her the way a man looks at a beautiful woman. He thought she had too many personal problems stemming from her childhood. She was a friend who had helped him bridge the gap from the rectory to the secular world. He knew he couldn't hide in her Wilton basement forever.

Lattimore pulled over to the curb and counted the number of stop signs he had passed. Senacal had told him he lived in a garage apartment behind a "pregnant" blue house, three stop signs down Marion Avenue from Union Avenue. He had passed only two so far. He chuckled at Matt Senacal's expression. In essence, the homes on each side of the hilly street were oversized. Only narrow driveways allowed the two-family structures to breathe. Like a rainbow, their colors varied from years of peeling paint.

He parked behind the pregnant blue house. A wooden door, in need of a fresh coat of white paint, led to Senacal's apartment above the garage. A light hung from a rusty bar above the door.

As Lattimore unpacked his car, Senacal yelled from the only window of his garage apartment. "What do you think, Virg? Do you like my place? It's like living on top of the world. I'll give you a hand bringing up all your shit." A blue-and-white sticker on Senacal's window read, BEWARE OF OWNER. Like Job, only Senacal could find peace of mind living on a pile of manure, thought Lattimore. Matt was one of a kind. He cared not what others thought of him and he spoke his mind with little or no invitation.

Senacal's single-room apartment was unfit for human habitation. His bed hadn't seen sheets since the day he signed his lease, and the kitchen sink swelled with stockpiles of dirty dishes. Lattimore was sure the clothes on the floor harbored vermin trapped beneath them. The air smelled worse than a city dump in mid-July. Empty hamburger boxes and cups lay everywhere. A film of dirt covered the window-panes, giving the world a permanent look of gray.

Senacal plopped the overhead projector and movie screen on the sofa and asked, "So what did you find out about the murders?"

"How can you live in such filth?" Lattimore's eyes searched the room for a safe place to sit. Finally, he dusted off a chair with an old sweatshirt he found under the kitchen table. "This place should be condemned and burned to the ground!"

Senacal just smiled and said, "Let's forget the soap commercial and get on with the murder investigation. What did you find out?"

Lattimore ordered the movie screen and overhead

projector to be set up while he reviewed the notes he had taken. Deciphering the FBI report had tested his priestly patience through two weeks of research.

Finally, Lattimore was set. He asked Senacal to sit down and be patient throughout his explanation. Then, the ex-priest carefully draped a large piece of white paper over the movie screen. The paper was marked with six red Xs.

"My overhead projector will flash a map of the eastern United States on the screen. The Xs already on the white paper will line up with the locations of the six murder sites as detailed in the FBI report. Are there any questions before I turn on the projector?"

Senacal felt like a schoolboy. He raised his hand to signal the start of class.

Click. The light from the overhead projector flashed a black-and-white map of the eastern United States on the movie screen. Lattimore approached the screen with a small metal pointer in his hand. His distorted shadow across the ceiling gave the apartment an eerie chill.

"You'll notice that of the six execution sites three are located in the Northeast as signified by this cluster of three Xs—one for New York, another for Vermont, and still another for Maine." Lattimore pointed to each X in the Northeast. "Oddly, the other three executions spread out like a fan from South Carolina, through Kentucky, and up into Wisconsin."

Lattimore paused for a second, then placed his pointer on the X for Fort Ann, New York. "The executions were committed consecutively in a back-and-forth pattern starting here at Fort Ann, New York, then out to Mount Horeb, Wisconsin, back to Bethel, Maine, then out to Fort Knox, Kentucky, back to Barnard, Vermont, then down to Rock Hill, South Carolina. If the pattern holds true, the next murder should take place in the Northeast." As the ex-priest spoke, his pointer danced back and forth across the map from one X to another.

Senacal spoke up. "The FBI made the same analysis at the Loudonville meeting, but the question is where in the New England area will the next murder take place. Do you know?"

"If you let me continue, you'll find it yourself."

"Wait a minute!" Senacal jumped to his feet, his heart pounded inside his chest. "You know where the next murder will take place?"

"Possibly." Lattimore remained calm. "But, please, allow me to continue." He motioned for Senacal to sit down.

Lattimore placed his Bible on Senacal's lap; it was opened to Genesis, Chapter 5.

"We know"—Lattimore raised his finger—"that the killer has more than an average knowledge of the Bible, and I'm sure he wants us to know that fact too. Therefore, I concluded that the order of executions had to have some biblical reference point. It was only an assumption, but I pursued it. So, I scanned the Bible looking for a passage that might suggest a reason for the back-and-forth pattern of the executions. Luckily, I found it in the Book of Genesis." He walked over to Senacal and pointed to a passage in Genesis, Chapter 5. He told Senacal to read it aloud.

"When Seth was 105, he had a son, Enosh and then lived another 807 years. He had other children—"

"Stop," Lattimore ordered. The ex-priest flicked off the overhead projector, turned on the ceiling light, and walked over to the screen. He reached for a wooden yardstick he had brought with him. There were six drilled holes in the yardstick. Each hole was labeled with the initials of one of the execution sites. He faced the screen and spoke with his back to Senacal.

"This is not exactly scientific by any stretch of the imagination, so please bear with me for a while. I do believe that each hole on this yardstick equals the inch-to-mile scale of the map on the overhead projector. Now, how old was Seth when he had a son?"

"A hundred and five years old. Pretty horny guy," mumbled Senacal.

Like a geometry teacher, Lattimore placed the yardstick vertically against the white paper covering the movie screen. He made sure that the bottom of the yardstick rested above the X for Fort Ann. Then he placed a black felt-tip pen into the hole in the yardstick labeled F.A. for Fort Ann. Holding the bottom of the yardstick firmly on the red X, he swung the top end of the yardstick clockwise, making a black curve on the paper.

"I believe he lived another 807 years?" Lattimore asked. He moved his yardstick out to the red X for Mount Horeb, Wisconsin, and readied himself for another geometric exercise.

Senacal said, "That is correct."

Lattimore held the yardstick vertically above the red X for Mount Horeb. Then, he put his felt-tip pen into the hole labeled M.H. for Mount Horeb and swung the top end of the yardstick clockwise, making another black curve on the paper until it intersected the first curve he had drawn for Fort Ann.

Lattimore pointed to the spot where the two curves intersected and said, "Both murders have this spot in common, but only as regards Seth's progeny. I caution you not to draw any absolute conclusions, just yet."

Senacal reached for the projector switch. He was impatient; he wanted to know the location where the lines met.

"No," Lattimore ordered. "Let's finish before we turn on the overhead projector."

Reluctantly, Senacal agreed. He read the genealogy of Seth, the third son of Adam and Eve, as Lattimore drew four other curves across the white paper covering the screen.

"When Enosh was ninety—Bethel, Maine—he had a son Kenan, then he lived another 815 years—Fort Knox. When Kenan was seventy—Barnard—he had a son, Mahalalel, and then lived another 840 years—Rock Hill."

The theory was bizarre—the creation of a cleric locked up too long behind seminary walls. Yet, Senacal knew Frank Lattimore was no madman. A virgin, yes, but not a madman. He knew Lattimore's theory rested on the prediction as to where in the Northeast the next execution would take place. Senacal checked the Bible to see who was next on Seth's progeny. "When Jared was 162, he had a son Enoch." If Lattimore was right, the next execution would take place 162 miles from where the six curves intersected on the white paper.

The yuppie priest flicked on the overhead projector and the map of the eastern United States once again flashed up on the screen.

Senacal strained his eyes to see where all six curves intersected. He yelled out, "They all intersect in northern Vermont!"

Lattimore turned off the projector and gave Senacal a map of northern Vermont. He held a similar map in his own hands. He knelt down next to Senacal and said, "Look to the right of center of coordinates B-3."

Senacal's eyes darted around the edges of the map putting letters and numbers together. Suddenly, his head jerked back and his eyes widened. He checked the coordinates again, then stared at the yuppie priest in bewilderment. "I don't believe it. I really don't believe it. They intersect in Eden, Vermont. There's actually a place called Eden?"

"There are more coincidences. Look northeast of Eden, below the Missisquoi River. What town do you see?"

"Enosburg."

"What's the name of Seth's son? You just read it."

"Holy shit," exclaimed Senacal. "It was Enoch."

"Find Eden again. What's the name of the river flowing through Eden?"

"The Gihon River."

"The Gihon was one of the four rivers that flowed from the Garden of Eden. Also, the Spring Gihon constituted the main water supply to Jerusalem. Now, look northeast of Eden, Vermont—"

"Wait a minute. Time out. I've got to think. Do you want a cognac?"

Lattimore walked over and placed his pointer down on Senacal's dirty kitchen table, then pointed at himself and said, "You bought a bottle of cognac, for me?"

"I was saving it for you and Ruthy to celebrate your deliverance from virginity. I even brought myself a six-pack of imported beer too. Your yuppiness is rubbing off on me, Virg."

Lattimore looked around the filthy room and shook his head. It was difficult for him to imagine Matt Senacal a yuppie.

Senacal returned from the kitchen area with Lattimore's cognac in a juice glass. The ex-priest hoped the glass had been cleaned.

"What you're saying, Virg, is that the numbers in the Bible referring to Seth's genealogy have a direct geographical reference to Eden, Vermont, and the six execution sites?"

"Yes, precisely."

"So using Seth's numbers, Fort Ann, New York, is 105 miles from Eden, Vermont, and Mount Horeb, Wisconsin, is 807 miles from Eden too. Is that correct?"

"As the crow flies. Remember, I used a yardstick and a felt-tip pen in my calculations, but it's close enough." Lattimore helped himself to another drink.

"The theory's a bit whacky," Senacal said, "but you've got my interest. I can see why it took you a couple of weeks to figure it out."

Lattimore sipped his drink and said, "Don't overlook the FBI. They got me started in the right direction."

Senacal flipped on the overhead projector and stared at the map while he rocked back and forth on the rear legs of his chair. "But let's go on. Maybe I can shoot some holes into your theory." He took a swig of beer. "Why did the murderer choose Fort Ann or Mount Horeb, or Bethel, Maine or Barnard, Vermont? I flunked geometry in high school, but I know a circle with a 105-mile radius from Eden, Vermont, goes through a hell of a lot of places besides dinky Fort Ann, New York."

Lattimore picked up his pointer and walked over to the map. "The FBI gave you the correct answer in their report. All the murder sites were chosen because of their proximity to towns, rivers, or cities mentioned in the Bible."

"But what about Barnard, Vermont? There's no Barnard mentioned in the Old Testament, is there?"

Lattimore paced a few steps before answering the question. "I wrestled with that one myself. However, there is a Bethel, Vermont, just a few miles north of Barnard. The killer choose Barnard because he already had a Bethel when he killed in Maine."

"And what about Fort Knox, Kentucky?" asked Senacal.

"The same reason as Barnard, Vermont. A few miles southeast of Fort Knox is Lebanon Junction, Kentucky. I don't think Lebanon needs a biblical introduction."

Senacal took a deep breath and exhaled slowly. The scope and detail of the executions frightened him, as did the image of a murderer who stalked his victims with a Bible in one hand and a road map in the other.

Lattimore turned off the projector, sat down, and sipped his drink. He didn't wait for Senacal's next question.

"You're probably wondering if any other combination of numbers in the Bible are applicable to the theory?"

Senacal smiled. "You're getting to be a good cop, Virg. Are there?"

"No. I doubt it. The census numbers of the twelve tribes of Israel are too large, and Noah's boat dimensions don't fit either."

Senacal stopped rocking on his chair. He tore off a few strips of his soggy beer label, rolled them into a ball, and flicked them indiscriminately into the air. He still missed a cigarette while having a cold beer. He looked at Lattimore and asked, "What about the clues of sixty-seven left, or sixty-five left, or sixty-three left and so on? What about them? Where do they fit into the Eden theory?"

"That's the spooky part. Do you want the long version or the short?"

"The short."

"The Bible recounts the tale of how Cain killed Abel out of jealousy and that the Lord was angry. God placed a curse on Cain and he could no longer farm the soil. The land would never be kind to Cain's descendants. He and his descendants became wanderers. God put a mark on Cain to warn anyone who met him not to kill him or seven men would die. Then, Cain left the Lord's presence and lived in a land called Wandering, which is east of Eden. All of Cain's descendants toiled as miners, toolmakers, and musicians. Kind of modern-day gypsies. They were scorned and pitied. Then Adam and Eve had Seth to replace Abel. God blessed all of Seth's descendants, not Cain's."

Lattimore stood up and paced in silence for a few seconds before he continued. "There are tales of great evil in the Bible. Revenge being, perhaps, the greatest of all evils. Christ, in the New Testament, tried to change this attitude with His gospel of love. 'Turn the other cheek' and so forth." He looked at

Senacal and said, "Pick up the Bible and turn to Genesis, Chapter Four, Verse Seventeen. I want you to read for yourself the motive behind Ken Newell's murder." Lattimore sat down and gulped his cognac as Senacal fumbled for the passage.

Cain and his wife had a son and named him Enoch. Then Cain built a city and named it after his son. Enoch had a son named Irad, who was the father of Mehujael, and Mehujael had a son named Methushael, who was the father of Lamech. Lamech had two wives, Adah and Zillah. Adah gave birth to Jabal, who was the ancestor of those who raise livestock and live in tents. His brother was Jubal, the ancestor of all musicians who play the harp and the flute. Zillah gave birth to Tubal Cain, who made all kinds of tools out of bronze and iron. The sister of Tubal Cain was Naamah. Lamech said to his wives, "Adah and Zillah, listen to me: I have killed a young man because he struck me. If seven lives will be taken to pay for killing Cain, then seventy-seven will be taken if any-one kills me."

Senacal flipped on the overhead projector and stared at Eden, Vermont. He mumbled, " 'Seventy-seven will be taken if anyone kills me.' " He tried to imagine what the murderer looked like. "Who's up there in Vermont playing Cain and Abel?" He thought of the Newell family; they had been numbers seventy, sixty-nine, and sixty-eight of the Curse of Lamech. That meant seven executions had preceded the Fort Ann murders. He turned toward Lattimore and said, "Who's up there?"

The effects of the cognac made Lattimore mellow; he shrugged his shoulders. "Who knows? New England is filled with biblical folklore like witch burnings, harvest moons, and of course, the Great

Awakening with its army of heel-stomping, 'you're all going to hell' ministers. You're the detective, not me. You'll have to go to Eden and find out for yourself."

Senacal walked up to the screen and pointed to Eden, Vermont. "Jared is next on the list and he was 162 years old when he had a son. If your theory's right, the next execution should take place 162 miles from Eden. Right?"

Lattimore was already clearing off a spot on Senacal's messy kitchen table. He spread out a road map of New England. He looked up at the kitchen ceiling and said, "If enough light can pass through that cemetery of dead flies you call a light fixture, you'll see a red circle has been drawn on the map with a radius of 162 miles from Eden."

Lattimore sipped his cognac and gave Senacal a few seconds to study the map. The red circle swung across southern Canada, into New York State past Albany, through Massachusetts north of Boston, out into the Atlantic Ocean, and back through central Maine.

Finally, Lattimore said, "What do you think, Virg? Throw out New York State and Maine because the pattern has been a different state for each execution. I doubt Canada and the Atlantic Ocean unless Noah's Ark is anchored off Portland, Maine. That leaves Massachusetts. Right?"

Lattimore poured himself another cognac.

"You're into that booze pretty good."

"I'll need it to meet your Liz Ruth tomorrow night. The thought of being a forty-five-year-old virgin is enough to drive any man to drink. However, let's find the Eden killer's next port of call. Pick a town along the red line through Massachusetts that has a biblical ring to it. That's what the murderer does."

"I'm not a Bible-reading man."

"You don't have to be with this one. You'll know it when you see it, just like the murderer will."

Senacal read off the towns above and below the red line. "Greenfield . . . Turner Falls . . . Millers Falls . . . Orange . . . Athol." Senacal's heart beat faster and faster. "Leominster . . . Boxboro . . . Billerica. Shit! Tell me what town it is! Maybe, I missed it."

"Patience, my good friend. I guarantee you'll shit when you see it."

Senacal's head popped up. "Virg, your language!"

"Sorry, I'm becoming a product of your environment. Please continue on your red line to Boston."

"Willington . . . Peabody . . ."

Suddenly, Senacal stopped. He took a deep breath. He couldn't believe his eyes. He checked the map again.

"You're shitting me," Senacal exclaimed to Lattimore, who had raised his juice glass of cognac. The red line had passed through Salem, Massachusetts.

"It's strange, isn't it? So very, very strange that the one name most synonymous with the Christian, Jewish, and Muslim faiths is approximately 162 miles from Eden, Vermont. Most authorities believe the etymology of the name 'Salem' is derived from the Hebrew, *shalom*, meaning peace." He paused, then said, "By the way, this Liz Ruth of Bergman's. She won't laugh at my virginity, will she?"

"What the hell does getting screwed have to do with the Curse of Lamech?"

"In a way Senacal, they're quite similar. We're both obsessed with a singular goal. You, with solving a murder. Nothing else matters to you. You're impervious to the filth you live in and you care little about the family that loves you. And I can think only of sex. A thirty-second thrill. Isn't that how long it lasts, Senacal?"

"On a good night, maybe."

Lattimore staggered to his feet and raised his glass. "So, let us drink to Matt Senacal, that he may someday learn how to love. Let us drink to the immortal soul of the innocent victim of Salem, Massachusetts, who possibly, at this very moment, is being stalked by our biblical killer, and there's nothing you nor I can do about it because nobody will believe the theory of a forty-five-year-old virgin. And let us drink to Liz Ruth, that she may be gentle and understanding in guiding me along the yellow brick road to manhood."

4

Salem, Massachusetts

April, 1986

THE 1986 class trip to the Thompson Museum in Salem, Massachusetts, was to be Sally Berthram's last. She was retiring in June from Worthington Elementary in Rochester, New Hampshire. Her January announcement to that fact had been direct, like Sally herself.

1/1/86

Dear "Bored" of Education,
Take this job and shove it. Sally Berthram is hanging up her yardstick in June. If you have a retirement dinner in my honor, send me a doggie bag.

Your best teacher,
Sally Berthram

Sally had never missed a class trip to the Thompson Museum in her twenty-eight-year teaching career. Once no school-bus driver would take her unruly class to Salem. So, Sally tied and gagged the three most troublesome boys to the front seat and drove the bus herself.

Why such an effort? Because Sally wanted her students to learn that Japan and China produced more than televisions, cars, and Ping-Pong players. "A day at the Thompson Museum is a nineteenth-century trip around the world," was her favorite metaphor at fund-raising time. The nineteenth-century mariners of New England had returned from China, Korea, Polynesia, and other exotic ports of trade with textiles, porcelain, weapons, musical instruments, religious artifacts, household items, and so on. "To build a museum filled with the world's treasures" was how the New England master mariners labeled it when the Thompson Museum of Salem was founded in 1823.

Sally Berthram wanted her students to experience life at sea in the eighteenth and nineteenth centuries by walking amid the extensive collections of ship models, paintings, portraits, maritime prints, scrimshaw, and navigational instruments. She wanted them to dream of life aboard the 330-ton *Fallmouth* as they gazed at the ship's eleven-foot replica on display in the main lobby. She wanted them to feel the salt breezes across their faces and the bobbing motion of the ship cresting the ocean swells. She wanted them to tremble during a sea squall and feel the tranquillity of the sea at dusk. Most important, she wanted her students to absorb through the cultural remnants of the museum, the adventuresome nature of these mariners who had sailed in the little known world beyond the Cape of Good Hope and Cape Horn and had returned to New England rich in experience and boastful of places they had traveled that few in America could even imagine.

They had been nineteenth-century astronauts, maurauders of the deep who had lived on the brim of life. Sally envied them. Sailing and adventure were in her bloodline. Her great grandfather was John Berthram, a noteworthy Salem merchant and one of the founders of the Thompson Museum. Sally cursed her century and her sex. She'd give anything for a trip back in time to sail in bloom to lands unknown.

Sally broke with tradition on this, her last class trip to Salem. Usually, a visit to Nathaniel Hawthorne's House of the Seven Gables was the day's first activity, followed by a visit to the Salem Witch Museum. Sally felt the witch trials of 1692 were exaggerated in importance, but she accepted America's thirst for the macabre. It brought added revenue to the Thompson Museum.

"Now, listen, you little shits," Sally yelled from in front of the bus. Her cursing like an old sea captain was tolerated by students and parents alike. Even her pipe-smoking in class was considered commonplace. Sally was an educational legend in Rochester, New Hampshire. She taught math on a Chinese abacus. Reading a sextant and astrolabe was a requirement for promotion to the sixth grade. Often she held classes at night to read the stars.

"I want you to keep your little asses glued to the seats while I go inside the Thompson Museum. It's not open yet, but I've received permission to visit the museum's Jefferson Room, where my great-grandfather's portrait hangs. The exhibit opens in a couple of days. I want a little time alone with him."

She turned and motioned for her chaperon to stand. "This is Ed Flynn." The man had to bend slightly from the waist so as not to butt his bald head on the bus' ceiling. "He's a former student of mine and he's in charge while I'm inside. I kicked his ass many a time when I taught him fifteen years ago. Now, his ass is as hard as his head. Ed's in the blacktop business. He's one of those bare-chested guys you see sneering at passing cars with steam spewing from his tar-crusted body." She walked down the stairs of the bus, paused, and looked back at her frightened class. "I dare any of you to make his day."

Curator Philip Morgan had arranged for Sally's early-morning visit because she had donated her great-grandfather's portrait to the Jefferson Room collection. His letter to Sally had mentioned that a security guard would meet her at the atrium entrance, a glass addition built onto the original museum in 1971. It was 8:35 A.M. The guard was five minutes late; Sally abhorred tardiness. She pounded the atrium door until a security guard appeared with a thermos cup of coffee in one hand and a doughnut in the other. He just stared at Sally for a second, contented to have a double pane of glass separating him from the irate woman dressed in denim on the other side. Reluctantly, he opened the door.

"You're late and you're getting crumbs on the clean tile floor," shouted Sally Berthram as she charged past the stunned security guard. She stopped under the archway leading from the atrium to the museum. She turned to the security guard. "Where the hell is it?"

He knew Sally missed the eleven-foot replica of the *Fallmouth*, one of Salem's famous nineteenth-century tall ships. He took a bite of his doughnut and explained. "It's in the cellar storage, being fixed and painted. You must be Ms. Sally Berthram. Mr. Morgan told me about your arrival this morning. My name's Todd Hutchinson." Some doughnut crumbs bounced off Sally's jacket as he spoke.

"I don't give a good crap who you are. I planned on my students seeing the *Fallmouth* today and I don't like shortchanging my kids."

Todd Hutchinson backed off a few steps for safety.

"Is the Jefferson Room one of the old rooms in the back?" Sally pointed toward the spiral staircase in the rear of the museum.

Hutchinson replied, "Yip. I'll check it out for you first. Then I'll continue on my morning rounds through the Jap and Chink galleries in the new wing of the museum."

Sally pointed her finger directly between his eyes

and said, "Go! I'll find it myself. You're not only stupid, you're a bigot, too. I never want to see you again for the rest of my life."

The museum lacked the warmth of the atrium and smelled like the ocean brine. Sally stopped for a second at the watercolor of the ship *Winnington* approaching Trieste. It stirred dreams of adventure in exotic ports. She had visited the museum many, many times over the years, but she still felt the thrill of that first visit with her grandfather when she was a child. He had filled her heart with a love for the sea, especially the nautical tales of her great-grandfather, John Berthram.

Sally zigzagged down a windowless hallway, around two wooden workhorses, an assortment of lumber, and a package of electrical wire curled up like a snake. To her right was a double door that had been painted white countless times over the last two centuries. She opened the door and squinted from the bright morning sun glistening off the freshly painted white walls. Then, she gagged twice from a putrid odor.

She covered her nose with a tissue and ran to a row of windows along the wall. The first window was jammed. She pounded the lock with the heel of her hand and freed it from its seal of caked paint. She lifted the window and took a breath of fresh air.

The room smelled like a latrine in midsummer. In seconds, the hallway reeked from the stench of urine and feces. Sally looked around the room. The checkerboard ceiling of oak beams showed no damage from a faulty toilet above. The room was immaculate. The schooners and brigantines stood tall in their glass cases. The pictures on the wall hung straight. A glass exhibit, supported by spindly mahogany legs, stood covered by a canvas drop cloth in the rear of the room. It was not an unusual sight for a room under repair.

Drippings, like small red rivers, flowed from letters and numbers written on the wall next to her great-grandfather's portrait. Sally forgot about the odor and approached the bloody message for a closer look. The inscription read, "2 Kings 9: 33–37. 56 left."

She touched the letters. The red liquid was thin and slippery. A chill ran through her body; it was blood.

"Gro-o-wl . . ."

She turned and saw nothing. Everything was still inside the room. She wondered if her ears were playing tricks on her. She looked out the window and saw nothing but a few naked trees. A dory sat peacefully on the floor with its cargo of lobster cages. An ominous quiet filled the room.

"Gro-o-wl . . ."

The sound was more muffled than before, but just as menacing. The glass exhibit covered with the drop cloth moved ever so slightly. Sally walked toward it, careful to be as quiet as possible.

She stopped just inches from the exhibit. The growling ceased, as did the scratching on the glass. Again, silence fell over the room. Small pools of blood dotted the floor under the exhibit.

Sally felt her great-grandfather's presence in the room. She had read of the dangers on the high seas, where retreat was impossible. She couldn't run from the imminent danger before her. She reached forward, grabbed the canvas drop cloth, and lifted it off the exhibit.

The glass exploded on impact from a charging Doberman pinscher. Sally had no time to run. Everything was a blur. The exhibit toppled toward her. Shattered pieces of glass slid across the hardwood floor. She pushed the charging dog to one side as she fell to the ground. She hit her head against the side of the dory just as a heavy object from inside the exhibit fell on her chest. The dog attacked. She closed her eyes and waited in horror for death, but it never came. She could hear the dog tearing at the object on top of her in a blind rage. She could feel the spray of cold blood across her face and the dog's warm breath on her neck. She prayed for the courage to remain perfectly still.

A minute or two passed like eternity. The growling stopped and the dog walked away, his temper and appetite satisfied for the moment. Sally slowly opened her eyes just enough to peek out at the heavy object on her chest. She couldn't see anything, her vision blurred from the blood smeared across her face. "Click, click, click . . ." The dog was near the windows behind her. She blinked a few times to focus better on the object on top of her, then she clenched her fists in fear.

She stared into the gnawed face of a dead girl whose left eye dangled from its socket. The girl's nose was torn from her face and her tongue lay pinched between her teeth. Sally closed her eyes and listened for the dog. She struggled to put the dead girl out of her mind. Whoever she was, she had saved her life; the dog had mistaken her for Sally.

"Click, click, click . . ." The dog was to her right, maybe ten feet away. Sally waited. She tried to see herself aboard the *Fallmouth* as it sailed across the Pacific toward Trieste. "Click, click . . ." The dog headed toward her. She felt its weight on her thighs, then it urinated on her left arm and walked away. Sally struggled to maintain her composure.

She remembered the oars in the dory behind her. Maybe she could use one to fend off the dog while she made her way to the door. She had to try something; she couldn't remain motionless much longer. "Click, click . . ." The dog headed back toward the windows.

She mumbled, "Now, Sally, now."

She tossed off the dead girl and pivoted to her knees. She slipped on the bloody floor and hit her chin on the boat. She noticed the girl's head was half-severed at the neck.

"Click, click, click . . ."

The dog turned toward her and charged. Sally grabbed the oar, but it was bolted into the side of the dory. She pulled on it as hard as she could. "Son of a bitch," she yelled. "Click, click, click . . ." The dog crouched to leap. Instinctively, Sally reached for a lobster cage sitting on the bottom of the boat and held it up in front of her like a shield. The dog slammed into the cage, its snapping jaws just inches from Sally's face. She pushed with all her strength and the dog and cage tumbled into the stern of the boat. Sally ran to the bow and rocked the boat back and forth to keep the dog off-balance.

She had little time to think before the Doberman would attack again. She needed a weapon. The boat had nothing she could use. Her eye caught a light fixture dangling from the ceiling behind the dog. A long screwdriver, left in haste by a electrician anxious for yesterday to end, lay on the exhibit below the light.

Sally stopped rocking the boat and stared at the dog. She wiped away the dead girl's blood from her brow. The beast growled, then it hopped over the first of three seats spanning the width of the dory. Sally began rocking the boat again; she needed time to gather her strength. A lobster trap sat on the floor between the second and third seats. Sally reasoned that the dog would have to get up on the seat to jump over the trap to attack her. At that point, she would have her chance to catch the dog off-balance. She stopped rocking the boat and held the bow of the boat firmly in her hands. The dog looked around the room, then sneered at Sally. It seemed as if it knew her plan. A few seconds passed in a stalemate. Cautiously, the dog hopped up on the seat.

With all her strength she twisted and jerked the boat to one side. The dog was thrown off the seat and slid across the floor, thrashing about in anger. She ran for the screwdriver while keeping a close eye on the dog. "Shit!" In her haste, she knocked the screwdriver off the glass exhibit. Desperately, she fell to her knees to find her weapon.

"Click, click, click . . ." The dog crashed into her back just as her hand reached the screwdriver. Sally gasped for air as the dog's powerful jaws tore into her right shoulder. Her body went limp; she thought she was going to faint. She could feel the dog's teeth sink deeper and deeper into her shoulder. She could feel the animal's hot breath on her neck. She knew in seconds the dog would tear the flesh from her shoulder, then wrap its powerful jaws around her soft neck.

She caught a glimpse of her great-grandfather's portrait on the wall and felt a surge of anger surface through the pain in her body. She reminded herself she was a Berthram, and Berthrams were fighters. She didn't want to die. She asked her great-grandfather for help and struggled to her feet. She knew she couldn't allow the dog to trap her on the floor. She had to get to her feet; it was her only chance. The dog clawed at her back as its feet left the ground. Her denim jacket was torn to shreds as the dog tightened its jaws around Sally's shoulder.

Her left hand reached back and felt for the dog's head, then her fingers searched out its eyes. Sally put her thoughts atop the mast of the *Fallmouth* on a cloudless day. She saw herself looking down on her great-grandfather, who stood proudly behind the wheel, his gray hair blowing in the wind.

The dog squealed as its eyes gushed out of their sockets and blood ran across Sally's back. Its jaws relaxed and Sally pulled the dog forward over her mangled shoulder and fell on top of it while sinking her fingers deeper into the dog's head. She drove the screwdriver up through the dog's chin into its mouth and through its tongue. She pushed up harder as the dog tried desperately to escape. The roof of the dog's mouth cracked; blood streamed from its nose. Sally kept driving the screwdriver further and further up into the dog's skull. She told herself that she was a Berthram and that she had to push harder. She didn't want to die. The dog stopped squirming; she felt the screwdriver pass through her fingers as it continued its path through the top of the Doberman's skull.

Salem Police Chief Stan Houle doodled the face of a dog on his police blotter as he waited for someone to answer the phone in South Glens Falls, New York. Finally, the ringing stopped.

"New York State Police. Officer Madden speaking. May I help you?"

"I'd like to speak to Lieutenant Schiff."

"Who's calling?"

"Tell him it's Salem, Massachusetts, on the line. I've got an answer to the telegram he sent me ten days ago." Stan Houle continued his doodlings while he waited.

"Police Chief Houle?" Schiff asked.

"We had a murder this morning. Kind of gory like you said it would be, so I called," Houle said.

"How many were killed?"

"One."

"Was the expression 'fifty-six left' written in blood on the wall?"

"Yes. How did you know that?"

"Never mind. You wouldn't believe me if I told you. In fact, I just became a believer myself this very moment. You didn't tell the FBI about my telegram, did you?" Schiff asked.

"No. I hate the bastards. Besides, they took over

the investigation and put the clamps on everything. The press wasn't even allowed near the museum. What's going on?"

"I'd rather not say. Was there a biblical reference preceding the expression 'fifty-six left'."

"Yes. How did you know that?"

"What was it?"

"2 Kings 9: 33–37. The passage describes how the Lord ordered dogs to eat up a woman named Jezebel. Is there a religious psycho running loose without a choke collar?"

"You could say that. Was a small sword with two lion's heads carved into it sticking out of the victim's chest?"

"Yes and no," Houle said. "There wasn't much left of the girl to even stick a pin into. But we did find a sword like you described in the room."

"Don't communicate with me over the teletype."

"Why would I want to communicate with you. I don't want the murderer to even know I have your phone number. Listen, this police business is getting to be too much. I've got to find a nice quiet place when I retire in a few years. A place where nothing much happens. What do you think of Vermont, Schiff?"

5

Eden, Vermont

April, 1986

AFTER JUST two weeks with Liz Ruth, Frank Lattimore felt good about his manhood and confident that his future looked bright as an ex-priest in a secular world. Thus, he decided to move out of Donna Senacal's basement and live on his own. Donna had blessed his decision. Their relationship had always been platonic, so Liz Ruth's sudden appearance in Frank Lattimore's life posed no threat to her. In fact, Donna had dreamily told Lattimore of her own recent happiness. On the night of her divorce ceremony, her mother had appeared smiling to her in a dream. It was the first time she had ever seen her mother smile. Donna had awakened convinced it was a sign from God to call off the divorce and stay with Matthew until her death. She was confident she and Matthew could work out their problems.

Senacal was too busy planning his Eden, Vermont, investigation to be impressed with Donna's proclamation. Lieutenant Schiff had shaken hands on an agreement. "It's my show," Senacal had said, "if I tell you where the next execution takes place, no FBI or state-police bullshit in the investigation. We got a deal?"

It had been a gamble for Lieutenant Schiff, who

always played his career close to the vest. If Senacal's plan went awry, his career was finished for violating every investigative rule in the state-police manual; but if Senacal and the ex-priest were right, his career could lead to a commander-major position.

Secretly, Senacal shared some of Schiff's doubts about his plan to trap the biblical killer in Eden. His renegade plan was as novel as the murders themselves. He could be the laughingstock of the department, or worse, be the victim of some grisly biblical sacrifice. He knew he needed Frank Lattimore with him in Eden. The ex-priest's biblical expertise and freedom from department regulation were crucial for a successful investigation. It was the third member of the team that worried him.

At first he thought Graham Twitchell was too old to be part of an undercover scam. Yet, the old man possessed certain qualities that would place him above suspicion. His small-town folksiness would endear him to the people of Eden, and his cantankerous nature was molded perfectly for the part Senacal had planned for him—an eccentric, self-made millionaire looking to invest in Vermont real estate. And then there was the matter of his age. Instead of a liability as he had first thought, Senacal reasoned it was an asset too. Who would suspect Graham Twitchell of being a make-believe undercover cop? Besides, having civilians along kept public bureaucracy from marring things up. Senacal liked operating on the fringes of the system.

From her Fort Ann home, Nel Twitchell yelled a few last-minute orders to her husband as she and Patton approached Senacal's waiting car. Frank Lattimore sat quietly in the back seat studying an old map of Vermont.

"I packed an extra sweater for you, just in case. It's the penguin knit," Nel chimed. "There's one in your suitcase for little Patton, too."

Graham Twitchell ignored his wife and kept walking toward the car. He nervously played with his Boston Red Sox baseball cap.

"I also packed some Kao in case you get the trots. Howdy, Mr. Senacal. Hope you boys catch a lot of fishes. My mother had a wonderful recipe for perches when my father brought some home from Vermont. I lived in Warrensburg until I was three, Mr. Senacal, then we moved to this house when my father went to work for the railroad. Big walleyes he'd catch, too, and pikes. I'll make some when you boys come home."

Twitchell rolled down the car window. "Shut your goddamn mouth!" On cue, Nel turned and headed back into the house. "You got to tell that woman where the dog died. I swear Nel was vaccinated with a victrola needle."

Senacal looked at Twitchell. "The trots?"

The township of Eden lay in Lamoille County, thirty-seven miles northeast of Burlington, Vermont. The 1980 census had counted 610 Eden residents spread out over sixty-six square miles of rugged mountainous terrain. Highways 100 and 118 were the main arteries through Eden. They brought the twentieth century to a people otherwise left isolated on the many dirt roads that knifed through the mountains.

Peckman's General Store stood near the intersection of the two state highways. The two-story blue building with white trim was the hub of Eden's social life. Daily, residents stopped to buy groceries and pick up their mail from the rural post office next door. The only place in town to buy gas was from the two pumps that sat like robots atop a cement island in front of the store. A white church, with a steep roof, was the only building visible from the front of Peckman's General Store. The church was windowless, with a double oak door. A large cross, holding a black figure of Christ, stood on the front lawn next to a sign that read: EDEN—SAINT MICHAEL'S CATHOLIC CHURCH—SUNDAY MASS 9:30 A.M. Only two buildings were visible from the rear of Peckman's General Store. One was a gutted mobile home that had been destroyed by fire, and the other was a stone vault in the Eden Cemetery, where, in winter, the dead waited for the cemetery ground to thaw. A green metal pole, in front of Peckman's General Store, held two signs. The top one read: HILL SLIPPERY WHEN WET. The bottom one read: EDEN TOWN HALL AHEAD.

Matt Senacal pulled his car over to the shoulder of Highway 100 just past Peckman's. His eyes danced across the empty fields of dead grass. He gripped the steering wheel tightly and said, "Is this it? Is this Eden? Did I miss it, Twitchell? I didn't even see a fucking cow for the last fifty miles, for Christ's sake!"

"You won't either. Most farmers keep their herds in the barn until the growing season starts outside. I'd say you'd have to wait about two or three more weeks. I didn't know you liked cows, Senacal. I could arrange for you to do some milking back in Fort Ann. Would you like that?" A twinkle glowed from Twitchell's eye. He pulled on his baseball hat and folded his arms.

Senacal turned and said, "I love you, too."

"Go straight ahead," ordered Lattimore from the rear of the car. He sat amid a library of books and maps about Vermont.

"Why? This goddamn place is no bigger than two sides of the same road sign," remarked Senacal.

"Just do as I say, Senacal. You want to catch your murderer, don't you? Then let's go. At the bottom of this hill, take a left onto Mine Road. I want to check something out."

On the corner of Mine Road and Route 100 stood

the Mount Zion Congregational Church. It was a small church that resembled a cake box with a silver roof and a red belfry. It listed slightly to the left on a row of movable cinderblocks, and its cement staircase was crumbling from neglect. The top section of the handrail attached to the church was missing.

Mine Road twisted through a thick forest tainted mauve with swollen tree buds tasting a hint of spring in the cool Vermont air. It was like riding on the back of a serpent. An occasional dirt path led to trailers of rusted metal surrounded by toppled stacks of firewood and smoky, orange oil drums. A dog or two waved their tails to welcome the intruders. The few inhabitants visible through the naked trees looked pale, like they had just awakened from hibernation with last fall's wardrobe glued to their unwashed limbs. Senacal checked his rearview mirror. He saw nothing but a cloud of dirt from the road's dusty blanket of winter sand.

Frank Lattimore inched forward to the edge of his seat; his eyes searched the treetops. Periodically, he checked a map of northern Vermont that lay stretched across his lap. Finally, he shouted, "That's got to be it. To your left."

"What the hell are we looking for, Virg?" Senacal asked.

"Belvidere Mountain."

The 3,300-foot-high mountain was nearly treeless compared to the smaller rolling pine hills around it. A network of old roads led down from the mountain, like ski trails, to two gray buildings connected by crisscrossing chutes at its base.

On Lattimore's order, Senacal turned onto a gravel road that led to the mountain. A heavy chain carrying a sign crossed the gravel road a few hundred feet from the gray buildings. The sign read, DO NOT ENTER.

Senacal jammed the car into park and wished for a

cigarette. "I've seen more damn signs than people since I've been here. How can I catch a schizo who thinks he's God if I can't find anybody."

Twitchell patted Senacal on the knee. "People are spread out up here. Not like the city where you all shit on top of one another in apartment buildings. My granddaddy use to say, 'If a man can't take a piss in his back yard without his neighbor's wife watching, it ain't home.' "

"I'm almost sure he's here," said Lattimore. "In a way, this mountain fits in with the biblical theme of the murders."

Senacal turned to listen to the ex-priest.

"You see, God told Cain he could never farm the soil again for killing his brother, Abel. If he did, the soil would not produce anything. The Bible mentions that Cain's descendants became miners and toolmakers." Lattimore gazed at the barren mountain. "Asbestos was mined here at one time, and it brought a decent amount of money to Eden. But it's illegal to mine it now. When asbestos particles are inhaled into the lungs, the result is often cancer. The biblical killer would look favorably upon this fact. To him, Belvidere Mountain is a reminder of the curse God put upon Cain's descendants."

While listening to Lattimore, Senacal had watched a red Dodge pickup stop near the entrance to the mine, then speed away after its driver made a quick study of Eden's latest visitors. Senacal was glad the nosy visitor had stopped. At least he was sure there were people living in Eden. He looked at his watch; they were late for their appointment at the Eden Town Hall.

A note tacked to the door of the town clerk's office read:

Dear Mr. Lattimore,
    The copy of Eden's zoning ordinance that you requested is with Mike Derkowski, owner

of Peckman's General Store. He is a member of the Eden Town Council. I also gave him a copy of the town's construction standards too. I thought your client would be interested in having it for future reference. We are pleased with your client's concern for the economic development of Eden. I will be back in my office tomorrow. Please feel free to contact me.

Sincerely,
Hannah Smith

The interior of Peckman's General Store looked more like a trading post than a grocery store. Two deer heads adorned the wall behind a wooden checkout filled with boxes of candy and chewing tobacco. A community bulletin board, cluttered with notices of junk and services to sell, leaned against an old, hand-cranked cash register. The four-aisle store was longer than twice its width. A small butchery, with rolls of cold meats on display, anchored one end of the store, and a frozen-food freezer with sweaty doors the other. The shelves were filled high with foodstuffs, thus giving privacy from nosy onlookers in the next aisle. Three NO SMOKING signs hung from the tiled ceiling.

A voice rang out from the rear of the store. "No dogs in my store!" A young black woman, dressed in a rainbow skirt, white blouse, and bracelets of braided jewelry, charged up the aisle from a back room separated from the store by a white curtain. Her mood was serious. "This is no barn. Out! Out," the woman yelled with arms flailing to scare Patton. Senacal clicked on his small concealed tape recorder and moved aside; Twitchell held his ground. The woman's jet-black hair was tied in a bun behind her head.

"He may defecate in your home, sir," the woman said to Twitchell. "But he will not in my store. Animals belong outside in the yard." Her enunciation was deliberate and her accent hinted a whisper of French. Twitchell remained undaunted.

A thin man wearing jeans and a red T-shirt suddenly appeared from nowhere behind the checkout counter. On his forearm was a heart-shaped tattoo of Cupid sitting on an anchor. The tattoo read: MARIE. The man didn't smile. He sipped a soda and carefully inspected the three men before him.

"Got yourself a spitfire here," Twitchell said to the man. "I like a woman with fire in her eyes. This one's a dandy ya got yourself here."

The woman pointed to the door and shouted. "Mo fine cause!"

Lattimore hadn't expected such a commotion in which to begin his charade. He caught Senacal's eye; the senior investigator nodded for him to begin.

"Mr. Derkowski?"

The man behind the counter slowly turned his head toward Lattimore.

"I'm Frank Lattimore of Federal Realty in Albany, New York. I wrote Hannah Smith earlier this month about our arrival. Today, she left a note at the town hall for us to see you about the zoning information I had requested." Lattimore pointed to Graham Twitchell. "My client is looking to make a substantial investment into the land for sale near Eden Lake. Do you have the information I requested?"

The store filled with silence. Marie Derkowski's finger still pointed to the door and her husband's eyes shifted back and forth between the three men. Senacal fumbled with a row of Life-Savers in a candy display next to the cash register. He tried to recall where he had heard an accent like Marie's. Lattimore was beginning to lose confidence in his acting ability.

Mike Derkowski spoke up. "Who's he?" He nodded in Senacal's direction.

"Nothing but my goddamn lawyer," said Twitchell.

"You can tell by his fancy clothes that I pay him well."

Derkowski chuckled.

To look like a lawyer, Senacal had discarded his sneakers and cords and had brought some new suits under Lattimore's direction. For the trip to Eden, he wore a white herringbone linen suit with a light pink shirt and matching plaid tie and pocket square.

"Out! Out," the woman screamed while staring at Twitchell.

"She your wife?" asked Twitchell as he looked at Derkowski. The storekeeper nodded his head up and down. "Then I'll compromise." He picked up Patton and looked at the woman. "If the dog shits now, then you can throw us both out. I won't mind. I've been crapped on a lot in my life."

Mike Derkowski's icy look melted into a broad smile. Twitchell seized the opportunity and extended his arm and the men shook hands.

"Da conay," said Marie Derkowski as she angrily stormed out of the store.

While the conversation at the checkout centered on condominiums and the history of the deer mounted on the wall, Senacal was curious about the room from where Marie Derkowski had earlier emerged. Her appearance was too impeccable for a woman to have been working in the back room of a grocery store. Senacal passed a few customers in the aisle; he hoped soap was on their shopping lists. He circled the end of the aisle near the white curtain and checked the mirror on the wall to see if Mike Derkowski was watching. The store-owner was busy with Twitchell and Lattimore. Senacal knifed through the curtain.

The back room was filled with bottle cases, broken shopping carts, and cobwebs just as Senacal had thought. There were no doors leading outside the store either. Senacal circled around a large cooler and noticed a small path leading through a stack of empty boxes to a small wooden door. He saw a crack of light appear from under the door. He clicked on his recorder and opened the door.

"A tiny room in the rear of Peckman's General Store is Marie Derkowski's private temple. I'm sure she's a Haitian and a follower of voodooism. Bottles, charms, trinkets, and gourds are hanging from the ceiling. Place smells like a garlic patch. Chalk drawings are sketched on the floor. Four candles light the room. A picture of a snake with large red eyes is hanging on a wall with the words D-a-m-b-a-l-l-a W-e-d-o written above the snake. The word H-o-u-n-f-o-u-r is painted on another wall. Tall drums are in the corner and an altar with eggs, cornmeal, and melons stands in the middle of the room. A red robe and a headpiece, shaped like tin horns, are stuffed into a straw bag on the back of the door. What the hell's a voodooist doing in Eden, Vermont?"

Senacal peeked through the curtain; Derkowski was still talking to Twitchell and Lattimore. He cut through the curtain and headed up the nearest aisle. In his haste, he forgot to turn off his tape recorder.

"Must get cold up on Granite Peak," said a soft voice from behind him.

Senacal turned and stared into the cherub face of a middle-aged woman wearing a red nylon jacket with the words EDEN EMERGENCY SQUAD written over her heart. Her head was crowned with a curly mix of brown and gray hair. She wore a warm smile.

"Are you talking to me?"

"Well, you're the only bald man standing in the aisle," the woman replied.

Senacal smiled and patted his head. He was use to the teasing his baldness inspired.

A beautiful girl in her early twenties walked down the aisle toward Senacal. There was an athletic bounce to her walk. A pair of faded jeans fit tightly over her firm hips. The girl dropped her groceries into the empty shopping cart of the woman talking to Senacal.

"Is he trying to pick you up, Momma?" The young girl eyed Senacal's wardrobe. "You must be one of them hotshot businessmen from Boston." She cocked her head and playfully stared at Senacal. A small queue of blond hair fell across her forehead.

"The name's Mary Kenite," said the older woman, "and this is my daughter, Pleasant."

Senacal extended his hand in friendship. He quickly glanced up at the mirror; Derkowski was still talking to Lattimore and Twitchell.

"My aim's to please. That's why Momma named me Pleasant. Do you think I could please you, Mr. Big City?"

Senacal smiled back at the young woman. He was pleased with the effect his new wardrobe had upon women.

"Don't mind her," said Mary, "you know the saying. 'The sap runs free in the spring.' " She nodded toward the front of the store. "You must be with those two in the front. Are you? I hear they're thinking of buying land for condos near the lake."

A yellow caution light flashed before Senacal's eyes; he suddenly became curious as to why Mary Kenite had stopped to talk to him.

"Who's your informant?" he asked.

"Oh, it's a small town. Word gets around. Besides, I'm the postmistress of Eden and captain of the emergency squad. There isn't much I miss."

Senacal decided to play along with her game. "Well, you're right about them looking into condos. The guy with the dog in his arms and the cow stitched on his back is the one with all the money. His name is Graham Twitchell."

Mary Kenite looked at Senacal. "And you?"

"I'm just his lawyer. I tag along in case there's any legal hang-ups during the land auctions with liens, taxes, warranty deeds, quit claim deeds, memorandums of purchase, and so on. Don't worry. Any unpaid taxes on properties are paid at the closing. That's Twitchell's law." Senacal smiled at Mary and winked at her daughter.

Out of the corner of his eye, he saw a red Dodge pickup stop at the gas pumps outside the store. A young man, dressed like a cowboy with mirror sunglasses, studied Senacal's car as he filled his truck with gas. Senacal started up the aisle toward the checkout counter.

"Where ya stayin'?", asked Pleasant. She toyed with her finger between her teeth.

"At the Ski Top Motel in Morrisville. We'll be around for a few days. We have to have the property in question surveyed and I know Mr. Twitchell wants to talk to some people with the Economic Development Council of Northern Vermont about some other properties for sale."

"I'd stay away from Belvidere Mountain," cautioned Mary Kenite.

"Why?"

"It's a death mountain. Even the Indians feared the gods that lived in the hidden cave at the top."

Senacal arrived at the checkout and tossed a few rolls of peppermint Life-Savers on the counter. Lattimore had told him they were more lawyerlike for an ex-smoker than beef-jerky sticks. The cash register showed a gas purchase of only four dollars from the departed owner of the Dodge pickup.

The three men exited the store.

Frank Lattimore drove the fifteen miles back to the Ski Top Motel in Morrisville while Senacal tape-recorded his thoughts of the first day's investigation.

"Have immigration and naturalization check on Marie Derkowski. I think she's Haitian and smells of money. Also have INS check on other Haitian aliens living in the Eden area. Have Mike Derkowski's navy record checked out. The guy's about thirty-five."

"How did you know he served in the navy?" asked Lattimore.

"The tattoo, Virg. Cupid was sitting on an anchor."

"I knew that," boasted Twitchell from a sleeping posture in the front seat. "Told me he graduated from Cohoes High School in the mid sixties. That's near Albany. A lot of good Catholic Poles in Cohoes."

Senacal shook his head and added Mike Derkowski's biography to the tape.

"Have Alabama license plate number RNQ-348 checked out. It's a red Dodge pickup. Suspect checked us out at Belvidere Mountain, then at Peckman's General Store, where he bought only four dollars' worth of gas. He must be really curious about our arrival.

"Mary Kenite, the postmistress. She came down the aisle with an empty shopping cart. I have a feeling she may have seen me enter the back room of Peckam's. She's probably friendly with Hannah Smith, the absentee town clerk, because she knew we were here to purchase land. Pleasant, her daughter, is a horny young woman who is hot for the new Matt Senacal. Clothes do make the man. Money, too."

"Let me have all your tapes," said Lattimore. "I want to make copies for my own study. Besides, it's good to have duplicates in case . . ."

Lattimore looked up into the rearview mirror; Senacal nodded his approval.

The next day Senacal had Lattimore make an appointment to see Hannah Smith, the Eden town clerk. She hardly looked at Senacal during the meeting in the Eden Town Hall. Her main concern was Twitchell. She told the old man that a survey of the land he considered purchasing had to be filed with the town before either the Zoning Board of Appeals or the Eden Planning Board would consider his applications to develop the Eden Lake property. She also presented Twitchell with a copy of an environmental study made by the State of Vermont as to the presence of asbestos in the town of Eden. She said the report would assure Twitchell that Eden was free of asbestos except in the old mine on Belvidere Mountain. She claimed there was nothing to fear because the mine had been properly sealed off years ago. She assured Twitchell that Eden, Vermont, was as safe as the Eden of Genesis.

Two more days had passed nowhere slowly. Sandwiched between business appointments with local surveyors and the Economic Council of Northern Vermont, three other trips to Peckman's General Store had revealed none of the original cast of suspects from the first visit. A different part-time worker had been minding the store on each visit. Senacal's patience was wearing thin. It was time to tip his hand and offer himself as the carrot to the proverbial rabbit. But where? And to whom?

"Virg, I want you to leave for Saratoga tomorrow morning," ordered Senacal as he studied his tea at the Embers Restaurant. It was not your typical candlelight-and-gardenia-type restaurant, but the food was the best Morrisville had to offer. "We've been here four days already, so it would be expected of you to leave, anyhow. I'll send you any tapes I record—that's if I ever meet anyone to talk to."

"What about Marie Derkowski? Is she legit?" mumbled Twitchell through a mouthful of mashed potatoes.

"Yes. Schiff found out she entered America in 1977 as Mrs. Michael Derkowski. Mike must have met her when he was in the navy. Schiff is still digging to find Derkowski's naval record. He must have had a top-secret classification."

"And the red Dodge pickup?" After asking the question, Twitchell jammed a dinner roll into his open mouth.

"It belongs to a Gil Pixley from Uriah, Alabama."

"Where?" queried Lattimore. His voice was edgy.

"Uriah, Alabama."

The name jarred Lattimore's memory. Father Uriah had been the prefect of St. Steven's Seminary in Baltimore, Maryland, where Frank Lattimore had studied as a young seminarian. The man never smiled. It was rumored that prior to this priestly vocation, Father Uriah had served as a marine drill instructor.

"Uriah was King David's finest soldier," said Frank Lattimore. "David took his wife, Bathsheba, then placed Uriah on the front line in a war and he was killed."

Senacal leaned back in his chair and exhaled slowly. He was getting tired of all the biblical coincidences in the case. He just wanted the investigation to begin. He looked at Lattimore and gave another order. "Before you leave tomorrow, check out all the car dealers in the area and see if they have a red Dodge pickup for sale. I've noticed Pixley following us a few times. If he thinks I've seen him, he'll unload it for another car. See what you can find. There can't be that many dealerships around here."

Twitchell slurped his coffee and said, "Probably shook her tits up and down and King David wrenched his neck. Damn women. They break up a lot of good friendships between men. I had this buddy named Watson years ago. A real pisser. Drink like a fish. We'd go hunting in the mountains and get so drunk we'd forget about the deer. Nel didn't like his wife. Bitch, bitch, and bitch! That's all she'd do about Watson. Poor bastard dropped dead one day and Nel jumped for joy."

Senacal seized the moment. "Did Nel shake her tits up and down for Petteys?"

"Shit! Wouldn't that be funny? But I doubt it. Nel's tits just hang like balloons down around her hips. They haven't moved in years, and I doubt they ever will."

Twitchell left the restaurant and headed across the parking lot to the Ski Top Motel. He had to take Patton for his nightly walk. It was nine P.M.

Lattimore had never witnessed anyone consume as much food in one meal as Graham Twitchell. The man ate with the speed of a vacuum cleaner and seemed annoyed to have to breathe between swallows. He liked Twitchell, but found irritating the old man's habit of snorting and flicking his nose with his hand at the same time. He put Twitchell out of his mind and concentrated his attention on Senacal.

"Being with you the last few days has helped me understand your feelings better."

The statement surprised Senacal. He stirred his tea as he spoke. "What feelings? Cops don't have time for them."

"That's precisely my point. I never realized being a cop was so mentally exhausting. There's little time for yourself. I can see why it's impossible to punch a time clock at five P.M. and leave your thoughts and fears at the police station."

Lattimore was different than most men; he cared about people's feelings.

"Thanks, Virg. Murderers don't take holidays."

"But you should. You're too involved in your work. No man is an island, Senacal. What I mean is, you've built a stone wall around your feelings and you don't allow anyone in. And those who try, like Donna, you scare off with your sarcasm. If you don't change, you'll die a lonely man. What good is it being a famous detective if you don't have anyone to share it with? I admire your self-confidence, but I abhor the insensitivity you show toward those who love you."

Senacal said nothing. He knew he was a workaholic, but it was still bitter to be reminded of the fact. He really didn't want to pursue the subject any further.

Lattimore shifted the direction of the conversation. "I want to thank you for introducing me to Liz Ruth. I think we have a wholesome relationship. She's sensitive and gentle. I owe you for that."

Senacal's flippancy surfaced. "Go slow, Virg. She's your first lay, and most guys remember their first and forget their last. Your life as a priest will seem like a honeymoon compared to a marriage with the wrong woman. Don't put your personal life with Ruthie ahead of the investigation up here. You're my link with the outside world in Saratoga. I don't want you screwing up. I have to be sure we're both singing from the same hymnal because it's just Twitchell and I up here. I need your undivided attention."

Lattimore squeezed his cup of coffee. "There you go again. Don't you see? It's possible to be a good cop and be a sensitive and caring human being at the same time. Why do you fight it so much?"

Silence fell over the table. Both men searched the restaurant for a place to hide. Senacal desperately wanted a cigarette. Meanwhile, Lattimore reminded himself that he was no longer a priest and that free advice best be left behind in the rectory. He turned the conversation back to the investigation.

"Watch out for Marie Derkowski, she's very dangerous."

Senacal relaxed. He said, "Because she's into voodooism?"

"She's more than that, Matt. You said in your tape that a straw bag on the door of Marie's temple contained a red robe and headpiece in the shape of tin horns. Is that correct?"

Senacal nodded. The waitress came over and refilled Lattimore's coffeecup; he waited until she had left before he continued.

"I made a copy of your last tape today. The one describing Marie Derkowski's temple. I wanted to know more about the meaning of the headpiece with the tin horns, so I called a priest friend of mine in Bayonne, New Jersey. He had been a missionary in Haiti for many years. He told me Marie's a member of the Sect Rouge, the most feared sect of voodooism in Haiti. They meet only at rural crossroads and grab an unsuspecting victim who happens to pass by. They dress in red robes and wear headpieces in the shape of tin horns. They take their prisoner to a secluded spot, where secret incantations are spoken over him. The members of the Sect Rouge believe these words turn the victim into a beast. He is then carved into several pieces and his blood and flesh are consumed by the members of the sect."

After Lattimore had left, Senacal sat alone at the table nursing his warm cup of tea. He admitted to himself that the ex-priest was right: he was a cynic who enjoyed a good laugh at another's expense, especially Donna's. He did put up walls around his private world. He had been close to Kimberly, but that had begun to fade with the arrival of her first boyfriend. He had little patience with a moody teenage daughter. Or, maybe, that was just his excuse for not getting involved. He respected Lattimore's courage to be honest with him.

A large banquet room used for wedding receptions and meetings adjoined the restaurant with its own outside entrance. However, a knotty-pine hallway inside was used by the occupants of both rooms as a common avenue to the bathrooms. From Senacal's seat in the restaurant, he saw a restroom sign over a door near the bar. He felt a bathroom visit and a cold beer were in order before heading over to his motel room. He left a generous tip, which was his custom with Lieutenant Schiff's money, and headed down the knotty-pine hallway to the men's room.

Suddenly, the hallway came alive with the Word of God.

"I will perform miracles in the sky above and wonders on the earth below. There will be blood, fire, and thick smoke. The sun will be darkened and the moon will turn red as blood."

The woman's voice came from the banquet room; Senacal put his ear to the wall and listened.

"Praise the Lord," chanted a crowd of disciples.

The woman continued her sermon in a loud evangelical voice. "Peter spoke those words of the Prophet Joel after the Lord entered him from the tongue of fire above his head. He was happy and spoke in many languages. Your Pentecost is at hand, my fellow sisters."

The female voices chanted again, "Praise the Lord."

The preacher shouted, "Who will be first to receive the Holy Spirit?"

A few seconds of silence followed a loud applause. Senacal could hear some women encouraging someone to stand up.

"Come, child. Don't be shy. Luke, Chapter nineteen, Verse forty, says that Jesus answered the Pharisees. 'I tell you that if my disciples keep quiet in praising the Lord, the stones themselves will start shouting.' Sing out the praises of the Lord. Come, child. Jesus will heal."

A loud hand-clapping accompanied an electric organ playing the hymn "Lean on Me."

Senacal's mouth went dry as the hallway filled with the fear of God. A picture of Ken Newell's body sizzling on a gas grill in Fort Ann, New York, flashed before his eyes. He took a deep breath to relax. He was confident somebody in the next room had to know about the Curse of Lamech.

Like a thief in the night, he opened the hallway door leading into the banquet room. He had hoped his entrance would go unnoticed, but instead, he heard the rustling noise of people turning in their seats. He looked up and caught the cold stare of a woman dressed in a red robe. Her arms were out-stretched and her long fingers pointed to heaven.

The Reverend Leisa Dawkins was the pastor of the Mount Zion Congregational Church of Eden, and her message from the pulpit every Sunday morning was the same: women had played a greater role in the life of Christ than men.

"Who stood below the cross of Christ? His mother and Mary Magdalene did. Where were his male disciples save John? Scared and hiding, afraid of what the Romans might do. Who broke through the Roman guards and comforted the Lord? A woman. Veronica was her name. Did Simon of Cyrene want to help Jesus carry his cross? No, Luke tells us, 'They seized him and made him carry it behind Jesus.' And who went to anoint Christ's body on Easter Sunday? Who was not afraid of the Roman guards? Three women: Mary Magdalene, Mary, the mother of James, and Salome. Where were the men? Hiding in fear."

Reverend Dawkins lowered her arms and spoke to Senacal. "Come in. The Lord's here for everybody."

Senacal rubbed his chin and shifted his weight from foot to foot. Most of the fifty or so worshipers were women with silver hair and big pocketbooks tucked safely at their feet. The few men present stood next to invalids in wheelchairs. In the middle of the banquet room, a cross, with a red robe drooped around the crossbar, stood behind an altar covered with white linen. Written on the altar cloth were the words LUMEN CHRISTI.

Leisa Dawkins responded to Senacal's hesitancy. "We have a doubting Thomas in our midst, sisters. He must place his hand in the wounds of Jesus to believe."

The women chanted, "Praise the Lord."

Embarrassed, Senacal sat down on a folding chair

in the last row facing the altar. Gradually, the congregations' attention drifted back to Leisa Dawkins at the altar. Senacal spotted Marie Derkowski, the Eden vodooist, sitting alone at the end of a row in front of him.

Leisa Dawkins looked more like a devil than a saint. A thick coat of blue eyeliner surrounded her eyes. Her long brown hair was streaked gray and her fingernails were painted white. She looked like a nightmare incarnate, Senacal thought.

A woman in tattered polyester, who had been standing in the aisle when Senacal entered the banquet room, walked slowly toward the altar.

"Speak, my child," Leisa Dawkins commanded the distraught woman before her. "All here are one in mind and heart, like the early Christians after they were filled with the Holy Spirit." Leisa Dawkins' voice was powerful; it stirred the crowd's enthusiasm and they began to mumble short prayers under their breath. She nodded toward the organist, a hulking young man with straight blond hair. There was no life in his eyes. He stared at Senacal as his beefy fingers played the old spiritual "Amazing Grace."

Gently, Reverend Dawkins placed her hands on the young woman's shoulders, then turned her around to face the congregation. The woman looked scared. She was short and her greasy hair was pulled back into a ponytail with a red rubber band. She twisted a dirty handkerchief around her fingers. Reverend Dawkins placed a white satin choir robe over her shoulders. The young woman cried. Senacal caught Mary Kenite, the Eden postmistress, smiling at him. She was sitting next to Hannah Smith, the Eden town clerk. Senacal coughed politely and clicked on his tape recorder.

Reverend Dawkins said softly, "Speak, my child. God is with you."

Struggling to keep back her tears, the young woman

said, "I married Sonny really young 'cuz we had to." Her voice trembled. Senacal noticed she had no front teeth. "We don't have nothin', so Sonny drinks a lot. And when's he drinks, he beats me real bad."

The women in the audience sang a verse of "Amazing Grace." "I once was lost, but now am found. Was blind, but now I see."

The woman struggled to continue; her voice cracked as she spoke. "I'd drink with Sonny 'cuz it wouldn't hurt. We'd drink and get so drunk I'd forget the kids. One day . . ."

"A-maz-ing Grace how sweet the sound. That saved and set me free!"

". . . Amy, she's my fourth child, opened the wood stove and her dress caught on fire." The woman broke down and wept.

Reverend Dawkins stretched out her hands over the weeping woman as two men ran to assist. Reverend Dawkins encouraged the suffering woman. "Say it, child. Release the sorrow in your heart. God will forgive."

"I couldn't reach Amy. I was drunk. I tripped over somethin'. Amy ran out the trailer and burned to death in the shed."

" 'Twas grace that taught my heart to fear, and grace my fears relieved." The singing grew louder. Some women in the crowd stood up and clapped their hands. Others locked arms and swayed to the beat of the hymn.

Senacal walked to the back wall and looked around. Marie Derkowski had left the room.

Reverend Dawkins closed her eyes and held her arms steadily over the crying woman. "The Lord's directing me to speak to this poor soul. I see the words of Luke, Acts four: twenty-nine. 'And now, Lord, take notice of the threats they have made, and allow us, your servants to speak your message with all boldness. Reach out your hand to heal.' "

With her eyes closed, Reverend Dawkins slowly raised her arms high into the air. The anxiety etched on the young woman's face began to dissipate, her body relaxed. The men on each side of her moved closer. Reverend Dawkins opened her eyes and moved her head in circles to draw the attention of her disciples. She shouted, "Grant that wonders and miracles may be performed through the name of your Holy Servant Jesus."

Swiftly, Leisa Dawkins dropped her arms and firmly placed her hands on the young woman's head. Like a cut tree, the young woman toppled backward unconsciously into the arms of the ushers.

The audience went hysterical. They joined hands and sang and embraced one another. The music was loud and still playing "Amazing Grace." Reverend Dawkins shouted about the crowd as the unconscious woman was carried away. "So I came to you full of joy, for it was God's will, and we enjoyed a refreshing visit with him."

Everybody applauded.

A sweet old woman, adorned with pearls and diamonds, looked up at Senacal. "Let it be said of the early Christians, see how they love one another." She kissed him and continued on her merry way.

Senacal shook his head in disbelief.

A wicker basket preceded the coffee and cookies. Senacal dropped a hundred-dollar bill into the basket.

"We have a Barnabas, sisters. We have a Barnabas in our midst," shouted the woman holding the basket. A few women came over and kissed Senacal. He knew his donation would draw the Reverend Dawkins to his side. He didn't care, it was Schiff's money anyhow.

"You're lucky she didn't say you were Ananias," said Leisa Dawkins from behind him.

Senacal turned. Up close, she was more frightful than from afar. Senacal paid her little attention.

"Who's Ananias?" he asked as he grabbed a cookie off a passing tray.

"He's an early Christian who deceived God and kept money from the sale of his land. The money was to be handed over to the church. He was struck dead by God before Saint Peter."

"Why? It was his money, not God's. Are you hoping these old ladies will hand over their purses to you in God's name? What's your take on a night like this?" He figured Leisa Dawkins was his best suspect since arriving in Eden. He would push her to the limit. "There is something I don't understand about you people. You claim to be all loving, yet your Bible is filled with killing and violence. Why does God allow people like Ananias to be so brutally killed?"

"You're not curious about Barnabas?"

Senacal smiled. "He was probably the good guy who dropped a fifty in Peter's basket. Religion is like most things. It's a con to make a buck."

He waited for her anger to surface, but she remained calm. The grin on her face widened into a warm smile. Her reaction surprised him.

"Would God approve of your scam tonight?" Senacal pointed to the woman who had fainted.

Leisa Dawkins' look became serious. "Why are you here?"

Finally he sensed a tone of anger in her voice. He said, "Like Pandora, I was curious and opened the wrong door."

Suddenly, he felt the presence of someone standing behind him. He turned. It was Mary Kenite and Hannah Smith.

"Thank you for your contribution tonight," said Mary Kenite politely. She bowed her head. "We call ourselves Lumen Christi—the Light of Christ."

Senacal looked over at the altar cloth.

Hannah Smith asked, "Are you a follower of Jesus?" The town clerk stood erect like a statue; only her eyes moved.

"Hardly," commented Reverend Dawkins. "I'm afraid our friend's contribution tonight is stained with the blood of Judas. He is not a believer of the Lord. But neither was Saul until the power of Jesus threw him off his horse."

"Don't judge me so quickly," said Senacal. He reached for another cookie.

"True words of a lawyer," said Mary Kenite.

"You're a lawyer?" Reverend Dawkins' question was followed by a smile. "My church in Eden is in need of one. Are you for hire? And by the way, what is your name?"

"Matt Senacal."

Mary Kenite spoke up. "Is the middle vowel of your name spelled with an e or an a, Mr. Senacal?"

Senacal thought for a second. "An a. It's S-e-n-a-c-a-l."

Hannah Smith asked, "What law school did you attend?"

Senacal knew Hannah Smith was testing him. "Fordham Law School, at night. I did it the hard way." He shifted his attention back to Leisa Dawkins.

"Why do you need a lawyer?"

"Something about a road easement on the corner of Mine Road and Route 100. The state is claiming that I must remove part of the church's cement stairway from the curb because they want to widen the road. I don't know what it's all about," she said, tossing her hands up in disgust.

"I'll take a look at your papers if you'd like." He smiled and raised a finger. "But I'd like an answer to my original question: why is the God in your Bible so vengeful? Why does He allow such brutal killings to take place in His name?"

Mary Kenite jumped at the opportunity to answer the question. "Times were violent in the Old Testament. There was always war. But God promised His Son to show a new way. The New Testament is a message of love. Christ said, 'Turn the other cheek.' I think God only tolerated the violence in the Old Testament."

Even Hannah Smith managed a slight grin of approval at her friend's answer.

The burly organist approached and stood next to Leisa Dawkins. His look was strange and his eyes cold. A chill ran through Senacal. A blue prayer book with a picture of Christ on the front cover was jammed into his shirt pocket. His head leaned slightly to the right and down; he said nothing. Reverend Dawkins reached out and grabbed the man's hand.

"This is my son, Mr. Senacal. His name is Tertius. Well, not really." She smiled at her son, but he showed no emotion. "My husband and I named him Jared at birth, but after the divorce, I named him Tertius."

Senacal forced a smile and extended his hand. He recalled that Jared was 162 years old when he had his son, Enoch, and that Eden was 162 miles from Salem, Massachusetts. Slowly and with his mother's prodding, Tertius shook Senacal's hand. His grip was like a vise.

"Do you know who Tertius was, Mr. Senacal?"

"Is this another biblical quiz?"

Reverend Dawkins laughed. "Tertius was the author of Paul's letter to the Romans. He wrote of the good news promised long ago by God through His prophets as written in the Holy Scriptures." She pinched her son's cheek. "He's my good news and salvation. So I call him Tertius."

Her son remained comatose on his feet.

Senacal decided he had seen enough. He checked his watch, then looked at Leisa Dawkins. "I'll be leaving Eden in a day or two with my client, Mr. Twitchell. If you want my help, it better be tomorrow."

"Fine. What time would be convenient?"

"Say ten o'clock in the morning?"

"Ten it is. Tertius and I will be waiting."

The cool night air felt good to Senacal as he walked across the parking lot toward the Ski Top Motel. He clicked on his recorder and taped his impressions of the Lumen Christi meeting.

"If Reverend Dawkins doesn't know about the Curse of Lamech, then nobody in Eden does. Tertius is a real wacko, if I ever met one. He's strong enough to break a man in two. Now, Hannah Smith! She's a clever bitch, and smart too. She should have known about the road easement case against the Congregational church. She probably has the deeds and survey in the town records too. Why didn't she speak up about it? She hardly took her eyes off me tonight, yet she ignored me like the plague in her office the other day. At least I know she and Mary Kenite are buddies. They must compare notes at night. That leaves Marie Derkowski, the voodooist. Where did she go? Why was she there? I could tell she wasn't caught up in the service. I don't think Lumen Christi and voodooism jibe. But that still leaves me with nothing. I better speak to Mike Derkowski. He's an arrogant bastard, but he may give me some answers about his wife, Marie. Check with Schiff again on Derkowski's naval record, especially . . ."

In one quick movement, Senacal clicked off the recorder and pulled out his gun. He pressed his back against the wall of the motel. The door to his room was ajar; he heard nothing inside. Matt Senacal always locked doors; it had been part of life growing up in the Bronx. There was a key to enter his parents' apartment building, a key to open the mailbox, and two keys to enter their apartment. Doors were never left unlocked in Senacal's world.

He listened. Nothing but stillness. He kicked open the door and waited. He reached in and turned on the light. The room was in total chaos. Sheets, dresser drawers, clothes, pillows, and so forth were scattered everywhere. He checked out the bathroom: it was empty.

"The tapes." He hopped over the junk on the floor and ran to the nightstand between the double beds. They were gone. His life was in danger, as were Lattimore's and Twitchell's. He imagined Tertius and his mother sitting around the kitchen table laughing at his description of Ken Newell's murder. Luckily, Frank Lattimore had insisted on making copies of the tapes. There was no point in calling the sheriff's department. He didn't want to reveal his true identity. He went to his car for a flashlight.

He shook out the sheets and bedspreads, then rolled them up into a ball on one of the beds. He placed an old newspaper over the lamp near the window. He wanted just a dull light in the room while he searched for clues. He dropped to his knees with his flashlight.

From ground level, a beacon of light from his flashlight stretched across the top of the carpet. Carefully, from his knees, Senacal followed the light's path across the top of the carpet fibers. He noticed a shadow from a hairpin, then a toothpick. The toothpick was old and dry. He continued his search at carpet level. He noticed some ants hiking up and down the carpet fibers. He inched forward on his knees, constantly following the light over the top of the carpet. A pillow feather—some thread—a paper clip. Just as his neck began to hurt, his light bounced off a bright object partially hidden behind the front bed wheel near the wall. Senacal stood up and walked over to the front of the bed. He smiled as he picked up a pair of mirror sunglasses, the same kind worn by Gil Pixley, the owner of the red Dodge pickup.

The next morning, Senacal told Lattimore that he

would handle the search for Gil Pixley's truck and that the ex-priest should leave immediately for Saratoga Springs. He told neither Lattimore nor Twitchell about the burglary last night.

There were four used-car dealerships listed in the yellow pages of the Morrisville, Vermont, phone directory. On the fourth phone call, Senacal found a dealer on Nelson Avenue that had a Dodge pickup for sale. The salesman told Senacal that the truck was in excellent condition and that the price was right. Senacal insisted that the truck had to be rust-free and that he preferred vehicles formerly registered in the South, where the winters were mild and the roads salt-free. The salesman told Senacal he was in luck. The red truck for sale had been formerly registered to a man from Alabama. Senacal smiled to himself, thanked the salesman, and lied when he said he'd drop by later in the day to look at the truck. He hung up the phone and looked at his watch: he had a half-hour to get ready for his appointment with the Reverend Leisa Dawkins. Senacal felt the investigation was finally making headway. He sensed Lady Luck was on his side today.

Leisa Dawkins and Tertius were waiting for Senacal and Twitchell at the entrance to the Mount Zion Congregational Church. Seeing her out of a robe, Senacal couldn't help but notice that what Leisa Dawkins lacked in facial beauty was more than compensated for by a magnificent body. She wore a white blouse and a black skirt. A gold cross with a wine-and-grape motif rested comfortably on her buxom chest. Tertius wore the same clothes as last night, blue prayer book included. A chill ran through Senacal when Tertius' powerful hand engulfed his in a handshake. The large young man appeared to possess both the strength and the personality to perform any one of the thirteen biblical executions. For a brief second a picture of Tertius laying Ken Newell's headless body on the gas grill in Evelyn Newell's living room flashed before his eyes.

After the introductions, Leisa Dawkins nodded for her son to speak.

"The Reverend William McKenzie was the first pastor of the Mount Zion Congregationalist Church, who commenced his labors on April 16, 1823, and was dismissed from his charges on August 19, 1825. The original congregation numbered fifty-two. If you'd follow me, I'd be glad to start the tour inside." The boy drawled his rehearsed words like an old phonograph record.

Like a robot, Tertius turned and opened the front door of the church and held it for his mother and her guests. Leisa Dawkins smiled approvingly as she passed her son. His face remained expressionless.

"Nice speech, son," Graham Twitchell said. He patted the young man on the shoulder as he entered the church. "Smile a bit. It don't hurt. A guide's got to smile and relax the tourists."

Slowly, Tertius' black eyes rose to greet Twitchell.

"You may begin, Tertius," said Reverend Dawkins. She took her son's hand and squeezed it.

The short tour of the church was show-and-tell time for Tertius. Senacal was surprised at the clarity, if not the stiffness of his speech. The boy had obviously been well disciplined. Senacal also sensed Leisa Dawkins' flirtations. When their eyes met, she smiled like a schoolgirl and on one occasion gently brushed her large breasts against his arm.

Leisa Dawkins' office was in the rear of the church. It was small and cluttered with an oak desk, a gray filing cabinet, and two folding chairs. On the wall hung pictures of former pastors and town fathers. Senacal's attention was drawn to a saying framed in glass and hanging directly behind the oak desk. It read: "No great ambition to depart from their old customs, nor a great desire for reforms." Reverend Dawkins sat down at her desk.

"That was a mighty fine tour, Ter . . . Tis . . ." Twitchell stammered over the pronunciation of Tertius. He looked at Reverend Dawkins. "Why didn't you call him John or Peter? Something simple."

Leisa Dawkins smiled. "He was baptized Jared, but he's called Tertius now."

"I knew a Jared," said Twitchell as he gazed at the ceiling in thought. "Jared Fairbanks of Victory Mills. That's a small village south of Fort Ann. Jared used to run a flea market on the weekends. Had about twenty vendors there in the park near the firehouse. Sold stuff most people trip over in their basements. Tried to sell my wife, Nel, there one day, but nobody wanted her."

Leisa Dawkins took a deep breath to suppress her anger. Like a judge, she sat ready to condemn Graham Twitchell. She pointed to the sign above her desk. "Read it," she ordered. A few seconds passed, then she lectured the old man.

"Lydia Howland of Eden wrote that of the men of Eden in the nineteenth century. She was the town historian and a participant at the Seneca Falls Convention in New York in 1848. She was involved in the drafting of the famous Declaration of Sentiments, which in the spirit of the Declaration of Independence declared that 'All men and women are created equal.' If I were your wife, God forbid, and I heard your remark about selling me at a flea market, I'd have slapped your face until it bled profusely."

Senacal watched Tertius move in behind Twitchell while the young man's eyes remained fixed on his mother's irate face. Senacal's eyes darted back and forth between Leisa Dawkins and her son, worried that any second the boy would lash out. Senacal cursed his judgment in allowing Graham Twitchell to be part of the undercover operation.

Suddenly, Twitchell raised his hands and stood up. The old man was unaware that Tertius stood just inches behind him. "I apologize. I know I can be a crusty old fool sometimes." He switched his attention to Senacal. "I'm going to walk over and take a stroll around the property for sale near Eden Lake. I'll be waiting for you in the car. Know you have some legal matters to discuss, anyhow." He apologized again to Reverend Dawkins, turned, and bumped into Tertius.

The young man's eyes were still fixed on his mother. Leisa Dawkins nodded and her son moved aside to allow Twitchell to exit.

Leisa Dawkins sensed Senacal's discomfort in the presence of Tertius. She pointed her finger and ordered her son into the church. He obeyed on command like a dog his master. Senacal cleared his throat loudly as he reached inside his pocket and clicked on his tape recorder.

"Tertius is really quite harmless but you're not the only person he frightens," said Reverend Dawkins. "Yet, despite his outward manners, he has an active mind considering what he experienced one evening when he was a child of ten." Leisa Dawkins stared at Senacal for a few seconds before she continued.

"That night my husband gagged Tertius and tied him to my bedpost as he raped me in a drunken rage. Tertius stood within inches of my face. I looked into my son's eyes as I was abused and saw the spirit of life leave him, forever. As you see him today, is how he's been since that horrible evening."

Senacal struggled with his urge to run. "I'm sorry," he said. His mouth turned cottony dry.

"You're sensitive, Mr. Senacal, unlike most men. I'll show you all the church's legal papers and then maybe you can help me as you promised last night."

As Leisa Dawkins rummaged through a very messy desk drawer filled with papers, pens, and paper clips, Senacal noticed a road map being tossed about. He recalled Lattimore's description of the biblical killer as a person with a Bible in one hand and a road map in the other.

"Here it is!" She handed Senacal a brown folder containing the church's documents and pulled her chair around to his.

Senacal examined an old church survey for a minute. "This goes back to 1959. You'll definitely have to get an update." He felt Leisa Dawkins' firm thigh against his leg. She smiled coyly. He ignored her advances. "Can't Hannah Smith help you with this legal matter? I'm sure she has all the town records like deeds, abstracts, road easement variances, and so on."

"Hannah Smith despises me, Mr. Senacal. She often tries to instigate my dismissal with the church synod. But I pack the house on Sunday morning and the church coffers are full. This church has never been richer. We now have enough money to begin giving the church a face-lift. Eventually, I'd like to hold my Lumen Christi meetings here when the renovations and addition are completed."

"Then why was she at your meeting last night?"

"To keep tabs on me. To find anything that could lead to my dismissal."

"And Mary Kenite?"

"The mail lady. It wouldn't surprise me that she reads everything before it's delivered. A real snoop. Tells Hannah Smith everything that goes on in Eden."

Senacal steered Leisa in a new direction. "You never did answer my question last night about your vengeful God. Why is there so much violence in the Bible?"

Reverend Dawkins sat back in her seat. "My dear Mr. Senacal, man is the author of evil, not God."

He sensed her uneasiness with his question, yet he decided to push the issue further. "But there are times when horrible and bloody killings take place in the name of God."

Reverend Dawkins' playful mood ended abruptly. "Those are rather strong words, Mr. Senacal. What horrible and bloody killings are you referring to?" She studied his eyes and waited.

Senacal struggled to keep his composure. He wondered if Tertius was listening as he smiled to cover up his nervousness. "Like the Crusades? You know, if you don't convert to God, then . . . chop goes your head!" Senacal slapped his hands and smiled at Leisa Dawkins.

Her playfulness returned. She ran her fingernails down his arm. "Don't blame God for those atrocities. God is forgiving, that's what counts. There are a lot of crazy people in this world, in case you haven't noticed." She briefly squeezed his arm against her breasts.

"I've noticed. In fact, I think Eden has their fair share, don't you?"

She laughed. "Do you think I'm crazy?"

"Well, we're all a little crazy. Take Graham Twitchell. There's a nut with a bag full of money."

"Come on, now." She stared directly into his eyes. "Who do you think is crazy in this town?"

"Anyone who lives here for more than a week."

"I love it! I love it! Come on, tell me. Who do you think is really crazy in this town?" She was insistent, squeezing his arm tightly.

"Well, to be honest with you most of the people I see as I drive about. They seem so forlorn living in such isolation. Why anyone would want to live in Eden is beyond me. There's nothing here. Maybe some kind of curse keeps them here."

Leisa Dawkins' mood changed once again. She released her grip on Senacal's arm.

"Mr. Senacal, your curiosity about Eden is quite unusual for a well-dressed lawyer just passing through. Maybe you're really a writer or maybe a detective?"

"Just curious," Senacal said, smiling. "I grew up in a small town and couldn't wait to leave. I guess I'm always wondering what makes people want to stay."

Reverend Dawkins' face smoothed. She ran her hand along the inside of his thigh and kissed him softly on the cheek. He had made love to women in the past for information, but he told himself to be careful of Leisa Dawkins.

"Do you like women with large breasts like mine, Mr. Senacal?" she whispered.

Suddenly, Senacal saw a large figure standing in the door; it was Tertius.

Reverend Dawkins went into a rage at the sight of her son. "Back, I said. You go to your seat in the front pew until I command you differently. I said, go!"

Tertius turned on command and walked down the dark corridor back to his pew.

Leisa Dawkins nervously pulled at her skirt in an attempt to gain her composure. "As time passes, he's getting harder and harder to control." She stood and retrieved an old book from her desk drawer. The gold lettering on the cover read: *The History and Legends of Eden*. Its author was Lydia Howland. Senacal looked up at Leisa Dawkins. "Is this the same Lydia Howland?" He pointed to the sign on the wall behind her desk as he looked over his shoulder to be sure Tertius had gone.

"Yes, the poor woman. Her intellect was trapped in the wrong century."

Senacal browsed through the book in silence while he waited for Leisa Dawkins to initiate the conversation.

"I thought you might enjoy the book," she said as she walked closer to Senacal. "You're a handsome man, Matthew Senacal." She kissed him gently on the lips, then walked over and closed her office door as she continued talking. "The book is only a loan. You must return it to me tomorrow night. I will arrange for Tertius to be elsewhere." She put her arms around his neck. "I do the Lord's work, Mr. Senacal. I help His children reach salvation. But I'm also a woman who needs the warm feeling of a man's naked body on top of her." She guided his hands over her breasts, then kissed him hard on the lips.

Senacal pulled away from her. He imagined Tertius knocking down the door and finding him in the arms of his mother.

"Are you surprised at my passion, Matthew?" Leisa Dawkins acted embarrassed by her question.

"You're a woman. It's that simple."

"But I'm a minister of the Lord."

"You're a woman first, a minister second."

"You're not scandalized? You're not shocked? I'm suppose to be above the ordinary. Sometimes I feel divine, like a spirit. Then at times, like now, I feel so human and sinful."

Senacal watched Reverend Dawkins slip into another one of her multiple personalities. Her look was distant. She was talking more to herself than to him. "I know I've lived in another time. I sometimes get very cold when others are hot and sweaty."

Senacal looked at his watch. "I must go, Leisa. May I call you Leisa?"

The lines of her forehead swelled in anger. "I'm a minister of Jesus. I'm his apostle, like Paul. Always call me Reverend Dawkins."

Senacal was relieved to be safely outside the church. The warm spring sun felt good across his shoulders. He concluded that Leisa Dawkins, with the aid of her son, was capable of carrying out Ken Newell's execution. At the car, Senacal flipped his car keys to Twitchell, who had been patiently waiting with Patton.

"Here." Twitchell handed Senacal a folded yellow note. "I found this on the car windshield after I left the preacher woman's church."

Twitchell slid into the driver's seat as Senacal opened the note and read it.

Dear Mr. Senacal,

You're in great danger. I know you entered my temple. I know of the evil that lives in Eden. Wait for me on Knowles Flat by the moon house tonight at ten o'clock. Come alone and tell no one.

Marie Derkowski

Senacal took a deep breath, then read the note again. He remembered Frank Lattimore's warning about the Sect Rouge, the worst of Haiti's voodoo cults. He wondered if Marie Derkowski would be waiting for him tonight dressed in a red robe and a headpiece shaped like tin horns.

"Why don't you take us over to the post office, next to Peckham's General Store?" Senacal said, getting in alongside Twitchell.

Senacal removed an envelope from the glove compartment and addressed it to Frank Lattimore in Saratoga Springs, New York. Into it he placed the tape of his conversation with Leisa Dawkins.

In front of the small red post office Senacal got out of the car and was ready to drop his tape into the blue jaws of the mailbox when Mary Kenite appeared from inside her office wearing her Eden Emergency Squad jacket.

"I'll take that for you, Mr. Senacal. I'm packing up the mail now. The truck will be here from North Hyde Park at any second." She reached out her hand with a smile. Mary Kenite always wore a smile on her face.

Senacal recalled Reverend Dawkins words: "It wouldn't surprise me that she reads everything before it's delivered."

Senacal snapped his fingers and said, "Forgot the lien copy. Damn it!"

"What?"

"Nothing." He turned and circled the car. "I'll mail it with some other stuff from Morrisville. Thanks, Mary."

The postmistress zippered up her jacket, nodded blankly, and went back into her office.

"You fixed her grits," Twitchell said, pulling out of the lot.

Twitchell sped off south toward Morrisville.

"Go ahead and read the book that crazy preacher woman gave you," Twitchell said. "Patton and I are enjoying the drive." A grin widened on his face.

"Enjoying what?" Senacal looked out the window to his right. "The scenery's shitty."

"The car. I'm enjoying the car. You told me to drive, so I did. I haven't driven a car since my left eye went bad back in '64. Nearly blind in it and the good one's got cataracts." He patted Senacal on the knee. "You're in good hands. Not much traffic today."

The History and Legends of Eden by Lydia Howland was fifty-six pages long and divided into three sections: Ecclesiastical, Biographical, and Political. The author had autographed the book with a bold sweep of her hand on the inside front cover. The Ecclesiastical section was disappointing. Senacal had hoped for a description of the Lamech cult, but instead, it gave a boring account of the history of Eden's churches. The Biographical section contained the stories of Eden's settlers like Noah Lloyd, Samuel Reed, and Hezekiah Farrington. He read of Samuel Reed's struggle with a mountain lion and of Noah Lloyd's wandering into a supposed lost cave on Belvidere Mountain. The Political section on the War of 1812, Abolitionism, and the Civil War was interesting, but of little help in solving the Curse of Lamech question.

Suddenly, the car jerked to a stop in front of the North Hyde Park Post Office, which lay approximately halfway between Eden and Morrisville on Route 100.

"What's up?" Senacal asked as Twitchell opened the car door to get out.

"Give me the tape!" Twitchell extended his hand.

Senacal put Lydia Howland's book down and reached for the envelope on the dashboard. "I don't know if its such a good idea mailing the tape from here."

"It ain't."

"Well, then why the hell do you want it?"

Twitchell snatched the envelope from Senacal's hand. "Just give me the damn thing."

The old man climbed from the car and entered the North Hyde Park Post Office.

Senacal shook his head in dismay. He had grown fond of Graham Twitchell since he had met the old man during the investigation of Ken Newell's murder in Fort Ann. It was like having a grandfather as a partner.

As his head swirled with images of his upcoming meeting with Marie Derkowski at the moon house, Senacal looked down on the seat next to him. Lydia Howland's book had flipped open and the sun, pouring in through the windshield, exposed the inside back cover. His attention was drawn to an ink drawing of four identical markings that looked like golf tees. Three were drawn side by side and tilted left of center. A fourth one was drawn directly above the three and also tilted left of center. The ink was similar to Lydia Howland's signature. Senacal's curiosity was aroused. He checked the inside front cover; there was no ink drawing, just the author's signature. He discovered the back cover was softer and thicker than the front cover.

Gently, he began tearing away at the inside back cover when the car door opened.

"Thought she was lying," said Graham Twitchell as he pulled on his Red Sox baseball cap and sat down in the car. He flipped the envelope containing the tape on the dashboard. "The guy in this Post Office told me the mail doesn't get picked up here in North Hyde Park by truck until 4:15 P.M. Then it goes to Eden. That's about four hours from now. Mary Kenite lied. Snoopy bitch, isn't she? I don't trust her, but she's not as nutty as the preacher woman. She's a looney. Right, Patton?" The dog barked from the rear seat.

"You got a knife?" Senacal asked. "I want to take this back cover apart. I think there's something in here."

"Better wait until we get back to the motel. You'll need a razor blade for that."

Senacal turned on the desk lamp in his motel room and opened Lydia Howland's book. The lining peeled off the back cover easily with Twitchell's razor blade and revealed an envelope placed in a space hewed out of the back cover of the book.

Great care had been taken to place the document in its century-old crypt. Senacal carefully removed the contents from the envelope. It was a six-page letter. The pages were yellow and stiff. The writing was legible; Lydia Howland had printed her message. Senacal placed the pages side by side on the motel dresser and read aloud for Twitchell to hear.

July, 1871

Winter will come in my absence. The weight on my conscience is too great to carry to my grave. My pen is my weapon, the words it bears are but buried in this sacristy tomb. May God forgive me for the fortitude I lack. If such be read, may he that read it have the strength of Samson and the wisdom of Solomon to right the wrong of the Tribe of Cain.

124

Nathaniel Howland and Jonathan Edwards, both born in 1703 of the year of the Lord, were boyhood friends in East Windsor, Connecticut. As mere children, they read Latin and Hebrew and the most abstruse writings in English. They remained loyal to God and themselves through manhood. Jonathan Edwards attended Yale Divinity School in New Haven at the age of fourteen and became one of the most original and acute thinkers yet produced in America. Nathaniel Howland's life was less auspicious behind a plow, though equally fervent in the pursuit of God's truths through the study of mental philosophy.

Nathaniel revealed to Jonathan his sin of incest shortly after having heard the latter's terrifying sermon in Enfield, "Sinners in the Hands of an Angry God." He told Jonathan about his recurring dream where God held him over the pit of hell by his heels and spat a hot green bile upon him. He saw Cain, Abel's brother, grasping at the right hand of God, and he heard Cain pleading with God to raise him from the grasp of Satan.

He confided in Jonathan that his salvation warranted a new genesis because of his terrible sin. Nathaniel reasoned that if God had not struck Cain dead for his terrible deed against Abel and if God said to Cain, "If anyone kills you, seven lives will be taken in revenge," then there was hope for his immortal soul in following the life of Cain. Jonathan blessed Nathaniel's interpretation of the dream, and Nathaniel left with his followers, the Drews, the Densons, the Farringtons, the Worthingtons, the Prescotts, and the Trombleys up the Connecticut River, past Fort Drummer and deep into New Hampshire Province. They named their community Eden, where they prospered in progeny and faith.

As God spoke to Cain so Nathaniel followed the precepts of God in Holy Scripture. "You can no longer farm the soil. If you try to grow crops, the soil will not produce anything," says the Lord in Genesis. So, Nathaniel and his followers mined the Mountain Belvidere for its brilliant stones and copper. They traded with the Indians for corn and killed the abundant fowl and beasts of the forest for meat. As Genesis says, "Then Cain built a city and named it after his son," so it was done in Eden like at Mamre. Nathaniel died in 1758 of western fever, contented in the spirit of the Lord.

Enoch, Nathaniel's first son born in Eden, followed the way of the Lord as prescribed by his father. As civilization encroached upon the Eden area, Enoch decreed that a vow be taken by the young to marry only within the Tribe of Cain. The Lord said in Deuteronomy, "When you make a vow to the Lord your God, it is a sin not to keep it." Enoch founded the Soldiers of the Sword and granted them the power to kill all who weakened and broke the vow. These soldiers were the most formidable of this new Tribe of Cain.

Irad, my grandfather, followed not the way of Nathaniel but of King Manasseh of Judah. Irad became drunk with power. All lived in fear of the Soldiers of the Sword. In the tradition of Jephthah's daughter (Judges 11:30–40), the first daughter born in a new year into a family of the Tribe of Cain was sacrificed to God. Like King Manasseh before him in Scripture, Irad built altars for the worship of Baal in Enoch's city and made an image of the goddess Anath. Irad died in 1828. I remember his death.

There was much licentiousness and debauchery about his funeral bier.

Methujael, my father, surely burns today in the fires of Sheol. He postulated the teachings of Irad and had the Soldiers of the Sword kill many of the Tribe of Cain who tried to leave Eden. He sacrificed his third son, my brother Judah, as a burned offering to Baal. He practiced divination and magic. Fear ran rampant throughout the Tribe of Cain. To my knowledge all was kept secret from the gentile town folk. The white powder of the mountain was in great demand. My father's wealth was the reward of the devil. He demanded my blood-stained wedding sheets the day following my marriage to my beloved, Joash. If clean, he would have had me stoned to death by the Soldiers of the Sword as directed in Deuteronomy 22: 20–21. I was spared the fate of my dearest friend, Marian. Methujael died in 1861. Satan rejoiced on the occasion of my father's arrival in hell.

Methushaell, my younger brother, incurred the wrath of God for continuing the teachings of our father. Pestilence among the Tribe of Cain was widespread. Dysentery and whooping cough spread like seeds borne on the wind. The white powder covered the mountain, leaves stopped budding and trees stood like scarecrows, hunched over near death. Men died young, clutching loved ones. Methushaell's power waned. The Soldiers of the Sword were weakened from disease and could not prevent the young from escaping. Men in good health joined the Union army. Others, by railroad, sought the 160 acres in the Dakotas and Nebraska promised by the Homestead Act.

I prayed for Methushaell's death. I begged

the Lord not to bear him a son so as to end this awful pagan cult. God punished me and begot Methushaell a son, Lamech.

"If seven lives are taken to pay for killing Cain, seventy-seven will be taken if anyone kills me," saith the Curse of Lamech in Genesis. Only thirty or so gathered this morning at his baptism in the City of Enoch. The mark was placed on his forehead with a red-hot iron as God did to Cain in Genesis, "So the Lord put a mark on Cain to warn anyone who met him not to kill him."

The child Lamech never cried. The smell of burned flesh permeated the city. Drunkenness and lewdness followed as the child lay sleeping on the stone altar. I prayed for the anger of God to strike the mountain down into a mere mound of sand. I prayed that the pools of water rise and rend assunder the city and that all present drown. I pleaded with God to break His covenant with Noah. All my wishes went for naught.

My breathing is hard, my sojourn on earth almost over. I pray till my death that Lamech die from disease, famine, or flood. If he is murdered, I fear a revival of paganism and idolatry among the descendants of the Tribe of Cain.

Pax vobiscum! Let 2 Kings 20:20 be my epitaph.

Lydia Howland

The blue numbers on Senacal's car clock read 9:45 P.M. The moon was full and Peckman's General Store was dark. The lights were out even in the Derkowskis' apartment above the store. Senacal took a left onto Route 118 West. His directional signal echoed in the empty night. His thoughts raced ahead of his car. Where did Gil Pixley fit into the family tree of the

Tribe of Cain? Was he a Howland relative from Uriah, Alabama? And what about Leisa Dawkins and Tertius? Were they descendants of Nathaniel Howland? He hoped Marie Derkowski would help solve some of these mysteries.

He pulled over alongside an old cemetery and wondered if one of the crooked gravestones was Lydia Howland's. Belvidere Mountain stood tall and ominous in the distance, its secrets covered by darkness.

Knowles Flat veered left off Route 118, just past the cemetery. The road was anything but flat; it weaved downward like a spiral staircase through a thicket of trees. He could barely see the sky. Suddenly, like emerging from a tunnel, the sky opened up and the land leveled. The moon house stood alone on the right.

A silvery square in the middle of the roof reflected the moon like a mirror. The house was white with black trim. It sat alone at the end of a long gravel driveway. A blue pickup truck with a white cap was parked in the front parallel to the house. A doorless shed stood in ruins off to the right.

Senacal watched the house from the road for signs of life. Nothing. He checked his side mirror. He was alone. Only Belvidere Mountain stood in the rear. He watched the blue minute hand on his car clock roll forward. It was 10:16 and no sign of Marie Derkowski. He drove slowly down the gravel driveway.

On closer inspection, the house had fallen into disrepair. The roof sagged like an accordion and the windows in the upstairs bedrooms were missing. A few screens lay broken on the porch roof. The land around the house was treeless, and a toppled rock wall lined the fields at woods edge. A collapsed barn overgrown with high grass gave sad testimony to a time of prosperity long gone.

Senacal got out of his car and drew his gun. Shadows from the bright moon dotted the landscape like pieces of a giant puzzle. He was careful not to slam the car door. Before leaving Morrisville, he had told Graham Twitchell that if he wasn't back in two or three hours, the old man was to leave Eden as fast as his spindly legs could carry him.

The hood of the truck with the white cap was warm. Senacal looked up. The reflection of the moon off the roof was from a strip of aluminum flashing. He walked to the back of the house. He remembered Lattimore telling him how the Sect Rouge waited in ambush at night for its innocent victims. The garbage can on the side of the house was empty, as was a can of soda lying under a shrub near the back of the house.

The back stairs creaked; he cocked his gun. He paused. No noise sounded from within. He checked the shadows of the house for hidden voodooists, then cursed the day he first heard of Eden, Vermont. The door was unlocked—a fact strange to Senacal but not an uncommon practice in rural America. He slowly stepped inside.

His shadow stretched across the floor and up the newly paneled wall. The room was bare, save for a rolltop desk filled with papers and rocks. Oddly, an apple crate filled with more rocks sat on the floor next to a pair of scuffed hiking shoes. There were no curtains on the windows, just shades, which were rolled up.

Senacal opened the door that led from the back room into the hallway. His eyes quickly scanned the house. Loose plaster littered the floor, and holes in the walls allowed a view of the front living room and kitchen. A doorless refrigerator stood near a kitchen window. The banister leading upstairs was broken in sections. The house smelled musty. Senacal walked back into the paneled room and turned on the ceiling light.

There was no point in being secretive. He was sure he was alone. He looked around the room for biblical letters and numbers on the walls. There were also no signs of a voodoo temple anywhere. Nothing. He walked over to the messy desk.

A physical map of the Acadian Peninsula from the Gulf of Saint Lawrence to Lake Ontario was thumbtacked on the wall over the desk. Lake Champlain, the Connecticut River, the Hudson River, and the Saint Lawrence River were clearly labeled in black letters. The word "Chester" was penciled in just left of Cape Cod. A red line connected Quebec and Lake Champlain. The map meant nothing to Senacal, but he thought it might to Lattimore. He carefully removed it from the wall and folded it.

A handwritten chart with three distinct columns was taped to the desk. Each column was headed by the symbol for some chemical compound. Under each heading were technical words and numbers initialized in different colored inks. Senacal mumbled, "What the hell does all this mumbo jumbo mean? AL_2O-Hexagonal, s.g. 4, h. 9. C-Octahedrons, s.g. 3.5, h. 10. TIO_2-Tetragonal, s.g. 4.2, h. 6.5." The word "Chester" was written in the column labeled AL_2O.

Carefully, Senacal peeled off the paper chart and placed it in his pocket.

The desk was damp around an empty soda can. He remembered Mike Derkowski drinking a soda the first day they met in Peckman's General Store. If this room was Mike Derkowski's rock laboratory, what was he studying? Senacal wondered.

He checked the desk drawers. Nothing unusual for a scientist of sorts—a square-faced hammer with sharp edges, a few cold chisels, some paper and pens. A binocular microscope and Jolly Balance scale sat on the floor. Senacal reached inside the wastepaper basket and retrieved a crumbled piece of paper. It was a phone message: "Hardness test TIO_2, usually equal to somewhere between apatite and orthoclase, but sample equal to quartz. Unbelievable! Knife-point test showed same results—big $$$$. Burlington-G.E. at 10:30 on 4/30."

Senacal was sure of one thing. Mike Derkowski showed more intelligence and ambition in life than being a grocery store-owner in Eden, Vermont. He took the note with him, turned off the lights, and went out the back door.

Senacal had no sooner walked down the back steps than he heard a car engine start. He ran to the front of the house and dashed up the gravel driveway. The car disappeared under an umbrella of trees just as the moon returned to light up the countryside. He was sure Gil Pixley had paid him another visit.

He turned and stared at the blue truck with the white cap parked in front of the moon house. It had to be Marie Derkowski's truck. He recalled touching its warm hood earlier. He walked to his car, opened the trunk, grabbed his flashlight, and walked toward the truck. He checked the shadows near the house to be sure he was alone. He heard his heart pound like a piston inside his chest.

His flashlight revealed the keys still in the ignition. He listened for any noise under the white cap in the back. Nothing. The crushing of driveway stones under his feet echoed loudly in the stillness of the night. He shone his flashlight through the side windows of the cap roof, but only his reflection bounced back. He banged the side of the truck and listened, his gun ready and cocked. His thoughts switched to Salem, Massachusetts. He recalled reading in the police report how an innocent girl was torn apart by a Doberman pinscher.

All was quiet around him. Senacal doubted any

dogs were under the cap roof. A picture of a faceless figure wearing a red robe flashed before his eyes. He walked to the back of the truck. The latch that lifted the door of the truck cap was securely in place. He held it tightly with one hand and readied his gun with the other. He heard something. He listened more carefully. It came from his feet, like a faucet dripping. He directed his light down and noticed a small pool of blood had gathered near his feet. Also, blood had splattered across his leather shoes. He took a deep breath, looked around for a second, and pulled up the truck cap door.

It was Fort Ann revisited. Blood covered the entire truck bed, and a piece of human scalp was stuck to the rim of a spare tire. The hair of the victim was long and black, like Marie Derkowski's. There was no body and the smell of exhaust fumes was strong. Senacal's attention was drawn to a yellow sheet of paper stuck to the wall of the truck: "ISH. 47: 10–11. 55 left."

Back at his car, Senacal pulled out a small Bible from under his seat. His eyes followed his finger to Chapter 47 of the Book of Isaiah. "You felt sure of yourself in your evil, you thought that no one could see you. Your wisdom and knowledge led you astray, and you said to yourself, 'I am God—there is no one else like me.' Disaster will come upon you, and none of your magic can stop it. Ruin will come to you suddenly—ruin you never dreamed of!"

Only in Vietnam had Senacal felt so scared and so alone as now. Marie Derkowski was killed because she knew the horrible secrets of the Curse of Lamech. But who told her of the Tribe of Cain? She was a Haitian. He doubted she had any direct bloodline to Nathaniel Howland. He sensed his own danger and Twitchell's. Even Lattimore was unsafe in Saratoga Springs. It was pointless to continue acting as a lawyer; he was sure the biblical killer knew he was cop. His fears and uncertainties led to anger. He looked at Belvidere Mountain sticking up into the starry night. "You hold the secrets, you bastard! But you're not getting my ass without a fight."

The Derkowskis' small apartment above Peckman's General Store was a mirror copy of the moon-house laboratory. A few pieces of old furniture were lost amid crates of rocks, camping gear, and discarded outdoor clothing dropped at the point of disrobement. Senacal barged past Mike Derkowski without an apology for waking him up.

"What the hell's going on?" Derkowski demanded desperately. It was 11:45 P.M. Senacal ignored the question and checked out the lone bedroom facing the front of the store. He looked out the window. There was a harvest moon in Eden, Vermont; everything was still.

Senacal threw Derkowski his pants. "Put them on and sit down." The storekeeper demanded a reason for the nocturnal assault on his apartment.

"Your wife's dead; she's been murdered." Subtleness had never been a Senacal virtue, especially at times like tonight when he had little time for condolences.

At first, Derkowski showed little emotion to his wife's death. Then slowly, his jaw dropped and he sat down on the arm of the living-room couch. "What are you saying? Where is Marie?"

"I said she's dead, but I don't know where the killer took her body," Senacal said as he continued to study Derkowski's face for signs of sorrow. "Well, I do have some idea, but I don't have time to go into it. I'm a senior investigator with the New York State Police. I'm sorry about your wife. I'd like to ask you some questions."

"You're what?" Deep furrows appeared on the

store-owner's brow as he struggled to keep his thoughts on Senacal's words.

"I'm a cop with the New York State Police."

"I thought you were a lawyer?"

"It was just a cover."

"I want to see some ID!" Derkowski said as he walked to the phone. "How do I know you're telling me the truth about Marie? Maybe you killed her. I'm calling the police." He lifted the phone off the receiver.

"Put it down," ordered Senacal as he showed Mike his police identification.

Derkowski said nothing. Slowly, he put the phone back down.

"I don't have time for any bullshit," Senacal stated coldly. He pointed at Derkowski as he spoke. "I am sorry about Marie, but I can't bring her back. I think she tried to help me tonight, if that's any consolation. There's a wacko family up here in Eden that goes around chopping up people in the name of God. I want Marie to be their last victim." Senacal waited for Derkowski to lift his head from his hands before he continued speaking. "I know Marie was a voodooist. I've seen her temple downstairs. Did anyone in Eden know about it?"

Derkowski shook his head, dazed. The pain of his wife's death was etched on his face.

"Are you sure?"

"Yes. She was a loner." His voice quivered. "Where is her body now? I want to see her."

Senacal sensed Derkowski's feelings were genuine, but there was little time for solace. He again told Derkowski he wasn't sure where the murderer had taken his wife's body.

"I saw your wife last night at a women's meeting in Morrisville," said Senacal. "The group's called Lumen Christi. What do you know about it?"

Derkowski shrugged his shoulders. "Marie just started going, so I don't know much about it. She goes to the meetings with Hannah Smith twice a month. That's all I know." He spoke as if his wife were still alive.

"Was she friendly with Hannah Smith? Is that why she went with her?"

"Not particularly."

"Then why did Hannah bring her?"

Derkowski hedged a bit with the question. "I asked her to. I thought it might give Marie an opportunity to make new friends. Hannah Smith owns Northern Vermont Realty Company. She sold me this store and the Trombley farm near by." Senacal recalled the name "Trombley." The Trombley family had accompanied Nathaniel Howland from Connecticut to Eden, Vermont.

"Did Marie have any friends? Did she ever visit any neighbors around here?"

Derkowski thought for a second. "She would visit with an old lady down Highway 24, near Bean Mountain." Derkowski pointed toward the back of the building. "Marie hated Eden. She talked about a great evil she saw in one of her trances with Damballah. He's some kind of god or angel that possesses her. She wanted to leave Eden. I told her that my research was almost completed and we'd be rich." He put on a flannel shirt that had been thrown over a chair.

Senacal spoke up. "What was the name of the lady near Bean Mountain?"

"I don't know. Marie never told me. The woman comes into the store every once in a while with her son."

Senacal laid out the map of the Acadian peninsula he had taken off the wall of the moon house. "What's this all about? What are you doing out there?" Senacal pointed in the direction of the moon house.

The store owner walked over to his desk in the

corner of the cluttered living room and retrieved a small white box from the bottom drawer.

He opened the box and dumped a brilliant red stone into his hand to show Senacal.

Senacal said nothing.

"It looks like a ruby but it's not," said Derkowski. "The stone is rutile, a mineral that's normally brittle and in abundance in northern Vermont. But this stone has the strength and beauty of a real ruby. I found it while digging on Belvidere Mountain."

Derkowski gently put the stone on the coffee table and cried.

Highway 24 was called Bean Mountain Trail by the Eden residents because it had never been paved. The town fathers had deemed that the road didn't warrant blacktop because so few people lived in the area it served. Senacal had surprisingly little trouble finding the dirt road in the night; it headed south behind Peckman's General Store. He put his gun down on the passenger seat and drove over the Gihon River, which was no wider than a king-size bed.

There was no life along Highway 24, just thick brush on each side of the road and an occasional naked tree stretching its bare limbs across the starry night. The old lady on Highway 24 fit somewhere into the puzzle, but Senacal wasn't certain where. He wasn't even sure where she lived, but he had to find her and talk to her about Marie's knowledge of the biblical murders. Time was running out; he was sure he was the next victim of the biblical killer. Derkowski had told him that the old lady and her son lived alone somewhere off a logging road near Bean Mountain. Senacal figured the old lady was either a mother figure to Marie or maybe a fellow voodooist, or both. He just hoped she wasn't a believer of Sect Rouge. If she was, Highway 24 was a perfect stage to seize a lone traveler in an unfamiliar setting.

He passed alongside Bean Mountain. It was a hill compared to Belvidere Mountain. He checked his rearview mirror a few times to be sure he was alone. The sounds of the night grew louder around him. The road surface changed from dirt to crushed stones as he surveyed the terrain for a logging road. He had traveled about a mile or so when his headlights flashed a message from a white sign. It read, HYDE PARK. "Shit!" He realized he had traveled too far. He looked for a place to turn around. A pair of animal eyes glistened in the dead grass to his right. He spotted a dirt path, turned around, and headed back to Eden.

The moon lit up the woods. Senacal drove slowly and peered through the leafless trees for a house or trailer or shack, anything that might house an old lady and her son. Silence was his only companion in the night. He was back on Highway 24 and its smooth roadbed. He stopped by a turn in the road just past Bean Mountain. A logging road, no wider than a car, turned off the highway to his left. He had missed it coming down earlier. The logging road was rocky in the middle and worn brown from traffic on the edges. It angled straight up a small hill, then disappeared down the other side.

Senacal hated Life-Savers, but he ate one anyhow. He turned up his brights and sat quietly studying the logging road. He had thought of Vietnam more in the last few months than he had in the nineteen years since he had left Da Nang for the States. Unlike some Vietnam veterans, Senacal had no trouble accepting the bitter American attitude toward the war. To him it was a job, and he did it. "Fuck it," was his definition of Vietnam.

Yet, Eden, Vermont, triggered bad memories. Perhaps it was the fear and uncertainty of the biblical killer as it had been of the Vietcong. He was at home in the Bronx or Long Island but not in the jungles of Southeast Asia or in the woods of northern Vermont. His thoughts switched to his kids and Donna. Maybe Lattimore was right, he thought. Maybe it was wrong to put up walls around his feelings. Yet loneliness had its reward: you had only yourself to worry about. At least Lattimore had him thinking about himself. He drove slowly up the logging road. He was determined to find the old lady Marie Derkowski had confided in. It was 1:21 A.M.

The light from his high beams danced off the bare trees ahead of him. Branches swiped his windshield and fenders. His muffler scraped against a rock in the middle of the trail. "You're making more noise than a goddamn army, asshole," he mumbled. The road dipped and turned. He completely lost his sense of direction. Often he was blinded by the glare of his own headlights. His sunglasses slid off the dashboard to the car floor. There was no place to turn, the road was lined with thick brush and fallen timber. He stopped the car and waited a few minutes in silence. It was 1:35 A.M. He had traveled fifteen minutes to nowhere. His hands were moist. He put the car in reverse and turned to back his way out to Bean Mountain Trail.

He heard a deafening blast as his back window exploded. A cold voice made its presence known on the road behind him as Senacal froze in fear.

"Get da fuck out."

Senacal felt helpless, like a hostage captured in a foreign land. He exited the car with his hands up and turned around. The man was old but tall and strong, with a full salt-and-pepper beard. He wore a green camo parka and matching bibs. He approached Senacal and ordered him to turn off the car lights, then nudged him forward without saying a word. They walked in silence for a hundred yards or so.

Senacal was sure he had met the biblical killer or at least one of the members of the infamous Soldiers of the Sword as described in Lydia Howland's letter. The man with the gun said nothing.

A faint light appeared to his right at the end of a dirt path. An old yellow trailer with a flat tin roof sat precariously on cinder blocks. A dog, tied to a pine tree, barked at their approach. The smell of burned garbage rose in smoke from a rusty oil drum. Stacks of firewood littered the front yard. Senacal's captor nudged him up the wobbly front steps.

"Get in," ordered the man at gun point.

The trailer was narrow with low ceilings stained yellow with age. The smell of cigarette smoke permeated the stale air. A kitchen anchored the front of the trailer and two tiny bedrooms lay at the end of a dark hallway in the rear.

Senacal stood in the middle of the living room. The room was filled with old, overstuffed green furniture and a small portable television. There was little room for anything else. A small wood stove stood boldly on a concrete hearth. The only light in the trailer came from a ceiling fixture in the kitchen.

The floor of the trailer shook as an old woman appeared from the dark hallway to his left. She didn't look at Senacal, but headed for the lone green chair in the room. Her gray hair was pulled straight back alongside her head. Her face was old and wrinkly. A blue terry-cloth bathrobe was tightly wrapped around her frail body. Her feet were naked and badly swollen.

The captor's gun barrel nudged Senacal forward until he stood directly over the woman. She slowly raised her head. She folded her hands on her lap before she spoke. Senacal felt the woman was about to condemn him to death. His attention was drawn to a chain saw sitting idle in a corner. He took a deep breath to calm himself. He waited for the woman to speak.

"What are you doing on my land so late at night?"

The clarity of the old woman's voice surprised Senacal. He replied, "I had to see you about a common friend. Marie Derkowski?"

The woman stared into Senacal's eyes for the truth. After a few seconds, she motioned for him to sit down on the couch. She rubbed her knotty hands together. "Are you Mr. Senacal? Marie had told me of your coming to Eden."

"Yes, I am." Senacal paused for a second before continuing. "Mike Derkowski, Marie's husband, mentioned your friendship with her. I had to talk with you tonight. It's important."

Again the old lady studied Senacal's eyes for a few seconds before she spoke. "You are either very brave or very stupid to come out here tonight. Either way, state your business."

Senacal heard his captor stir in the kitchen. He imagined a shotgun aimed at the back of his head. He decided to be honest and direct. He had a feeling the old lady knew more about the reason for his visit than she was saying.

"I'm a New York State Police investigator. There have been a series of brutal slayings performed in execution style throughout the United States in the last few months. I happen to believe they are connected somehow to Eden. I came up here undercover to have a look." He slowly turned to his captor and asked permission to remove Marie's note from his inside jacket pocket.

He gave the note to the old woman, then spoke as she read it. "I think Marie knew about the murders. She was killed tonight." Out of nervousness, Senacal glanced over at the chain-saw case in the corner of the room.

The old woman crumbled the note and covered her eyes with her left hand and wept in sorrow.

"I thought it had ended in 1927," the old woman

said as she wiped her tears with a crumbled tissue she retrieved from her bathrobe pocket. She looked at Senacal through moist eyes. "I'm Adah Howland, Lamech's wife."

Senacal's mouth went dry. His heart pounded against his rib cage. He felt weak at the mention of Lamech's name. He readied himself for death. He was sure the man behind him was about to walk over and blow his brains out with his shotgun. He called himself asshole three times in succession for having ever heard of the name Eden, Vermont.

Adah Howland pointed to the man behind Senacal. "This is my son, Jabal, Lamech's son."

Senacal was lost for words. He proclaimed to himself the title King of Assholes. He grinned feebly at Jabal. It was the best he could do under the circumstances. Jabal's face was expressionless, as if chiseled in the best Vermont marble.

"Put the gun down, son. Bring Mr. Senacal's car to the house for him."

Jabal left the trailer and Adah Howland went to the kitchen to make coffee. Senacal had difficulty accepting his reprieve from the jaws of death, but he had enough presence of mind to reach inside his jacket and click on his tape recorder. Adah returned with the coffee and Senacal gulped it down to please her. He dared not say he preferred tea over coffee. His heart still beat rapidly as Adah offered him some fresh corn bread.

"How much do you know about the Howlands?" asked Adah as she neatly folded her bathrobe over her legs.

He told her about his finding Lydia Howland's letter.

"Then let me bring you up to date since Lydia's death."

Senacal figured the woman to be at least in her eighties.

"I was fourteen years old when my marriage to Lamech was arranged by my father, Joseph. Lamech was then nearly fifty years old. He had taken a wife in Plymouth, New Hampshire. Her name was Zillah, as all names in the direct line of Nathaniel Howland matched the names mentioned in Cain's family. Lamech was a gentle man and loved Zillah dearly. He had spent much time in Plymouth, but the Scriptures had to be fulfilled. He had to take two wives. I had two sons by Lamech, just as the Bible proclaims. Jabal, whom you met tonight, was born in 1922, and Jubal was born in 1927, just two months before Lamech's death." Adah paused for a sip of coffee.

Senacal asked, "Was Lamech killed or did he die a natural death?"

Adah's eyes looked up as if searching the ceiling for the answer. "Up to a few weeks ago, I would have said he died by drowning in the great flood of '27. Lamech, as I said, was a gentle man. When he spent time with me, he would bring his daughter, Naamah, with him from Plymouth. She was my equal in age, yet I loved her as a sister." Adah stared straight ahead. "Don't think harsh of me, Mr. Senacal, that as a young girl I slept with a man older than my father. We did as parents directed in those days."

Senacal nodded his understanding.

"Naamah was beautiful and full of life. On such visits by Lamech, we'd play together like young girls anywhere. She helped me care for Jabal and clean the house and so on. Then, upon leaving Eden in the spring of 1927, Lamech and Naamah drowned in the flood. Their horse buggy was found on the banks of the White River near Sharon. Hundreds died with them that spring."

Senacal moved to the end of his seat. "Are you sure he died from drowning?"

"My father was a Soldier of the Sword. He investigated Lamech's death and said it was so. His body was found partially decomposed. He proclaimed the death as accidental and that the prophecy of killing seventy-seven need not be fulfilled. After that, the Tribe of Cain ceased to exist."

"What about Naamah? Did they ever find her?"

"No. But many lost loved ones forever in the flood."

"Did Zillah, his other wife, have other children by him?"

"The biblical Zillah had a son named Tubal Cain, but Lamech never told me he had a son by her. Perhaps she was pregnant that spring as I was with Jubal. But that's just a guess."

Senacal moved to the edge of his seat and paused a few seconds before he spoke. "There is one part of Lydia Howland's story that confuses me. Maybe you can help. She made reference to a hidden city built by Nathaniel Howland for his son. I understand why he built it—because Cain built one for his son, Enoch, and he wanted to do everything Cain did." Senacal lifted his palms heavenward. "So where the hell's the city? How can you have a city in a place that's got more deer than people. Do you know the location of this mysterious city?"

Adah Howland's eyes returned to the ceiling in thought. Her chin quivered slightly before she spoke. "I never entered the City of Enoch. I was to be married there, but my father persuaded Lamech to forsake its location. I was told it was a place of great horror. The morning of my wedding I was taken by foot to a clearing surrounded by tall oaks and elms. I was married to Lamech before a marble statue that stood near an apple tree cut in the shape of a cross. It was so beautiful there. I always felt the City of Enoch had to be somewhere nearby. After the ceremony, I was taken to await Lamech. He came to me some hours later."

"This is hard for me to ask, but I must. . . ."

Adah raised her hand to stop him. "I know what it is you seek." A look of sadness settled over her tired face. "You're concerned that my sons may have continued the lineage of the Tribe of Cain. Fear not. I castrated them when they were very young so this horrible cult would end with their deaths. Jubal, my youngest, lives in Saint Albans, and works for the Central Vermont Railroad. He despises me for my decision to deprive him of manhood. Jabal has stayed with me. He understands the Howlands must die without progeny."

Senacal felt a lump in his throat. He wondered how young boys were castrated. Or old boys, for that matter. His body quivered from the sadistic images that flooded his mind. Jabal opened the front door, walked into the kitchen and took off his camo fatigues. Senacal waited for Adah to speak.

"Jabal," cried Adah to her son, "write down Jubal's old address in Saint Albans and give it to Mr. Senacal. Jubal has begun the Curse of Lamech."

Senacal heard Jabal fumble through the kitchen drawers. Senacal hoped Jabal's loyalty rested with his mother and not his brother.

"Did you know Marie well?" asked Adah while she waited for her son.

"No, I didn't. I only met her a few days ago. She got real upset about my friend's dog in her store."

Adah smiled. "She was normally quiet, but gifted with the supernatural powers. The day you arrived, she appeared at my door in a trance. The irises of her eyes were hidden under her eyelids. The calves of her legs trembled. Her body stood pitched forward. She was dressed in a white gown and spoke through her loa, her Damballah. She hissed as she told of your coming to avenge the serpent in our midst. She chanted the name of Lamech and began to draw lines in ashes on the floor of the trailer. The symbols she drew were those tattooed on Lamech's forehead at his baptism."

"Like four golf tees leaning left of center?"

"Correct. How did you know?" Adah played with her gold wedding ring.

"Lydia Howland drew them on the inside back cover of her book. Go on. What happened next?"

"She carried on, speaking mostly Creole and some English. She knew I was Lamech's wife, but she told me I was safe from my husband's avenger. She promised you would free the loa of Eden. Then, she tired and fell asleep. When she woke up, she had forgotten everything. She pleaded with me to tell her what she had said. We were friends, so I did. I believe that is why she wanted to speak to you tonight. I believe Marie is not dead; she brought you here tonight. She guided you to my house."

Senacal had little time to digest Adah's story. He jumped at the sight of Jabal's hairy arm passing over his shoulder.

"Here's my brother's old address. He is very bad. If he started the revenge of my father, bring him here and I will kill him."

Senacal forced a quick smile at Adah's son, then turned to the old lady and said, "I know you and Jubal feel that Jabal is behind the killings, but—"

"No! I'm Jabal; my brother's Jubal," said a voice from the dark corner of the kitchen. Senacal reminded himself not to make the same mistake twice. Jabal Howland seemed to be a man of little patience.

"I'm sorry. Once again. I know you and Jabal feel that Jubal is behind the killings, but did Marie say who she thought might be the serpent of Eden?"

Adah pulled on her robe. "Marie feared the Preacher of Tongues and her insane son, who walks in a trance. The preacher has been here only a short time, and her ways are different." Adah looked at Senacal and raised a crooked finger at him. "Remember. I, Adah Howland, sinned greatly by making my sons impotent. I am old and the Howland progeny ends with my sons' deaths. They may not father a successor to the kingship of the Tribe of Cain. Jubal is filled with hate. He is capable of revenge. Yet, of Lamech's other wife, Zillah, I know nothing. I'm sure Naamah died, yet a son may have been born to Zillah by Lamech. You must end this horrible cult. You must find the one who has started the Curse of Lamech and dash his head against a stone in the name of God."

Even though it was late, Senacal checked in on Twitchell when he arrived back at the Ski Top Motel. The old man was O.K., but was indignant at the suggestion that he not travel with Senacal to Saint Albans in the morning. "I'll follow ya in a damn taxi if I have to," argued Twitchell. Patton barked in agreement with his master.

Senacal felt it was too late for a debate; he was tired and wanted to catch a few hours' sleep before meeting Jubal Howland in the morning. He waved good night and went to his room.

The shower's hot water beating down on his face failed to cleanse the picture in his mind of Marie Derkowski writhing on the floor of Adah Howland's trailer. Senacal had always been a disbeliever, a critic of miracles, black magic, or any supernatural power that defied human reasoning. Yet Marie Derkowski had learned of the Howland family's secrets while in a voodoo trance. She even saw the markings on Lamech's forehead. It was strange—so very, very strange, like everything else about the case, thought Senacal. He agreed with himself that he was too tired to think. He dried himself off and slipped into a pair of red briefs and opened the bathroom door. He immediately froze in place.

Pleasant Kenite stood between the motel's double

beds in her lace underwear. She was beautiful, her thighs silky and muscular, her stomach flat and firm, and her large breasts nearly bursting over her black bra. Her blond hair lay softly across her shoulders. She played with Senacal's gun in her hand.

"Don't you believe in phoning first?" asked Senacal.

She ignored his humor and gently stroked the barrel of his gun. "I saw the light on." She walked toward him, her smooth hips undulating like the ocean surf. "I thought the big-city lawyer might be lonely. You did tell me where you were staying. Remember?"

Senacal recalled their meeting in Peckman's General Store. "How did you get in? The door was locked."

She stood with her face inches from his. Her warm body smelled of a light perfume. "A key, how else? The owner's son is an old friend and he's on duty tonight at the main desk." She giggled like a schoolgirl and ran the tip of her tongue across her upper lip. She eyed Senacal's body carefully. "The bulge looks good in red."

"The better to hold on to, my dear," Senacal said. He kept his eye on the gun.

As she reached up and kissed his neck, she placed the gun firmly against his groin.

Senacal jerked to attention. "I hope the damn thing's not loaded."

She laughed, then said, "Take off my bra."

Senacal's chest warmed to the feel of her large naked breasts. She moaned softly and slid her hand inside his briefs.

"Fondle my breasts." She closed her eyes and moaned softly into Senacal's ear.

He obeyed her command. He felt his sexuality blossom in her hand, though he feared his testicles had a limited future. He slid his hands inside her panties and pulled her hips against his body.

She pulled the trigger of the gun. "Click." At the sound, Senacal's heart skipped a beat. "Click, click . . ." The gun was empty.

Quickly, Senacal grabbed Pleasant's hand and twisted the gun free. She fell backward on the bed; her blond hair blanketed her face.

"Where are the bullets?"

She laughed at his question and pointed to the dresser. He loaded the gun and stared at Pleasant sprawled on the bed.

"Why did you come here tonight?"

She sat on her legs. "I saw your light on." She playfully toyed with a finger in her mouth.

"Where were you coming from?"

She brushed the hair off her face. "First I was with Mamma on an emergency call, then I was with my boyfriend until now. He's a wham-bam-thank-you-ma'am sort of lover. I like my sex slow. I thought a big-city lawyer over forty could keep it in neutral longer than the young bucks around here."

Senacal struggled to keep his mind on the investigation. "Where did you learn to unload a gun?"

She laughed and stood up on the bed. Her naked breasts bounced firm against her chest. "Hell, I'm a country girl. I dropped my first deer when I was thirteen, a year after my cherry was plucked." She spread her legs and slowly slid her fingers down inside her panties. "Now, are you going to put your toy gun down and take out your six-inch shooter, or am I going home feeling like a jilted bride on her wedding night?"

"How are you with a chain saw?"

"Brum-m-brum-m," Pleasant chanted loudly as she bounced on her knees.

She was the most uninhibited woman Senacal had ever met. She jumped up and down on the bed, laughing as she cut down an imaginary forest. She was crazy and beautiful and lacked a conscience.

Only in dreams do forty-five-year-old men get seduced by horny young blondes.

She tossed her panties into the air and beckoned for him to join her on the bed.

He checked the door to be sure it was locked, then mumbled, "Go for it, asshole." He yelled, "Geronimo," and tackled her to the bed.

6

Saratoga Springs, New York

SENACAL'S TAPES and Lydia Howland's book and letter arrived by express mail to Frank Lattimore's condominium in Saratoga Springs about the time Senacal and Twitchell were halfway to Saint Albans from Eden. A letter from the Sacra Congregatio de Religiosis in Rome, Italy, accompanied the Eden package to the priest's home.

Lattimore had been expecting the onionskin letter from Rome. He sipped his coffee in thought before he read it. He had met Matt Senacal at Donna's divorce ceremony on the evening of March 20. It had been a momentous day for him: not only had he become involved in a multiple-murder case, but that night he had mustered the strength to write his procurator general in Rome to seek official dispensation from the priesthood.

The letter from Rome was written in Latin; it was dated April 14, 1986. Lattimore looked at Bergman's calendar hanging on the side of his refrigerator. It was April 28. Officially, he had been an ex-priest for the past fourteen days. It felt good, but he couldn't have done it alone. Senacal had given him the strength to make the decision, and Liz Ruth had provided the human tenderness he had so desperately sought for years.

"Contrariis quibuslibet non obstantibus," said the letter. "It is not pleasing to stand up against those who are contrary." Frank Lattimore was free to begin his new life. He carefully put the letter in his desk and opened Senacal's package from Eden. Two of the three tapes in the box were of Senacal's conversations with Leisa Dawkins. One of them had been recorded at the Lumen Christi meeting, and the other had been taped at the Mount Zion Congregational Church. The third tape was from Senacal's conversation with Adah Howland. For the next hour, Lattimore listened to the tapes and meticulously placed the information into his computer.

Next, he read Lydia Howland's letter. It was informative, and her knowledge of the Bible was praiseworthy. But it was her strength of character that impressed Lattimore the most. Like himself she too had struggled with a vow. She too had been torn between her professed loyalty to her religious family and that of her conscience and the greater good of mankind. Lattimore felt a genuine empathy for her spiritual plight.

Lattimore found the closing of her letter strange. "Pax Vobiscum: Let 2 Kings 20: 20 by my epitaph." Why request an epitaph in a letter she knew might never be discovered? Was it a clue of some kind? He reached for his Bible and quickly found the quote. "Everything else that King Hezekiah did, his brave deeds, and an account of how he built a reservoir and dug a tunnel to bring water into the city, are all recorded in the history of the Kings of Judah." The quote seemed out of character for such a sensitive and intelligent woman.

He scanned Lydia Howland's letter for other clues. Near the end of her letter a sentence read, "I prayed the city and all present drown. I pleaded with God to break his covenant with Noah." Lattimore wondered if water had been commonplace in the City of

Enoch. He laid out a highway map of Eden and studied the area around Belvidere Mountain. Two small creeks flowed down the mountain into the Gihon River. But it was not enough to draw a valid conclusion. Two Kings 20: 20 had to signify something more.

He scratched out combinations of numbers for 2 Kings 20: 20 on a yellow pad. "20 × 20 = 400, 2 × 20 × 20 = 800, 2 + 2 + 2 = 6." The number 6 startled him. He stood up and paced back and forth in front of the living-room window.

It was called "germatria," the study of assigning numerical values to the inspired words of the Bible. Lattimore had dabbled with its intricacies in the seminary, spending much time on the infamous Anti-Christ or Beast in Chapter Thirteen of Revelations. "The Beast was allowed to make proud claims which were insulting to God. . . . It began to curse God, His name, the place where He lives. . . . It was allowed to fight against God's people and to defeat them, and it was given authority over every tribe, nation, language, and race. All people living on earth will worship it." The Beast was so real to the apostle John that he had left its identity for man to recognize in Revelations 13: 18. "Here is wisdom. Let him that hath understanding count the number of the beast; for it is the number of a man and his number is 666."

Lattimore sat down and put a harness on his imagination. He reasoned that Lydia Howland was no prophetess capable of identifying a biblical killer 115 years after her death. He was sure that 2 Kings 20: 20 had significance in the case, but he would have to be patient and wait.

He reread the letter again. "That's odd," he mumbled as he leaned back in his chair. His curiosity was aroused by an unusual simile in the letter. " 'Then

Cain built a city and named it after his son,' so it was done in Eden like at Mamre."

He knew Mamre was a plain near the city of Hebron in south Palestine. He wondered why Lydia Howland would compare Mamre to the City of Enoch. He tapped a pencil on his desk and stared blankly at the cars speeding up and down Route 50 outside his condominium. He processed the word "Mamre" through the biblical rollodex in his memory. A few quiet seconds passed. Only the tapping of his pencil was heard. "Macpelah," he screamed. He tossed his pencil into the air.

"What's the biblical significance of Macpelah?" had been the very first question Senacal had asked him upon their introduction at Donna's divorce ceremony. Cave of Macpelah had been written on the elevator wall in Mount Horeb, Wisconsin. According to Genesis, Macpelah was the land east of Mamre and the burial site of Abraham and Sarah. Was Nathaniel Howland buried at the location in Eden once called Marme? Maybe its location would prove useful in locating the city built by Nathaniel Howland for his son, Enoch. His questions had few answers, but he was sure Lydia Howland's letter would help him solve the biblical riddle.

Senacal had mentioned at the end of his Adah Howland tape that Marie Derkowski had been the latest victim of the Curse of Lamech. Lattimore added her name to his computer list of victims. She was number fifteen since the Fort Ann execution of Ken Newell on January 4.

Lattimore sipped his coffee and studied the details of all fifteen deaths. He still found some of the methods of execution repugnant: a gas grill, beheading, a wild dog, a chain saw, and the ever-present two-foot sword with two lions' heads carved into an ivory hilt. His research had revealed that the sword was a copy of an Assyrian type dating back to 3000

B.C. After reading Lydia Howland's letter, he concluded the sword had probably been the official weapon of the infamous Soldiers of the Sword.

His computer clicked up more facts he had accumulated about the murders from information given him by Senacal. The killer had cited six different books of the Bible at the eight murder scenes. Deuteronomy and Leviticus had been used twice. Lattimore saw no significance to these facts, nor for the number of killings per location. However, he concluded that at least two teams of killers were necessary to carry out the executions. He figured one team probably roamed the New England states, while another team was responsible for the peripheral states, like Wisconsin and South Carolina. Some individual members of the cult may even have been sent out months in advance to entrap a victim. He had learned from Senacal that Thomas Gilcrest, father of the young man who had discovered the decapitated bodies in Mount Horeb, had told the FBI that his son had become infatuated with a female student named Nina Sadler. Witnesses had seen Harry and Nina leave the University of Wisconsin campus together on January 20, but Nina had disappeared thereafter. Her college personnel file had been fraudulent.

The clicking sound of Lattimore's cursor announced the arrival of a new title from the bottom of his screen—*The Original Seven*. Counting down from seventy-seven, Ken Newell was victim number ten, and his parents were numbers nine and eight. That left seven unaccounted murders. He wondered who they were and in what manner they had been killed.

The word "suspects" appeared next to the green monitor. The list totaled five: Mike Derkowski, Mary Kenite, and her daughter, Pleasant, Gil Pixley, and Hannah Smith. Lattimore typed in the new suspects mentioned in Senacal's tape: Leisa Dawkins and her son, Tertius, and Adah Howland and her sons Jabal and Jubal. That totaled ten suspects in all.

Lattimore's mind drifted toward a disturbing fact in the case. It always seemed to surface when he reviewed the facts of the case. It was the tape, Demons Beware. Senacal had found it in the Newells' stereo on the morning he investigated young Ken's murder. There had been no other rock albums or tapes in the house. Lattimore was sure the murderers brought the tape with them and played it while they sacrificed Ken Newell on a gas grill. He wondered what kind of person would want to listen to their favorite music while executing a young boy in cold blood.

Frank Lattimore jumped at the touch of Liz Ruth's warm hands touching his shoulders. He had forgotten about her asleep in his bed. Her hands felt warm and reassuring. She kissed his neck and slid her fingers through the thick hairs on his chest. His nipples swelled to her touch. He relaxed and put Eden out of his mind.

She nibbled his earlobe and whispered, "You got time for a quickie?" She growled. He laughed. As a priest, he had always thought sex was vile, an act performed in drudgery by married partners to make babies only. Liz Ruth had taught him differently.

He showed her the letter from Rome. "It's official. I've been an ex-priest for the last fourteen days."

"I'm kinda glad you were a celibate all these years. The priesthood's a good training camp for lovers. Who knows, if you hadn't become a priest, you might have ended up like Senacal."

He held her in his arms. Her body felt warm through the white silk nightgown he had given her. "Be nice. I owe a lot to Senacal. He fixed us up."

She gently kissed him on the lips. "I'll give the bastard credit for that."

Frank Lattimore's lovemaking was rudely interrupted by the piercing sound of his front door bell.
The ex-priest scurried out of bed, put on his pants,
and slipped into his Docksides. The priesthood had
conditioned him to react quickly to the sound of a
bell.

"Hurry back. There's more where that came from,"
teased Liz Ruth from under the silk sheets.

As usual, Lieutenant Schiff wore no smile as he
led FBI Agent Robert Hawkins and a man with a
jagged scar across his forehead into Lattimore's apartment. Agent Hawkins managed a weak smile when
he was introduced to Frank Lattimore, but the stranger
said nothing. He opted for a view of the Saratoga
Springs Performing Arts Center from the picture window in the living room. He wore a neatly trimmed
crew cut and nervously played with some loose
change in his pocket.

Lieutenant Schiff spoke up first. "I called the FBI
yesterday after Senacal had phoned about a letter he
had found describing the activities of the Howland
family. I figured we had reached a point in the
investigation where secrecy was no longer important. As it turned out, it was a good thing I called
Agent Hawkins."

"Coffee anyone?" Liz Ruth didn't wait for an answer; she proceeded directly into the kitchen with
her robe flowing in her tailwind.

Schiff looked at Lattimore and said, "Ask her to
leave. We have important matters to discuss."

Schiff represented the strong authority figure Frank
Lattimore had succumbed to all his priestly life. Obedience was the hallmark of a good priest. His first
instinct was to submit to Schiff's request and ask Liz
Ruth to leave. But he reminded himself he was no
longer a priest. He stared at Schiff and said, "I don't
work for you or the FBI. So please don't come in
here telling me how to run my personal life. I think

you owe the lady an apology." It felt good standing up to authority for the first time in his life.

"Bravo!" cheered Liz Ruth from the kitchen.

Schiff managed a wry smile and said, "I apologize. I'm a bit uptight about Senacal and Twitchell being alone undercover in Eden with a wacko killer running loose who thinks he's God."

"Are they all right?" Lattimore asked as he sat down at his desk. His computer was still on. He had forgotten to turn if off in the heat of passion with Liz Ruth.

"I think so. Senacal called this morning and said he and Twitchell were driving to St. Albans, Vermont, to check out a guy named Jubal Howland. He didn't have time to give me the details."

Agent Hawkins spoke up for the first time. "The FBI is ready to throw its entire support behind your Eden, Vermont, theory but we'll have to move quickly. It's becoming more and more difficult to keep the press quiet about the killings. If it becomes headlines, we're afraid the killer will go underground."

"How have you kept it out of the papers?" Lattimore asked Hawkins.

From the kitchen, Liz Ruth jumped at the question. "Sex and taxes. The FBI bribes the hell out of the newspaper owners by saying, 'Don't print the story and we won't audit your taxes or print the picture of you and your bimbo in the bathtub.' "

Agent Hawkins glared at Liz Ruth as she strutted toward the bedroom with her coffee in one hand and the morning newspaper in the other.

The sound of change jingling in the stranger's pocket filled the room. He turned from the window and looked at Lattimore. "Congratulations. You're quite a detective."

The stranger was short with square shoulders and

a resonant voice. Lattimore smiled back, then looked at Agent Hawkins for a formal introduction. The stranger didn't wait for protocol.

"I think we've wasted enough time already. My name is Sam Canfield. I'm a retired lieutenant colonel in the United States Air Force. Two years ago in Wyoming, I witnessed the execution of seven fellow Air Force personnel." He stopped and rubbed the scar on his forehead for a second or two. "I don't know if witness is the proper word. At the time, I was temporarily blinded. Yet, the sounds I heard . . ." His voice momentarily trailed off when Schiff raised his hand for him to stop.

Lieutenant Schiff and Agent Hawkins looked at each other to see who would speak first. Schiff took the lead. "When Mr. Canfield approached the FBI Agent Hawkins thought it best that we fly here to speak with you directly. He thought his story might give a clue to the identification of the Eden, Vermont, killer."

"This is the first you've spoken about this?" Lattimore asked Canfield, confused.

Canfield lowered his head for a second and rubbed the scar on his forehead. "Fate dealt me a second chance to make good. You see, after I retired from the Air Force, I became a cop with the Louisville Police Department. On February 17th of this year, I was called to assist the Fort Knox Police on an unusual homicide. As you know two decapitated soldiers had been burned in General Patton's jeep in the Patton Museum in Fort Knox. They had been torched by an army flamethrower and a small sword was stuck in each soldier's chest. I just knew the murders had been performed by the same killers as those of the seven Air Force personnel in Wyoming. There were just too many similarities in both instances. I had agreed to a military cover-up the first time the killers struck in Wyoming. After seeing those two dead soldiers in the jeep I knew I had to call the FBI and tell them my story."

Frank Lattimore slipped a tape into his recorder and asked Canfield to start from the beginning. He knew time and patience were required for Canfield to tell his painful story.

"There's not much to tell. I was assigned to drop six Air Force Academy cadets over the Eden Valley Reservoir in Wyoming. After the drop . . ."

Lattimore moved to the edge of his chair and cradled his coffee mug tightly in his hands. "You said Eden?"

"Yes I did. It was the first time the Academy ever used the Eden Valley Reservoir as a survival training site. It was a superior's idea to drop them there. The six cadets had been insubordinate, so that was their punishment. The Eden Valley Reservoir is quite a distance from the Academy in Colorado Springs, Colorado."

Agent Hawkins unfolded a map of Wyoming and handed it to Lattimore. A red circle in the southwest section of the state highlighted the Eden Valley area. Lattimore noticed there was a town called Eden just south of the reservoir near a high mountain called Granite Peak.

Agent Hawkins looked at Lattimore and said, "When Lieutenant Schiff called me yesterday and explained your Eden, Vermont, theory I just knew the Wyoming murders had to have been committed by the same person this Senacal was tracking down in Vermont. How often does the name Eden pop up twice in a criminal investigation? In fact I'd like a list of your Eden, Vermont, suspects. I'll run their names through the computer. One of them just has to be linked to Eden, Wyoming, in some way."

Lattimore nodded. He was absorbed in his own reverie. There was something familiar about Canfield's story, but he couldn't quite put his finger on it. He was sure it would come in time. He asked Canfield to continue with his narrative.

"After the drop, my plane suddenly developed an engine problem. I circled around for awhile looking for a place to land. I saw a narrow plateau near Granite Peak and went in for an emergency landing. The ground was bumpy and the plane broke apart, but we survived. I received a large gash across my forehead that caused my blindness. Lieutenant Jenkins began leading me to safety through the woods when we smelled the burning kerosene."

Lattimore listened but his mind wrestled with trying to recall the familiar facts in Sam Canfield's story. Whatever it was, he knew he had heard it before in connection with the case.

The vision of a boy holding his dog on Highway 13 in Vietnam flashed before Sam Canfield's eyes when Lattimore asked him about the kerosene odor he had smelled. Even after twenty years, he still found the flashback difficult to accept. He rubbed his hands for a few seconds and continued with his story.

"The smell reminded me of napalm. It was a real putrid smell. I told Lieutenant Jenkins to head in the direction of the smell. It's funny . . ." Canfield paused; his eyes moistened as he struggled to continue. "I don't know why I gave that order. I knew something was very wrong. I could feel it as we walked through the woods and the smell grew stronger. I often thought afterwards, I should have told Jenkins to turn around." Canfield cleared his throat. "Anyhow, we traveled for fifty yards or so until we came to a large open quarry. Jenkins told me that the six Air Force cadets we had dropped over the Eden Valley Reservoir were lined up parallel to each other, naked on a stone altar in the smoky quarry. They were gagged, and hooded guards carrying small swords surrounded the altar. Then a man in a rainbow cloak stood on a stone pulpit and delivered a crazy speech. I'll never forget it as long as I live. He talked about a god named Baal who would rise out of the earth and spread fear all over the earth. He then said something about a group called the Soldiers of the Sword who would be feared all over the earth too." Canfield paused and rubbed his scar in thought for a few seconds. "In one part of the sermon the preacher said, 'The revenge of Lamech must soon begin. May the headless bodies of our enemies be left to the birds and wild animals.'

"Then those sounds . . . and later I saw them. It was horrible," Canfield almost whispered.

"What happened to Lieutenant Jenkins?" asked Lattimore.

"He buried me under some leaves and tried to rescue the six cadets. I told him it was foolish, but he said it was war and it was his duty." Canfield paused for a second. "I spent the night under the leaves. The murderers continued chanting and singing until dusk. Miraculously, my vision returned with the morning sun. I creeped over to the quarry. All that remained were seven headless bodies on the stone altar. When I finally reported back to my superiors at the Academy, they ordered an immediate cover-up. They officially reported that the training plane had crashed and the bodies had burned beyond recognition. I only had a few months left before retirement, so I went along with it."

Canfield looked into Lattimore's eyes. "Don't judge me harshly. Cover-ups are common in the military. You get used to lying. Who would believe the real story, anyhow? Sometimes I wonder if it ever happened myself."

After Canfield had finished his story, Lattimore turned and punched the code name 'Suspects' into his computer.

He had to silence the nagging question in his

mind. What was the fact in Canfield's story that was so familiar to him? A list of Eden suspects appeared on his monitor. Under each name were facts about the suspects he had taken from Senacal's tapes. Next, he played back Canfield's story on his tape recorder. Maybe the missing fact was in his computer under a suspect's name? As the three men hovered around him, Lattimore listened to the tape and studied the facts on his monitor at the same time.

Lattimore talked to his computer as he studied the screen and listened to the recording of Canfield's story. "Come on baby. Tell me who killed all these innocent people." A few minutes passed in silence as new information rolled up from the bottom of the screen. Then a calm came over Frank Lattimore. He sat back in his chair. He pointed to the name of an Eden suspect on the screen and said, "Gentlemen, this is your Biblical killer."

7

St. Albans, Vermont

SENACAL DROVE slowly through St. Albans' main street and studied the silver car that had followed him from a distance across Vermont. He turned into a nearby shopping mall and parked in front of a fast-food restaurant. A branch office of a Vermont bank stood directly behind the popular eatery. He cautioned Twitchell not to look around but to casually walk into the restaurant. If Gil Pixley had been following them halfway across the state, Senacal didn't want to arouse his suspicions now.

"Their burgers make me fart. Even Patton gets heartburn," Twitchell moaned as he pulled the small dog from the car.

"You can't bring Patton inside a restaurant," Senacal said.

"Let them try to stop me. Patton goes wherever I go. Besides, I'll just tell them Patton is my seeing-eye dog."

Inside, Senacal quickly surveyed the restaurant. "Get that table in the corner," he ordered. The table commanded a view of Route 7 and the mall. Senacal made a quick inspection of the mall parking lot but saw no sign of the car that had followed them.

"Can I get you anything?" Senacal asked.

"Get me a coffee. Hot and sweet, just how I like my women."

"If you ever had a hot, sweet woman she'd kill you."

"That young filly nearly broke your back last night. I saw her. She was in and out of your room as quick as a wink. When I was your age, I'd of had her begging for more."

Senacal returned and fifteen minutes passed in idle talk but no sign of Gil Pixley or his silver car appeared. Senacal noticed another entrance into the mall farther up Route 7 from where he sat.

"Give me the keys," Twitchell said.

"Uh!" Senacal's mind was on Pixley's whereabouts.

"I'll flush him out for you." Twitchell stood up and grabbed the car keys off the table. "He's not stupid enough to let you see him. He's waiting behind the bank for you to leave, then he'll follow you. Saw Broderick Crawford flush out a crook from behind a roadside diner on *Highway Patrol* once. If it worked for Crawford, it'll work for me. Wait by the drive-in out back. I'll deliver Pixley to you. Hell of a good television show, that *Highway Patrol*. Don't know why it went off the air. *Perry Mason* was another good one."

Twitchell was out the door and into the car before Senacal had decided to allow him to leave. Patton jumped into the passenger seat beside his master. Twitchell turned into Route 7 and headed toward the other end of the mall.

Senacal slammed his fist down on the table. "Damn it!" A silver car pulled out from the bank behind the restaurant and followed Twitchell out of the mall.

When the old man approached the other mall entrance, he flipped on his directional signal and turned quickly back into the mall. On cue, the silver car followed Twitchell's lead. Having lured his prey into the trap, the old man stepped on the gas pedal and zigzagged around three parked cars as he raced across the half-full parking lot. A few bewildered pedestrians ran for cover behind their cars as Twitchell led Pixley back to Senacal.

"The old man's crazy," Senacal mumbled as he watched Twitchell turn the mall parking lot into a drag strip. Senacal hopped over the food counter, showed his police identification to the restaurant manager, and waited for Twitchell to arrive at the drive-in window.

"I told you I'd flush him out," said Twitchell as he rolled down his car window. "Just like Pete DePaolo in the 1925 Indy Five-hundred. First driver to go over a hundred miles per hour, and he did it on bricks too!" Twitchell raced the engine a few times for Senacal's pleasure. A boyish glow flashed across the old man's face. Patton barked proudly next to him.

"Remind me to have you arrested when we get back to New York," said Senacal. He motioned Twitchell to park behind the bank, then he hid behind a green dumpster. He didn't have long to wait. Pixley circled the drive-in ramp and unwillingly picked Senacal up.

"Pull over there!" Senacal pointed his gun toward the bank parking lot where Twitchell waited. "No cute stuff or your balls will end up as scrambled eggs all over your car muffler." A look of pain appeared on Pixley's face.

Gil Pixley was a bowl of Jell-O in blue denims. His face was round and soft like a baby's bottom and his engraved silver belt buckle was hidden below his stomach fat. His pudgy hands gripped the steering wheel in fear. He hadn't blinked since Senacal entered his life, nor had his head moved an inch. He looked like a clown in his black cowboy hat and rattlesnake-skin hatband. His facial color was pure white.

Senacal flipped his police identification wallet on the dashboard and Pixley squeezed the steering wheel tighter.

"Where are my tapes?"

At first Pixley was too scared to speak. His voice quivered as he told Senacal they were in his motel room back in Morrisville.

"I've got a rope in my trunk," Twitchell yelled from in front of Pixley's car. "We could lynch the stealin' bastard from this here oak." Pixley's eyes bulged at the sight of Twitchell laughing. Senacal waved the old man back to his car.

"Why did you break into my motel room?" Only silence answered Senacal's question. "Come on. I don't have all day." He nudged Pixley in the ribs with his gun. The cowboy jumped and his hat fell over his eyes.

"I thought you knew about the money," Pixley said.

"What money?"

"My great-granddaddy's money. Or maybe I should say St. Albans' money. But after all these years probably Saint Albans doesn't know its their money either."

"For Christ's sake, take your goddamn hat off your eyes."

"Can I take my hands off the wheel?"

"How else are you going to fix it? With your nose."

Pixley placed his hat back on his head.

Senacal carefully scrutinized Pixley's body for a weapon, then said, "Is that all fat under your shirt or a machine gun?"

Pixley said he carried no weapon. However, Senacal searched under the seat to be sure. The suspect seemed innocent enough, but Senacal reminded himself to be cautious.

"Now, why have you been following me around for the last few days?" Senacal asked.

"I told you, because of the money. I thought you were looking for it too. Those tapes are awful." Pixley's face shriveled up in disgust.

"Why did you follow me out to Knowles Flats the other night?"

Pixley nodded. "I thought you were after the money." .

It was obvious that Gil Pixley had a story to tell. Senacal leaned back against the car door. "All right, just spill it, son."

"My mother was a Young before marrying my daddy, and her granddaddy was Confederate Lieutenant Bennet H. Young. Did you ever hear of him, sir?" Pixley moved his head for the first time and looked at Senacal. His eyes bulged at the sight of Senacal's gun.

"No," replied Senacal between tight lips. "Robert E. Lee is about the extent of my Civil War history." He waved his gun at Pixley to continue.

The southerner's head swiveled back to center position, his hands still squeezing the steering wheel like a sailor's to a life raft. "My great-granddaddy and about twenty-five Confederate soldiers descended upon St. Albans from Canada." Pixley ventured a glance toward Senacal. "It was the most northern invasion of blue-belly territory by the Confederates in the whole Civil War, and my great-granddaddy was in charge of that invasionary force." Pixley's face beamed proudly.

Senacal said, "Be careful. You're in blue-belly territory now."

Pixley cleared his throat and coughed to collect his thoughts. "The Confederates under the command of Lieutenant Bennet H. Young, my great-granddaddy, robbed two hundred thousand dollars from three banks in Saint Albans, but were caught shortly thereafter in Canada. However, only seventy-five thousand of the stolen money was recovered."

Senacal shook his head in disbelief. "And you're here to find the other $125,000 that has rotted away like soggy leaves since the Civil War?"

"Wait! Let me explain. On May 23, 1904, my great-granddaddy was the grand marshal of the Cedar Creek, Virginia, parade celebrating the anniversary of Virginia's secession from the Union. My grandmother was there and later wrote down in her diary about the reunion her daddy had that day with a John S. Marmaduke, one of the twenty-five in the St. Albans raid. It seems Marmaduke headed east with the $120,000 after my great-granddaddy headed north to Canada. He placed the money in a lead box, sealed it with wax, then buried it behind a marble statue in a clearing in the forest. He told my great-granddaddy that the clearing was near a mountain surrounded by tall elm trees with an apple tree shaped like a cross in the middle of the clearing. Marmaduke was sure the marble statue would be there after the war. So he buried it ten steps behind the statue, but we lost the war."

Pixley paused and sadly shook his head back and forth. Water crested over his eyelids.

"What the hell are you crying about? The damn war ended over a hundred years ago, for Christ's sake!"

Pixley regained his composure and continued. "I found my grandmother's diary a short while back and thought I'd try to find the marble statue. I started in Eden because that's where Marmaduke was captured and later sent to Johnson's Prison Camp near Lake Erie. After the war, he was afraid to return to Vermont for fear of a reprisal, so he waited until 1869 before he went back, but had no luck finding his treasure. That money's worth a million today, if it's in good shape."

Senacal sifted through Pixley's story. The reference to a marble statue in the woods coincided with Adah Howland's description of her wedding site. He observed Gil Pixley one more time. He figured the man was incapable of even mustering the strength to swat a fly, nevertheless kill Marie Derkowski. Yet, he had a motive and did break into Senacal's motel room.

"Who else did you follow in Eden?"

"Mostly you! Three men in a car usually means ya'll priests or gangsters. I thought ya'll looked like big-city mobsters."

Senacal wasn't amused. "Who else did you talk with?"

"The town clerk was nasty. She just stared at me through her thick glasses when I asked for old maps of the area. She was suspicious of my request. I asked the postmistress too, but she laughed and said the whole state was one big marble statue. I think the store-owner knows about the clearing. He's always studying rocks and does a lot of hiking up near Belvidere Mountain." Pixley paused for a second and stared through the windshield. "You know, St. Albans has a lot in common with Cedar Creek, Virginia."

Senacal ignored Pixley's last remark. "What about Reverend Dawkins and her son?"

"I don't know them." Pixley shook his head.

"Her son's a big guy. Walks like Frankenstein and built like a shit brick house."

Pixley's eyes nearly fell to his puffy cheeks. "Yes! I saw him running bare-chested along Mine Road one night. It was cold. He certainly looked strange."

Pixley's knuckles were white from squeezing the steering wheel. Senacal told the cowboy he'd not arrest him if he left Vermont immediately. Pixley agreed without an argument.

"It's real strange," Pixley said as he stared through the windshield. "My great-granddaddy raided this town on the same exact day and year that his hometown of Cedar Creek was under attack by Union General Philip Sheridan. It was October 19, 1864. Confederate General Jubal Early suffered twenty-nine hundred casualties during the campaign."

"Who was that Confederate general?"

"Jubal Early." Pixley looked at Senacal. "Jubal was a descendant of Cain who loved music."

The Central Vermont Railroad Building in St. Albans had the charm of an icehouse in January. Red towers with green slate roofs jutted up like mountain peaks at each end of the three-story building. The windows, shaped like skeleton keyholes, lined up across the three floors like crowded clothespins on a laundry line. Senacal and Twitchell ignored the building's homeliness as they walked up the stone steps in search of Jubal Howland's new address.

"Let me do the talking," Twitchell argued. "You don't know a goddamn thing about the railroad. Half my retired friends worked for the D and H and I've heard their old stories a thousand times over."

"I want you in the car with Patton," Senacal said. "This isn't a game. We're dealing with a psycho."

Twitchell stopped on the top step and faced Senacal. "And I'll kiss your ass if you can con a good railroad man into giving you Jubal Howland's address without saying you're a cop. You don't know the difference between a 'nosebug' and a 'boomer.' "

The argument continued until the pair stood outside an office with the word "PERSONNEL" written in black on the door's frosted glass.

Senacal sighed. "O.K., you win. But, remember . . ." He pointed a finger at Twitchell. "This investigation is mine. If I decide to butt in, then move aside. If you don't, you kiss my ass."

"And if I get that crazy Jubal Howland's new address, then you kiss mine." Twitchell opened the door and walked in. Senacal followed.

The office was large and empty save for one gray desk occupied by a slim middle-aged woman. She looked up at the loud intruders and walked to a mahogany gate that separated the office from the visitors' section. She waited for the men to state their business.

Twitchell bent his body from the waist. "Excuse us. I was wondering if I could speak to the man in charge." His broad smile was not warmly received.

The woman's face was chiseled in stone. She looked directly into Twitchell's eyes. "There is no man in charge. There is, however, a woman in charge, and she's standing before you."

Senacal laughed to himself at the thought of Twitchell kissing his ass.

"I'm sorry," Twitchell said. "No offense. Railroads is usually a man's world, except for his kin. Was your daddy in railroads?" Twitchell reached for his red handkerchief and blew his nose loudly.

The woman remained undaunted by Twitchell's hygiene. "Yes, he was, as a matter of fact."

"Betcha he was a hogger? Was he?" Twitchell smiled as he waited for her answer.

"Yes, he was."

"Which line?"

"Maine Central."

"Oh, what a pretty run. Right up the Connecticut River through Lancaster, Groveton, Colebrook, and West Stewartstown. Right into the Canadian sunset." Twitchell flailed his arms about to dramatize his excitement. "Betcha ya rode with him when school was out? The window music is beautiful up there in the summer."

"Yes, I did!" A red glow flushed her cheeks; her body relaxed.

"Use to take my daughter too. I'm an old D and H man myself. Retired in '66. Use to head into Rutland twice a week. Not as pretty a run as your daddy had, though."

The woman smiled broadly. "Well, what can I do for you?" She stared at Senacal for the first time.

"This here's my son-in-law, Matt Senacal. I'm Graham Twitchell from Fort Ann. And you are?"

She again blushed. "Agnes Connelly."

"Am goin' to call you Aggie. O.K.?" A twinkle glowed in Twitchell's eyes.

She nodded shyly.

"Matt here's my watchdog. My daughter wouldn't let me drive up here alone to look up an old railroad friend, so she nagged Matt here to take me. She was afraid I'd drive right into Lake Champlain and drown. It's the eyes."

Agnes Connelly laughed quietly behind a clenched fist. She found Twitchell delightful. "You and my father are so much alike. He's in a nursing home up the hill on Route 105." She looked at both men for a second before she continued. "Who is your friend? Maybe I can help. Is he retired from the Central Vermont?"

"His name is Jubal Howland," Twitchell said. "I have an old address, but he moved."

Stiffness returned to the woman's body. She darted her eyes coldly back and forth between the men. "You have a very strange friend, Mr. Twitchell. He makes me very uncomfortable when he comes in here, which isn't often, thank God."

"It was his childhood," Twitchell said with a hint of compassion in his voice. "His dad was a drunk and used to beat him up badly. He's a loner."

"It's not that, Mr. Twitchell. He's a religious fanatic. He's always preaching about some prophecy of the Bible that he must fulfill. He has a horrible symbol carved into his forehead—"

"Like golf tees," interrupted Twitchell.

"Yes. He once told me God put it on his forehead thousands of years ago. The man's definitely sick."

"Once you get to know him, he's not bad. May I have his address?"

Agnes Connelly argued with herself aloud. "Well, it's irregular. But seeing nobody cares much about Jubal and you're an old railroad man, I'll get it for you. Will you please excuse me?" She smiled and left for a small room in the rear cluttered with gray filing cabinets.

"You are the world's biggest bullshitter," whispered Senacal out of the corner of his mouth.

Twitchell whispered back, "Goddamn proud of it, too."

Agnes Connelly returned with Jubal Howland's file. "Here it is. Savage Street. That's all it says. There's no number."

"What's Jubal do on the Central Vermont?" Twitchell asked. "Used to be a gandy dancer when I knew him."

"He still is. Claims he likes to wander because God condemned him to a life of wandering. Real schizo is that troubled man. Plays the harmonica all the time."

"Where's he working today? I'd like to surprise him."

"Hold on." Her footsteps echoed loudly off the high ceiling as she walked to her phone.

"What the hell's a gandy dancer, a whore?" asked Senacal under his breath.

Twitchell replied softly, "It's a track repairman. Now, shut up. You're supposed to be my henpecked, candy-ass son-in-law. You better get puckered up 'cause my ass is ready for a big juicy kiss."

Agnes smiled at the men while she waited on the phone. She hated to see them leave; they had been her only visitors all week.

"He left this morning for Burlington," she said as she hung up the phone.

"A frog replacement?" Twitchell queried.

"Yes. He'll be there all day, then he's scheduled for two days off. He'll probably be wandering about the countryside fulfilling God's prophecy."

Jubal Howland's home on Savage Street needed no number. A circular piece of red plywood was nailed between the bedroom windows of a small dilapidated house overlooking the Central Vermont rail yard. The front porch was wrapped in torn plastic and the flat roof listed slightly to starboard. Written in black on the circular piece of red plywood was the reference: "Gen. 4: 21." Senacal reached for his Bible under the car seat. It read, "His brother was Jubal, the ancestor of all musicians who play the harp and the flute."

Twitchell put a leash on Patton, then turned to Senacal. "It's shit time for Patton. Got to take her for a walk. Hate to think what it's like inside. If I lived here, I'd burn the house down with the son of a bitch inside."

The street was short with oak trees lined up in single file on each side. Jubal Howland's house was the last one on the right next to a vacant lot littered with rotting timbers.

Senacal removed his gun and held it inside his herringbone sport jacket. Gently, he kicked a garbage can on the path to the side door. It was empty. Either Jubal was a light eater or the garbage was picked up yesterday.

He knocked on the door to lessen neighborly suspicion, though he was sure Jubal Howland was in Burlington. He knocked again to be sure. Nothing. He reached for the glass knob; the door was unlocked and he walked into Jubal Howland's temple.

In the living room, rows of lighted candles stood

side by side on the empty shelves of a metal book-case. Their reflection danced across the living-room ceiling like a flickering rainbow. A hearth oven of mud brick stood in the middle of the room, and a column of smoke from burning incense billowed up to the ceiling, filling the room with a sweet odor. An icon over the living-room fireplace showed devil fig-ures with spears and grappling hooks attacking peo-ple ascending Jacob's ladder to heaven. The sole piece of furniture in the room was a concrete bench, like that found in a cemetery, placed behind a large harp with a curved top. A few colored mats of bam-boo were scattered about the living-room floor. Senacal took a deep breath, reminded himself he was deal-ing with a real sicko, and headed upstairs. He read-ied his gun in case. His mouth turned dry. He wondered if Jubal Howland was as big as his lum-berjack brother, Jabal.

The upstairs was one large room, except for a door leading to a sun parlor. The walls were white with the letters and numbers of biblical references painted in red. Senacal recognized one of the references; it was Genesis 22: 6–10—Ken Newell's epitaph. He also recognized Marie Derkowski's, hers was the last painted on the wall. He climbed the last few steps, turned around the shaky banister, and instantly crouched to fire his gun. His heart skipped a beat.

A human skeleton dressed in green priestly vest-ments was propped up on a stone altar. It was held to the back wall by wire snaked through its empty eye sockets. A gold pointed hood adorned the skull. Bony toes were barely visible beneath the dusty cha-suble. Behind the skeleton lay a small mound of human skulls stacked randomly one on top of the other. There were about a dozen or so. Senacal studied the skeleton before lowering his gun. His eyes darted around the room to be sure he was alone. He wondered who the skeleton was. He suddenly felt very nauseous.

He kicked open the sun-parlor door. It overlooked the Central Vermont rail yard where a large grain elevator dominated the dreary scenery. Senacal smelled gasoline. He walked past a blue couch cluttered with old newspapers, an electric heater, and rolled-up maps neatly stacked and bound by rubber bands. A picture of a triumphant David with Goliath's bloody head at his feet hung on the wall opposite the couch. He spotted a chain-saw case in the corner. He flicked it open with his foot. Chunks of dried flesh and black hair had hardened on the chain bar. "Marie Derkowski," Senacal mumbled.

He was curious about the pyramid maps on the couch. He toppled the mound with his pen and scattered the maps out until they were lined up like a row of pencils. His eye caught the words, "#2 Mt. Horeb." He peeled off the rubber band; it was an aeronautical map of southern Wisconsin. A red circle was placed around the figure of an airplane at the intersection of routes 92 and 18. Mount Horeb was a mile or two from the airport. "Shit. That's it." Senacal exclaimed.

He grabbed another map labeled "#4 Bowman Field." He tore off the rubber band. The map was of the vicinity around Louisville, Kentucky, and a red circle designated Bowman Field, a small airport southeast of Louisville. It was just ten miles or so from Fort Knox, the site of the fourth execution.

"He's a goddamn pilot," Senacal said aloud. "A modern wanderer! No wonder the killings were executed so quickly one after the other. Jubal Howland carried the severed heads of his victims back to Eden on a plane."

He paid little attention to the skeleton priest on his return visit downstairs. The living-room air was thick with incense; he coughed as he ran past the harp into the kitchen looking for a phone to call Schiff. The kitchen was bare, almost medieval in appearance. A kerosene lantern sat on a wooden shelf alongside a few black frying pans, a metal can of olive oil, and a burner similar to the kind used in a chemistry lab. There was no sink, no refrigerator, and no stove. Bushels of onions and dried fruits sat on the dirt floor.

Senacal yelled, "Where the hell does this fruit cake keep his phone?"

He searched the walls and ceiling of the living room for phone wire. Nothing. He opened a small door under the stairs.

The cellar was dark. He felt for a wall switch as he descended. "Click." From the stairway, he saw a large picture of an airplane's instrument panel tacked to a brown Peg-Board over a workbench made of particleboard. As Senacal approached, he noticed the colored photos of a Douglas DB-7 light bomber and a Boeing B-17. Both planes were of World War II vintage and stapled to the floor joists. The workbench was littered with aeronautical charts. He opened one; it showed the direction of air masses across the eastern United States from Canada and the Gulf of Mexico. Another showed isogonic lines dividing the United States into magnetic zones. A phone hung on the Peg-Board. Senacal reached for a clipboard that contained copies of flight logs that had been arranged in chronological order dating back to August 10, 1985. The last entry was for today, April 27, 1986.

Jubal Howland had left his aerial calling card. Quickly, Senacal studied the columns. "Departure point: Burlington, Vermont. Takeoff: 1655. Destination: Coventry, Vermont. ETA 1810." Coventry lay east of Eden on the New Hampshire border. Senacal picked up the phone. He was anxious to announce to Schiff the identity of the Eden killer.

Senacal was quiet during the hilly ride in the snow across the Green Mountains of Vermont to Coventry. An early-spring snowfall had begun falling over northern Vermont. It was called "poor man's fertilizer" by the local farmers. Its flakes were large and moist and floated like a host of butterflies to the ground.

"Put on your damn wipers or you'll kill us all," said Twitchell. Patton barked approvingly at his master's suggestion.

Senacal flicked on the wipers but remained lost in his reverie. He stared blankly ahead at the horizon. His mood confused Twitchell. The old man had expected his friend to be excited over the discovery of Jubal Howland as the biblical killer. Instead, Senacal sat quietly behind the wheel with the look of Atlas carrying the world's woes on his shoulders.

"Ya got a burr up your ass or did ya forget how to talk?" snapped Twitchell.

Senacal patted Twitchell on the knee and managed a quick smile. A sign on the right read BELVIDERE CENTER AHEAD. The snow began blanketing the shoulder of the road.

"It just doesn't make any sense," Senacal argued. "They said Lattimore solved the case. He identified the biblical killer after listening to some witnesses the FBI found. How could Lattimore have known?" Senacal slammed his hand down on the dashboard. "And worse yet, Schiff left orders for me to wait at the Ski Top Motel until he and Lattimore arrived. It's pure bullshit." He again slapped the dashboard.

"Did Lattimore say Jubal was the murderer?" Twitchell asked. He reached for Patton, who had become frightened from the noise of Senacal's temper tantrum.

"That's even more bullshit. Schiff left instructions not to tell me in case I'd try to capture the son of a bitch before he and the FBI arrived. Did you ever hear such bullshit in your lifetime?"

Twitchell patted Patton on the head. "Sounds like Lieutenant Schiff knows you pretty damn well. If I were him, I'd have made the same judgment call. You're a pretty lousy team player, Senacal." Twitchell's attention was drawn to a green road sign on his right. "Here's Route 118 ahead. A right will take us back to the Ski Top Motel. A left will bring us over to Coventry and Jubal Howland. Let's see what kind of a team player you are. My money's on a left-hand turn to Coventry."

Senacal vaguely heard Twitchell's bet. Through the falling snow, he saw Belvidere Mountain straight ahead. It seemed to burst upon the horizon directly from the pits of hell. Senacal focused his anger on the peak. The mountain stood in contradiction. On the one hand, it produced beautiful stones and harbored treasures left by maurauders in war. Yet, it witnessed horrible scenes of death deep within its bowels. She stood tall above the land, a pinnacle of evil, like a lighthouse, sending its ominous message of death to all who knew her secrets. She was Senacal's Armageddon.

"Fuck you," Senacal yelled in anger at the distant mountain. For a few precious seconds, he had lost touch with the reality of his surroundings. There were no icy roads where his thoughts had traveled.

"Stop!" Twitchell braced his hands against the dashboard.

The flashing red light was above Senacal's car before he was aware of its message. Instinctively, he hit the brakes hard, forgetting for the moment the icy road. The car didn't stop; it slid through the intersection of Route 118. Patton howled. Senacal released the brake and turned the steering wheel sharply to the left. The back of the car swung around to the front as if pulled by a rope. It slammed into the metal guardrail and became airborne. Senacal heard Patton whine as Twitchell fell across his lap. He grabbed the old man and held him tightly. He could taste blood in his mouth. His hands were wet. He looked down at Twitchell's bleeding head, then slumped across the steering wheel into unconsciousness.

8

City of Enoch

IT HAD been a flippant remark said in jest about Senacal's baldness, but it had placed Mary Kenite in Colonel Sam Canfield's grisly account of the Wyoming executions. "How's the weather up on Granite Peak?" Mary Kenite had asked Senacal in Peckman's General Store. Unfortunately for the postmistress, Senacal had forgotten to turn off his recorder upon exiting Marie Derkowski's voodoo temple. Lattimore had made the connection between the Granite Peak mentioned in Colonel Canfield's story and Mary Kenite's use of Granite Peak as a metaphor for Senacal's baldness.

Frank Lattimore studied Lydia Howland's letter on the air flight to Morrisville, Vermont, while Schiff and Agent Hawkins were busy with police matters. As information was received from the FBI, Agent Hawkins shouted the message back to Lattimore.

"Mary Kenite lives on a gravel road off Mine Road near Belvidere Mountain. I've dispatched agents from Burlington to Eden to put her house under surveillance."

"Mary Kenite was transferred to the Eden, Vermont, post office from Rock Springs, Wyoming, two years ago."

Darkness settled around the small airplane as it

streaked to northern Vermont. No word had been received from Senacal since he had called from St. Albans.

Lattimore spoke up. "Have you notified the Vermont police about our coming?"

Robert Hawkins turned slightly to catch Lattimore's eye. "Yes. They'll meet us at the Morrisville airport and hopefully we'll hook up with Senacal at the Ski Top Motel."

"Did you tell them about Mary Kenite?" Lattimore asked.

"What would I tell them?" replied Agent Hawkins. "I have nothing on her except that she lived near Granite Peak, Wyoming. After they hear your story—and hopefully believe it—then we can proceed as a team with the investigation. It's better that way. In the meantime, her house will be under surveillance by my agents. We'll keep tabs on her."

Frank Lattimore opened a highway map of Eden and marked an X on a gravel road off Mine Road. He was sure the spot marked the approximate location of Mary Kenite's home. The highway map was quite detailed, marking the locations of mobile homes, farm units, seasonal dwellings, dwellings other than farms, and so forth. The homes were all too crowded together along Mine Road for Mary Kenite's taste, reasoned Lattimore. The gravel road probably led to her home, secluded somewhere in the woods where she had the privacy to plan the biblical murders.

Lattimore reasoned that the key to convicting Mary Kenite rested in locating the City of Enoch. He was sure she practiced her evil sorcery there, as had her ancestors before her. He reasoned the City of Enoch had to be a cave or a quarry similar to the one Sam Canfield stumbled upon two years ago in Wyoming. He was convinced that Lydia Howland's letter provided the clues to the city's location. As before, he was drawn to her epitaph, "Let 2 Kings 20: 20 be my epitaph." He opened his Bible to the appropriate passage.

"Everything else that King Hezekiah did, his brave deeds, and an account of how he built a reservoir and dug a tunnel to bring water into the city, are all recorded in *The History of the Kings of Judah*. Hezekiah died and his son Manasseh succeeded him as King."

Lattimore stared out at the Vermont dusk in thought. His mind was absorbed in Lydia Howland's letter. He had read it so many times he practically had it memorized. He scribbled the words "Mamre and Macpelah" on a yellow pad. He was sure that Lydia Howland's comparison of Eden to Mamre connected the Howland family's secrets with the word "Macpelah" left on the elevator wall in Mount Horeb, Wisconsin. Macpelah was the burial site in Mamre of Abraham. Lattimore concluded that Nathaniel Howland, the founder of the Tribe of Cain, was buried in the City of Enoch.

Lattimore was curious how Leisa Dawkins knew about Lydia Howland, so he put Senacal's tape of his conversation with Leisa Dawkins at the Mount Zion Congregational Church into his recorder. He wanted to refresh his memory about how Senacal came into the possession of Lydia Howland's book. He played with the tape until he reached the part where Reverend Dawkins was about to scold Twitchell for his insensitive remark about selling his wife, Nel, at a flea market.

Leisa Dawkins had said, "Lydia Howland of Eden wrote that"—(she had pointed to a saying framed in glass above her desk)—"of the men of Eden in the nineteenth century. She was the town historian and a participant at the Seneca Falls Convention in New York in 1848. She drafted the famous Declaration of Sentiments, which in the spirit of the Declaration of Independence declared that 'All men and women were created equal.' "

Lattimore reached down and retrieved Lydia Howland's book *The History and Legends of Eden.* He reasoned that maybe the answer to Lydia Howland's riddle was in her book and not her secret letter. After all, she was a historian and 2 Kings 20: 20 referred to the history of the Kings of Judah.

He was impressed with the book's detail. "The settlement was commenced in 1808 by Thomas H. Peckman, Samuel Reed, and Isaac Jones. In 1809, its population 29; 1820, 219; 1830, 279 . . ." His right thumb released a few more pages. A heading read: Ecclesiastical. "The first religious meetings were held in a barn. The inhabitants were supplied with preaching by ministers who traveled from place to place, preaching and exhorting at every opportunity . . ." A few more pages passed under his inspection. He told himself to concentrate on the investigation and not dillydally, as was so often his habit with such readings.

A detailed map of Eden in 1880 appeared before his eyes showing the exact locations of residences, churches, and places of business. The town was divided into fourteen school districts, each district clearly marked by dotted lines. The physical characteristics of Eden were clearly marked on the map. Lake Eden was called North Pond at that time. Bean Mountain was clearly marked, as was Belvidere Mountain. His attention was drawn to a small drawing located north of the present-day Peckman's General Store in School District 6. The hand drawing, made after the book was printed, resembled three golf tees standing side by side and tilted left of center. A fourth one was drawn directly in the middle above the three and also tilted left of center. Below the symbol was the printed name of Hezekiah Farrington.

Lattimore had spent two years studying the ancient art of cuneiform at the Oriental Institute of the University of Chicago. Cuneiform writing was recorded on small, wet clay tablets with a three-sided prism point usually made of reed, wood or ivory. The writing was done in neat columns from right to left using about thirty-nine symbols. Lattimore recognized the drawing as the cuneiform symbol for "grain." He knew it had to be the symbol of the Tribe of Cain.

In jubilation, Lattimore shouted, "Bingo!"

Agent Hawkins and Lieutenant Schiff turned around from in front of the plane. The priest's face shone like a child's on Christmas morning.

"Sorry," he said, "but I think I've found Nathaniel Howland's City of Enoch, or at least the entrance to it. I want you to have your agents pick up a woman named Adah Howland and her son, Jabal. They live near Bean Mountain. I'll need them as guides."

Hawkins stood up and started down the aisle. "What's all this about the City of Enoch? And who the hell's Nathaniel Howland?"

Lattimore raised his hand for Hawkins to stop. "Don't worry about it. You'll find all the evidence you need there to put Mary Kenite away for life. I'm not nuts. Remember, 'ya dance with the one that brung ya.' " He looked at Schiff and raised his eyebrows. "I'm all you've got. Trust me. I know what I'm doing."

Hawkins left the ex-priest to his tapes, books, and maps.

Hezekiah Farrington's name on the map had excited Lattimore because the name "Hezekiah" tied in directly with the biblical quote 2 Kings 20: 20. Yet, the name "Farrington" was equally revealing. In her letter, Lydia Howland had mentioned that a Farrington family had followed Nathaniel Howland from Connecticut to Vermont. He knew there had to be something special about the location of Hezekiah Farrington's home.

He opened Lydia Howland's book to a section

marked "Economics and Agriculture." The section listed a directory of local businesses. His eyes followed his finger down the page. "David Pratt's starch factory located on Road 7. Moses Gibson's sawmill located on Road 12. William King's sawmill located on Road 32. James Peters' grist- and sawmill located on Road 22. Hezekiah Farrington's saw- and gristmill and butter-tub factory was built by Mr. Farrington many years before this author's birth. The lumber mill gave employment to about fifteen hands, all friends and religious brothers, and turned out from five to eight hundred thousand feet of lumber annually. They added the business of manufacturing shingles and butter tubs and also erected the gristmill. . . ." Oddly, the words "by the waters of Shiloah" had been written by Lydia Howland in pen after the word "gristmill."

"How much longer?" Lattimore yelled as he packed up his books, maps, and tapes.

"About a half-hour or so," shouted the pilot.

"Speed it up, if that's possible with an airplane. This time Sennacherib will not be denied admittance to Jerusalem."

Senacal's world was a carousel of confusion. The gray Vermont sky spun like a top around his car as he lay slumped against the door. Pine needles danced down his shattered windshield in small rivers of melting snow. He heard voices from afar. He looked at his hands; they were red with Twitchell's blood.

A voice sounded from outside. "Mr. Senacal, are you O.K. in there?"

His dizziness lifted and his legs moved painlessly. He turned his head in the direction of the voice that had called his name. The wet dirt on the car window clouded his vision, but he recognized the cherub face of Mary Kenite, Eden postmistress and captain of the Eden Emergency Squad. However, he didn't recognize the other girl standing next to her. She had stringy black hair and wore an oversized flannel shirt with baggy painter's pants.

"Are you O.K.?" shouted Mary Kenite between cuffed hands.

Senacal nodded. He touched Twitchell on the neck below the ear for a pulse. He felt a strong beat.

Mary opened the car door and with the help of two other squad members slid Senacal out onto the ground. She took his pulse and examined his prone body. "No blood oozing, no bones sticking out. You look all right, Mr. Senacal. But let's be sure." She told one of the squad members next to her to examine Senacal while she walked around the crushed car to check on Twitchell. A blood-pressure cuff was placed on his arm while the girl with the baggy painter's pants prepared a stretcher to carry him to a waiting ambulance.

Senacal cursed his bad luck, but he was happy to be alive. He told the man attending him that he suffered no dizziness, nor did he think he had a concussion. He could see that he rested at the bottom of a small embankment just below where his car had crashed through the guardrail. Above him a yellow ambulance flashed a red light of caution to nosy motorists who slowed down for a curious peek. He noticed Pleasant Kenite standing next to a white van parked behind the ambulance. A magnetic sign attached to the side of the van read, EDEN EMERGENCY VEHICLE.

"Twitchell," yelled Senacal. He suddenly remembered his friend. He rolled to his side to get up but was stopped by the young girl with the baggy painter's pants.

Mary Kenite reappeared and directed her assistants to place Senacal onto a stretcher. She knelt down next to him and smiled broadly before she spoke. "Your friend will be O.K., Mr. Senacal. He has a bump on his head that may account for his mumbling about some meeting in Coventry. I'll call the hospital. They'll probably order an X ray taken, to be sure. You're both very lucky men not to be seriously hurt."

Suddenly Mary Kenite's attention was drawn to a Lamoille County sheriff's car that pulled up behind the white van. A young officer got out and was greeted by Pleasant Kenite, who began explaining to the policeman the details of Senacal's accident.

"It's Officer Mark Browner," Mary said as she struggled to her feet. "He's a rookie, Mr. Senacal. I'll assist him with the accident report so we can be on our way as soon as possible. If you feel up to it, I'll need your car registration from the glove compartment."

Senacal hardly heard Mary's offer of assistance. His mind drifted toward Jubal Howland. For a second he thought of asking the Lamoille County police officer to have Jubal Howland delayed for questioning at the Coventry airport. But he thought otherwise. Lieutenant Schiff had ordered him to report to the Ski Top Motel. He would be a team player for a change. He was sure Eden had no hospital, so the ambulance would probably take him and Twitchell to Morrisville anyhow. He could call from there and let Schiff handle the police matter of arranging for Jubal Howland's arrest and questioning. His thoughts quickly returned to the accident.

He complained to the girl with the baggy painter's pants that he was well enough to stand. After a quick blood-pressure check he was allowed to rise. He felt a stiffness in his left shoulder, but otherwise he was fine. The trunk of his car had been jarred open from the accident. He took off his wet sport coat and retrieved his gray nylon jacket from the car trunk. He remembered wearing the jacket last the morning of Ken Newell's murder. Fortunately, it had lost the stench of the boy's burning body. He walked around to the other side of his car. He found Graham Twitchell strapped to a stretcher. He knelt down next to his silent friend, who just stared off into space.

Suddenly Senacal sensed something wrong. Patton was not at his fallen master's side. Senacal looked in the back seat of the car and saw the dog lying on her side with her parched tongue protruding from the side of her mouth.

Senacal recalled Lattimore's words during dinner at the Embers Restaurant: "No man is an island, Senacal. What I mean is, you've built a stone wall around your feelings and you don't allow anyone in." Looking at Twitchell, he knew Lattimore was right. He felt close to Twitchell, much like a boy to his grandfather. It was time to show that love. He cradled the old man against his chest and affectionately stroked his forehead.

"Patton got killed, didn't she? She'd be here if she wasn't." Twitchell didn't need an answer to his question, just silence to confirm his fear. For a second or two he bit his lip. "Had her eleven years. Ever have a dog, Senacal?" He didn't wait for an answer. "Dogs are great. Always excited to see you. Your boss can kick you in the ass, your wife can nag you, but your dog will always wag his tail when you get home. Patton used to run around in circles in front of me. Sometimes, if I had a bag of groceries, I'd yell, 'Patton, get the hell out of the way!' If I'd shovel snow, Patton would be there next to me. Even digging up the septic tank, she'd stand there loyally smelling my shit." Large tears fell from his eyes and down the furrows of his craggy cheeks. Senacal reached out and held his friend in his arms. The old man cried.

Mary Kenite tapped Senacal on the shoulder.

Senacal wasn't sure how long he had been holding his friend.

"We best be going now, Mr. Senacal," said the postmistress.

Pleasant Kenite playfully winked at Senacal before she and the girl with baggy painter's pants reached down and lifted Graham Twitchell into the air. Senacal noticed everybody else had left the accident scene except a young man in jeans wearing an Eden Emergency Squad jacket. Mary told Senacal that the police would meet them at Saint Jude's Hospital in Morrisville and that the young man with the jeans would arrange for his car to be towed. She told him that she was experienced in these matters and that he had nothing to worry about other than his well-being and that of his friend.

"Where's the ambulance?" queried Senacal. He made a quick survey of the roadside. The yellow ambulance was nowhere to be seen.

"We only have one ambulance in Eden with the proper life-support equipment, Mr. Senacal. I ordered it back to the station in case a more serious emergency develops in our absence. You and your friend will be fine in the auxiliary white van we use for cases like Mr. Twitchell's. The trip to Saint Jude's Hospital is a quick one."

"Are you sure my friend is O.K.?" Senacal extended his hand to the stretcher. His attention was focused on Twitchell's well-being.

"I'm sure, Mr. Senacal. The van will be fine. In fact, I don't even think he needs an X ray. A good bowl of hot soup would probably make him feel as fit as a fiddle." An innocent smile creased her lips.

The floor of the van was covered with a clean piece of white padding.

Pleasant pushed aside a pair of ski boots on the van floor to clear a path to a metal bed securely bolted to the side of the van.

Senacal held the old man's hand. The two young girls strapped Twitchell into the bed. He was covered with a brown blanket, and a clean pillow was placed under his head.

Mary smiled, locked the van doors, and drove away.

"Am I in hell?" Twitchell asked from the floor of the van.

Senacal followed Twitchell's eyes upward. The van ceiling was covered with a large poster of a green serpent wearing black armor. Hot columns of steam spewed from the dragon's fiery mouth. A rock star dressed in black sequins held a sword to the beast's chest. A satanic smile glowed from the singer's face; his long black hair looked like it had been shampooed in starch.

A rock-'n'-roll poster on the ceiling of a medical-emergency vehicle? Senacal slapped his hands together. "You're an asshole," he mumbled. He cursed himself for being so stupid as to allow himself to be trapped inside a locked van. Why hadn't he been more suspicious of Mary Kenite? Suddenly he found a host of reasons to doubt her. If she and Jubal Howland were partners in the biblical killings, then she now knew about his trip to Coventry. He also realized she had to have seen his gun in the glove compartment of the car, a habit he had developed while on long car trips. He replayed how she skillfully isolated him and Twitchell at the accident scene. He told himself to remain calm and play along with her game. He again called himself asshole for being locked in a van without his gun.

The small window looking in on the driver from the rear of the van was covered up with a bumper sticker that read, SPELUNKERS DO IT BETTER. Senacal could hear the women laughing and talking in the front.

Ten minutes passed. Suddenly he felt the van turn

left. Rule out the hospital, thought Senacal. Twitchell just stared at the picture on the ceiling. The van stopped after a short ride on a dirt road. Senacal could hear Pleasant speaking to someone on the road. He crawled to the rear, but suddenly the van jerked forward and he fell backward to the metal floor. Twitchell managed a weak laugh and said, "You'd make a lousy sailor, Senacal."

He got up and looked out the rear window. A girl with brown hair stood on the side of the road. After the van moved on, she crossed the road and clipped a chain to a hook on a tree. A sign dangled from the middle of the chain. It read, NO TRESPASSING. The girl wore a black jacket and a pair of tan calf-length boots with red leather tassels at the top. Senacal sat down as the van bounced along the road. He felt his heart pound inside his chest. He hated the feeling of being trapped like a caged animal.

The van stopped and the back doors flew open before an old orange house with black shutters. The house looked like a pumpkin. Two dark windows, like eyes, were cut into the house above a doorless garage.

Mary Kenite got out of the van and greeted Senacal with her usual warm smile. "I hope the trip wasn't too bumpy, Mr. Senacal. I radioed the hospital and told them Mr. Twitchell was doing just fine. They said it wasn't necessary to bring him in but to keep an eye on him for a while. They know me real well at Saint Jude's, Mr. Senacal."

While she examined Twitchell once more, Senacal hopped off the back and casually walked to the front of the van. He was curious about Mary's conversation with the hospital. He saw the accordion wire of a radio receiver dangle from the van's dashboard.

The postmistress yelled to the girl with the baggy painter's pants who had followed Senacal to the front of the van. "Here, child!"

The young woman turned on command and along with Pleasant picked up Twitchell and carried him into the house.

"Isn't it beautiful up here," said Mary. "Pleasant and the girls live here. They use to live with me on Mine Road, but you know how noisy young girls can be. I do spend a lot of time up here, though. Come in when you're ready, Mr. Senacal. The soup's already on the stove. It's been simmering all day." She smiled and walked into the house through the pumpkin's mouth.

Senacal stood in the middle of nowhere with the disturbing thought that he was Mary Kenite's prisoner. He again cursed himself for being captured so easily. No one had even held a gun to his head. He looked around the countryside. He had no idea where he was, nor in what direction to run for help. The pumpkin house stood alone among the tall pines. He was cut off from the outside world with night about to settle over northern Vermont.

He opened the door in the back of the garage and walked into a den. The room was neatly decorated in a colonial motif, and a large fireplace took up most of the back wall of the room. Its mantel was filled with an assortment of knickknacks; pictures, school mugs, and candles. Peculiar to the colonial decor was a large picture over the fireplace of a Spanish conquistador sporting a thick beard. A brass plate announced the soldier's name: Juan Cabrillo— Explorer of West Coast—1542. Senacal wondered if Ken Newell's murder had been planned in the den.

Senacal felt someone behind him. He turned and stared into the black eyes of the girl with the baggy painter's pants. He hadn't heard her creep up on him. "Your shoes," she said. She pointed to a plastic mat near the door; it was filled with an assortment of footwear. She left as quickly as she had appeared.

Senacal found her very strange. She acted more

like an obedient child than a young adult. He placed his shoes beside the others on the mat. The house was very warm. He removed his jacket and carried it over his arm as he walked into the kitchen. Like the den, the kitchen was immaculate with plastic runners crisscrossing over an orange carpet. A vegetable soup was simmering on the copper stove. Senacal yelled, "Anybody home?" He tried to act as if he suspected nothing.

Twitchell's raspy voice sounded from the living room. "Yeah." The old man sat in an overstuffed chair holding an ice pack on his head. A large picture of Franklin Delano Roosevelt occupied center stage on the living-room wall. The picture showed FDR at his desk writing his famous "The only thing we have to fear is fear itself" speech. A brass plate on the frame read: F.D.R.—3, 3-'33.

Senacal turned his attention to his friend. "How are you doing?" He threw his gray nylon jacket over the arm of the sofa.

"Fine." The spark was gone from Twitchell's eyes. He missed Patton.

"What do you say I call a taxi so we can get the hell out of here?" Senacal said.

"This is Eden, Vermont," said Twitchell. "They don't have taxis."

Senacal shrugged his shoulders. "Where is everybody?"

A voice sounded from the kitchen. "The girls are changing for supper." It was Mary Kenite; she had slipped into the kitchen from a small laundry room. She stood over the stove with her back to her guests. "One of the girls will take you both back to Morrisville after we eat. That is, if Mr. Twitchell feels no dizziness."

While Senacal and Twitchell sat in the living room, four girls circled them like bees around a rose bush. Some carried clean clothes upstairs, others were busy dusting furniture or sweeping the plastic floor runner that connected all the rooms. They were children in adult bodies. He recognized the girl holding the chain along the dirt road and the girl with the baggy painter's pants. The other two girls were equally strange.

Mary shouted an order from the kitchen. "April, a clean tablecloth for dinner!"

A girl wearing a large sweatshirt and faded jeans skipped down the hallway with a clean tablecloth and spread it out over the dining-room table.

"They jump around like a bunch of fairies," whispered Twitchell to his friend. "Weirdest bunch of skinny broads I've ever seen."

"Obviously, you're feeling better?"

"Stop babying me, goddamn it. Ya think a little bump on the head is going to keep me down?"

Mary called her guests to a dinner made for a Trappist monk. The meal consisted of vegetable soup, corn bread, and a crusted meat pie. Water was the only beverage served. The china was a floral blue porcelain with matching blue crystal water glasses. The tablecloth and napkins were of the finest blue linen.

Senacal sat opposite the girl with the baggy painter's pants. She was his constant shadow all afternoon. He was sure she was under Mary's orders to watch him.

"My wife, Nel, makes a hell of a meat pie," Twitchell said to Mary. "Are you French?"

"No." Mary's cheeks flushed a pink red from the attention given her cooking. She smiled behind her raised water glass.

"The French like meat pies. For Christ's sake, on Thanksgiving, Nel's sister, Flo, will have a big turkey dinner with all the trimmings. But you've got to have a slice of Nel's meat pie first." Twitchell leaned forward over the table and whispered. "Nel's meat pie is better than Flo's turkey. Flo lets the damn bird dry up like a burned piece of toast."

Everybody laughed haughtily.

Twitchell's ability to make light conversation gave Senacal time to think. He thought maybe he had overreacted to Mary Kenite. After all, she had been very helpful in giving him and Twitchell medical assistance. Also, Pleasant could have killed him as they made love on his motel bed.

"Are you girls skiers?" Senacal asked. "I noticed a pair of ski boots in the van." Senacal motioned to Mary Kenite to pass him the soup. He hoped his feeling of optimism would last. The bowl was nearly empty. Mary looked at the girl with the baggy painter's pants and said, "Nina, would you please get Mr. Senacal some hot soup?"

The name knifed through Senacal's memory with razor-sharp clarity. The girl had no sooner risen to her feet than Senacal knew her exact identity. She was Nina Sadler of Mount Horeb, Wisconsin. She was Harry Gilcrest's girlfriend. She fit perfectly the description given the FBI by students at the University of Wisconsin. He struggled with his emotions. He put a piece of meat pie into his mouth to disguise the fear on his face. His mind raced recklessly forward. Did Twitchell recognize the name? Was this his last meal on earth? The thought of a chain saw cutting through his neck made him want to vomit. He looked up at Mary Kenite; she was waiting for his attention to answer his question about the girls' skiing. He was sure she read the fear in his eyes.

"Yes, Mr. Senacal, the girls are skiing instructors. Girls, tell Mr. Senacal where you ski." She tapped a spoon on the table twice. On cue, the girls stopped eating and focused their attention on Mary.

"I ski at Big Jay," April said, the girl who earlier had set the table. "There's a North Jay and a Little Jay, but I ski at Big Jay." She covered her mouth with her hand and giggled. The other girls laughed with her.

Mary looked at Senacal and sighed. "Girls will be girls."

Twitchell reached for another piece of meat pie and said, "Silliest bunch of women I ever met. They're like cackling hens!"

Everybody laughed, except Senacal.

Nina Sadler returned to the table with a hot bowl of soup. She placed it in front of Senacal. He had lost his appetite but thanked her with a smile.

He could only think of his escape. His seat commanded a view of the whole house. Suddenly, he remembered he had no shoes on. He glanced over at the plastic mat in the den. They were next to a pair of tan calf-length boots with red leather tassels at the top. His attention was drawn to his nylon jacket hanging over the arm of the living-room sofa. The sight of a dirt smudge on the sleeve acted as a switch that put his life on instant replay. He saw himself dirtying his jacket on a white van outside the store in Fort Ann, where he had stopped for tea on the morning of Ken Newell's murder. He looked out Mary Kenite's living-room window and saw the white van.

His thoughts flashed back to Fort Ann as his breathing became more difficult. He remembered standing before a wobbly card table pouring his tea when Gracie, the nosy cashier, called his attention outside to a girl with beautiful jewelry. He had caught a glimpse of the girl's leg entering the van. She wore a tan calf-length boot with red tassels. Senacal looked over at the boots standing next to his shoes in the den. His heart skipped a beat. He was having supper with Ken Newell's murderers.

Suddenly, his Fort Ann questions had answers. The bloody tablecloth had been put into the washing machine because of Mary Kenite's fanaticism for cleanliness. "April, a clean tablecloth," she had yelled to April before dinner. Plastic runners abounded everywhere. He had noticed Nina Sadler take great care to walk on one when she went for the soup. No wonder there had been no bloody footprints on Evelyn Newell's kitchen carpet. The girls had their shoes off when they severed Ken Newell's head with a chain saw. They had used plastic runners between the washing machine and Ken Newell's charred body. One of Mary's girls may have even put the clean towels on the stairway leading up to Evelyn Newell's linen closet. Senacal wanted to run. He was afraid to look at Mary for fear his eyes revealed his knowledge of the biblical murders.

He forced himself to listen to the conversation around the table. "I am a Shoshone Indian," said Nina Sadler to Twitchell, "and my people live in the Wind River Indian Reservation in Wyoming. It is very beautiful there, Mr. Twitchell. The mountains are our backbones, the rivers are our veins. We share the environment with the elk and deer and live as one. But not the white man. I grew up to hate the white man who raped the land and the soldiers who had killed my people."

When Nina finished her story about how she had met the Kenites and headed east with them to live in Vermont, Senacal rose from the table. He had to take action. All he could think of was the radio in the white van. Maybe with luck he could reach the county sheriff's office. It was a long shot, but so were his chances of seeing the morning sun.

"This old body of mine feels like it's been through a wringer," Senacal said as he walked a few steps into the living room. He stretched his arms and rubbed his neck. "Why do you have a picture of F.D.R. in your living room, Mary? I thought all you Vermonters were Republicans." He looked out the window. The dark clouds that had brought the afternoon snow had left; the sky was now alive with bright stars.

Senacal turned around. Mary stood under the archway between the kitchen and living room with a blank look on her unsmiling face. She spoke as if in a trance. "Franklin Delano Roosevelt could have been the Beast of Revelations." She folded her hands as if in prayer and walked over to the picture. She talked with her back to Senacal. "He had two of the three sixes, Mr. Senacal. His famous speech was prepared on March 3, 1933 on the eve of his inauguration. See the brass plate under his portrait. It reads: 3,3-'33. That reads six and six. He succeeded where no President or man had dared venture before. He could have conquered the world but he didn't. He had the world's most powerful army at his command but he failed to see God's Will in John's word. Truman followed Roosevelt and he had one of the three sixes too. He was the thirty-third President, Mr. Senacal. Three plus three is six. His picture hangs on the bedroom wall upstairs. He had the Atom Bomb at his disposal, but he never used it to destroy the world as God would have wanted."

She turned toward Senacal and snapped her fingers. Instantly the girls at the table stood up and bowed their heads. Their obedience to Mary Kenite was immediate. Senacal swallowed hard; his eyes darted back and forth between Mary and her followers.

She said, "All God's words in the Bible must be fulfilled. Did you know that, Mr. Senacal?"

Senacal wasn't sure what to say. He looked at Twitchell. The old man just raised his eyebrows and sighed. Nina Sadler walked over to the old man and ordered him to take off his baseball cap and stand up. He obeyed without a complaint.

Mary spoke up. "Well, Mr. Senacal, mighty son of Sargon the Second and Conqueror of forty-six cities around Jerusalem, is your tongue tied in deceit? Have you not a thought on God's prophecies or those of Baal?"

If there was even the slightest hope of escape, it now faded before Senacal's eyes. Mary Kenite had slipped into another one of her multiple personalities. She just looked at Senacal through bulging eyes with a cold stare. She appeared inhuman, capable of the most heinous of human acts. The four girls moved under the living-room archway and fixed their gaze on their leader, waiting for her next command to be carried out.

"I don't much believe in God or His prophecies," said Senacal. "But I hardly think He's the type to approve of murder."

The charade was over. He was sure Mary Kenite knew his true identity. He felt angry for allowing himself to be captured so easily. He regretted involving Graham Twitchell in the case.

Mary clapped her hands three times. It was followed by an ominous quiet. Twitchell and Senacal exchanged a quick glance of uncertainty. The girls stood at attention, their eyes glued to Mary.

The stairway creaked behind Senacal. Then it creaked again and again in regular intervals. Someone was coming downstairs. Senacal was afraid to look.

"It is the virgin Anath," Nina shouted. Immediately the girls fell to their knees.

Senacal took a deep breath and turned toward the stairs. Pleasant Kenite stood behind him; she was dressed in a white linen gown with a gold girdle tied around her shapely body. The look on her face was distant, like her mother's. Senacal shook his head and blinked several times in succession. He had trouble accepting the reality around him. He felt surrounded by an Amazon tribe of lunatics who had just awakened from a civilization long forgotten by time. They chanted names he had never heard before. Strange, weird, cartoonlike were the words swirling around in his head to describe the people who would shortly execute him in a brutal manner. Who are these people? His questions and fears went unanswered.

Pleasant spoke up. "Sennacherib has come to the City of Enoch. It is time to honor Baal. The spring sun has warmed the earth. The Curse of Lamech must be fulfilled."

Mary turned toward her young female followers. "It is time to clean up, girls. We have much to do tonight. April, a clean tablecloth."

Nina stayed behind and guarded the men at gunpoint.

Two girls tied Senacal and Twitchell together, back to back, and threw them onto the floor of the white van. Nina Sadler stood guard over them. A half-hour passed with little conversation exchanged between both men. Senacal noticed other young women scurrying back and forth in front of him. He concluded they must have been upstairs with Pleasant while he and Twitchell ate their last supper. He wondered how many young girls Mary Kenite had recruited for her lunatic plan of death.

Finally Mary appeared and hopped into the van. Senacal and Twitchell were pushed to the back. She sat on the bed Twitchell had earlier used, and stroked her sword with the same affection a mother caresses a newborn. Senacal was all to familiar with her weapon. It had two lions' heads carved into an ivory handle. The van began to move. Senacal could hear Pleasant talking on the radio in front. He figured she was talking with other members of the cult about the night's activities.

Mary Kenite's eyes remained distant yet a slight grin creased her fat lips. A black cape with a high satin collar lay drooped across her shoulders. Nina and April knelt on each side of their spiritual mother. The van had traveled about five minutes in silence when suddenly Nina began singing to music piped through a set of earphones on her head. Mary smiled approvingly. Nina shouted, "Singin', singin' blood is a streamin'." She snapped her fingers and tapped her foot on the floor.

Senacal looked up at the ceiling poster and shook his head.

"What kind of mumbo jumbo are they listening to?" shouted Twitchell to Mary Kenite.

A smile beamed from the postmistress's chubby face. She motioned to Nina to play the music aloud for Twitchell's benefit. Nina obeyed instantly. She attached a small speaker to the side of her radio and screeching voices filled the van. "Cop blood is a-flowin'. Singin', singin'."

Twitchell banged his foot on the floor. "Turn that damn thing off!"

Both girls looked at Mary. Obedience was mandatory for any member of her group. Permission was needed for everything, even to speak. Mary appeared amused by Twitchell's outcry. She motioned to Nina to lower the volume.

"Sounds like someone's squeezing their nuts, for Christ's sake," Twitchell complained.

April lowered her head. "Mother, may I speak?"

"Yes, my child, speak your mind. But, remember, they're wolves in lambs' clothing. They know not what they say."

April stood over Twitchell. "You're weird, grandpa. Real weird."

To Senacal the whole scene was bizarre. In minutes he was about to be ritually sacrificed. And by whom? By a group of crazy women arguing with an old man tied up on the floor of a white van. But maybe there was a method to Twitchell's madness, thought Senacal. Maybe he was trying to anger his captors into fighting among themselves. It was a typical television ploy, thought Senacal, but worth a try. He had nothing to lose. Senacal looked up at April and said, "Did you know you left behind your Demons Beware tape in the Fort Ann home of Ken Newell?"

The smile left Mary Kenite's face. The teasing and fun were over. She raised her sword over her head. Anger replaced her look of serenity. "Kneel," she ordered.

Both girls dropped to their knees before her.

"You both disobeyed my command. You were trained to carry out my orders, and playing music in the homes of God's sinners is strictly forbidden by my covenant."

Senacal imagined Nina Sadler's warm blood spilling over him as he watched Mary's sword shake above her head. He tried to defuse Mary's anger. "Where were your first seven executions, Mary? I know about the Howland family and the Curse of Lamech," he said.

Mary Kenite stared coldly into Senacal's eyes for a few seconds, then lowered her sword over the girls' heads. "Your sins are forgiven," she said. Gently, her sword touched their shoulders in a symbol of forgiveness.

They crawled beside their spiritual mother.

Mary pointed her sword at Senacal. "Like Daniel, you have the power to read dreams, but I know it's only trickery. I know you have returned to conquer the new Jerusalem, our City of Enoch, but you will receive no tribute in gold or silver this time. Baal in the Book of Kings has announced your coming."

Twitchell sighed. "Never knew a preacher who could talk straight English."

Mary Kenite ignored Twitchell's remark. Her real enemy was Senacal. "You're quite clever, Mr. Senacal, to have learned so quickly about the Howland family and the mysteries of the Curse of Lamech." She paused and stared at her sword for a few brief moments. "So, you're curious about the first seven executions? I'll tell you. You see, Mr. Senacal, for years I was waiting for a sign from Baal as to when to begin the revenge of my grandfather, Lamech. Then two years ago the Wyoming sky echoed a warning foretold by Baal in Canaan thousands of years ago. His warning said, 'The sound of wings has been heard over the land and our enemy has descended like locusts upon our land divided by rivers. Listen, everyone who lives on earth! A time is coming when Baal will rise from the land of Mot and the Soldiers of the Sword, a tall and smooth-skinned people, will be feared all over the world.'

"That day in Wyoming six soldiers parachuted over our camp while I was teaching my female disciples. Later, while the six cadets were being sacrificed to pay homage to Baal, a seventh soldier charged us in a vain attempt to rescue his fellow parachutists. I knew at that moment I had to return to Eden, Vermont, and begin the Curse of Lamech. You see, Mr. Senacal, in Genesis, Lamech said to his wives, 'If seven lives are taken to pay for killing Cain, seventy-seven will be taken if anyone kills me.' Don't you see? That day seven enemy soldiers fell from the sky. I had to kill them. I have no choice now either. I must kill seventy-seven to fulfill the Curse of Lamech, my grandfather. It's all in the Bible, and God's word must be fulfilled. Don't you understand that, Mr. Senacal?"

Mary Kenite slowly raised her sword above her head until it touched the van roof. Her eyes were glassy. Her mind drifted off to another world. Small beads of perspiration appeared on her wrinkled forehead. She was visibly upset.

Senacal sensed he was her next victim. Instead of defusing her, he had angered her more. He felt only for Twitchell and again cursed the day he had asked the old man to accompany him to Vermont.

Suddenly, Mary lowered her sword. April wiped the perspiration from her spiritual mother's brow. Mary looked at Senacal and said, "You will not die here, Mr. Senacal. Baal has sent you to us as a sign of his pleasure over the recent killings. Tonight, we will offer you back to him in a solemn ceremony."

Senacal's fear gave way to anger. He knew he had been granted a temporary reprieve from death. "Cut the bullshit! How the hell am I some goddamn sign?"

"Your name, Mr. Senacal. You told me at the Lumen Christi meeting that the middle vowel of your name was an a. At that moment, I knew you were Sennacherib, mighty son of Sargon the Second and conqueror of forty-six cities around Jerusalem. In the past, Baal spoke of you, as did the prophet Isaiah. Tonight your head will hang in place of the girl from Salem. We failed to bring back her head from the museum. The dog was anxious for its evening meal that night."

Nina and April giggled like schoolgirls.

Mary Kenite's double-talk confused and angered Senacal. He was sure of one thing only: He was going to die a horrible death in isolation from the world. A rescue by the police seemed so remote.

"Adah, Lamech's wife, told me Lamech was not murdered," Senacal said. He would try reasoning with her, though he knew it was futile. "He died in a flood in 1927. If he died by accident, you don't have to fulfill the prophecy you're so worried about."

"You are wrong, Sennacherib, mighty son of Sargon the Second and conqueror of forty-six cities around Jerusalem. My grandfather was killed by this very sword." She looked down at the sword on her lap. "Joseph, father of Adah and captain of the Soldiers of the Sword, followed Lamech and my mother, Naamah, from Eden in the rain. Joseph killed Lamech with this." She held up the sword in her hands. "My mother, Naamah, was a witness to the killing, but was swept away by the mighty floodwaters before Joseph could kill her. She clung to the sword in her father's chest as they were both swept down the Connecticut River toward the City of Sharon. The sword worked itself free from Lamech's chest just as she passed a tree still rooted to the earth. God directed this to happen. A group of Mormons found my mother and brought her with them to Wyoming, where I was born. She told me all the tales of the Howland family and I vowed to fulfill the prophecy of Lamech and continue the cult of Baal."

The van slowed to a near stop and turned left onto a bumpy road.

Senacal and Twitchell just looked at each other and said nothing. Senacal hoped the old man's death would be swift and painless.

Mary Kenite no longer paid attention to Senacal. Her face gave evidence of a new personality emerging from her sick mind. She tapped both girls on the shoulder. They put on black shrouds that covered their bodies to their knees.

Senacal and Twitchell were blindfolded and gagged. The cord that bound them together was cut. Senacal knew he'd never see Twitchell again. Nina grabbed Senacal and forced him toward the van's doors.

Mary Kenite chanted Senacal's future as the van slowed to a stop. "You are a prisoner in the new Jerusalem, the City of Enoch. You raped us of our riches once, but not again, great statesman of Assyria. The prophets foretold your coming. Your death will be performed by the goddess of war, who sits naked upon her horse and carries her sword of vengeance. Tonight, Baal will return from his deadly sleep in the land of Mot. You will be offered up in sacrifice to him."

The van stopped and the doors swung open. The

smell of burning torches filled the air. "Mother, Mother, Mother," chanted a host of female voices from outside. Senacal's blindfold only added to his horror.

"My children," Mary Kenite shouted like a preacher on Sunday morning. "As John said to the Lord on Mount Tabor, 'It is good for us to be here.' Benedicamus Domino!" She threw her arms up into the air.

"Deo gratias," came the reply of her followers. Senacal was tossed from the back of the van to the ground and kicked several times in the ribs and back. "Conqueror of our city," yelled a woman above him. He flinched at the coolness of her spit hitting his face.

He was pulled to his feet and forced to walk blindly between a gaunlet of a dozen women carrying torches. He wondered if Twitchell followed him in mock procession to their deaths.

"Where's your army, mighty son of Sargon?" yelled a voice from his left. A pair of hands shoved him forward. He felt cold. His clothes were wet from having been thrown on the damp ground. His captors began chanting in female voices, each side alternating ancient verses of prayer.

"Yea, the whisper of the stone. The murmur of the heavens to the earth, of the brightness in the stars. I understand the lightning, which the heavens do not know. A matter that men do not know, nor the multitudes of the earth understand. Come and I shall show it. In the midst of the mountain of me, God of Saphon, in the sanctuary in the mountain of mine inheritance, in the good place in the Hill of Power."

Finally, the chanting stopped. Senacal had traveled through hell. He had been prodded and pushed and continually spat upon.

The women were now silent. He could feel his heart pound against his ribs. He cringed at the thought of death by a chain saw.

The sound of footsteps approached and the women next to him moved aside. They untied him, removed his gag, and tore off his jacket and shirt in one quick swoop. He was shoved forward repeatedly, until he was thrown against a tree. His back bled from the coarseness of the bark. His arms were tied to branches above his head and his blindfold was ripped from his eyes. The torches turned the night into day and Senacal stared into the eyes of a dozen women bent on killing him. He recognized the black eyes of Nina Sadler among the crowd of women wearing black shrouds. They were like clones, tall and lean, with straggly hair. The women said nothing; they just stared at him with glassy eyes. He saw a marble statue to his left. It was chiseled in the shape of a naked woman with large breasts. The woman carried a ram across her shoulders, and a snake crawled between her legs. Lying next to her was a lion at rest.

Senacal looked up. The sky danced with a chorus of bright stars. The moon, full and tinted orange, was visible through the large umbrellalike trees surrounding the grove. He realized this was Adah Howland's wedding site. He realized this was the clearing where Confederate soldier John Marmaduke had buried the stolen St. Albans money. He searched for Twitchell in the crowd of worshipers but didn't see him.

An eerie chanting voice sounded in the night. The ring of women parted before him and formed a lighted aisle. Pleasant Kenite advanced through a corridor of kneeling women dressed in black. She wore the same outfit as at the house: a white linen gown with a gold girdle tied around her shapely body. Her blond hair was pinned back against her temples by ivory bodkins. She carried a long knife in one hand and a silver cup adorned with lions in the other. She stopped within a few feet of Senacal. Her eyes stayed fixed to his. The women in black chanted, "At Anath's feet bow and fall. Prostrate yourselves, honor her and say to the Virgin Anath, declare to the Progenitress of Heroes. 'The message of Aliyan Baal, the word of Aliy the Warrior.' "

The whole thing was bizarre, a Halloween party in April, a bad dream with no ending. He was an urban cop; he could accept death at the hands of a drug-dealer in a dirty alley in Queens, but not while tied to a tree in Eden. He hated their chanting, He felt cold. He pulled his arms in frustration, but succeeded only in tightening the leather cords around his wrists. "You're all nuts," he yelled in anguish.

A young woman stepped out of the crowd and gagged him.

Nina Sadler moved forward holding an alabaster jar on a gold tray. Pleasant placed the knife and silver cup on the tray in exchange for the jar. The other women chanted, "Put bread in the earth, place mandrakes in the dust. Pour a peace offering in the midst of the earth, a libation in the midst of the fields! Thy tree! To me let thy feet run. To me let thy legs hasten. For I have a word that I'll tell thee, a matter that I'll declare to thee. 'Tis the word of the tree."

Pleasant rubbed Senacal's body with the sweet-smelling ointment from the alabaster jar. Her touch was gentle. She stood only inches from his body. She rubbed his arms with long strokes as her breasts grazed his chest. The women repeated part of the chant. "For I have a word that I'll tell thee, a matter that I'll declare to thee. 'Tis the word of the tree."

She tore his pants from his body. He stood naked in the cool night; the women drew closer to the tree. She moved her oily hands over his navel, then his buttocks, and finally his penis. Senacal's body jerked to attention. His eyes bulged. A picture of Adah Howland castrating her sons flashed before his eyes.

211

He choked on the gag in his mouth. She gently stroked his penis, then dropped to her knees and anointed the rest of his body.

Senacal watched in horror as Pleasant retrieved her knife and silver cup from the tray. He was sure he was about to be castrated. The air smelled of a sweet perfume. The throng of women chanted a foreboding message into the night. "Pouring the oil of peace from a bowl, the Virgin Anath washes her hands, the Progenitress of Heroes, her fingers. She washes her hands in the blood of soldiery, her fingers in the gore of troops."

Senacal's body stiffened as he watched Pleasant slit his upper arm and catch his warm blood in her silver cup. The women repeated their chant.

Senacal struggled in vain to free himself, then closed his eyes.

Pleasant licked his blood and said, "Oh, Sennacherib, King of Assyria, Conqueror of the City of Lachish, Mighty Warrior who plundered Babylon. I am Anath, sister of Baal, widowed sister-in-law of nations and Mother of Warriors."

As she spoke, Nina Sadler released the shoulder strap of Pleasant's linen garment and untied her golden girdle. She stood naked before Senacal as Nina rubbed her body with the same alabaster ointment that had earlier drenched him. Slowly, Pleasant pressed her body against his and twisted her neck to suck his blood.

Her body was hot, almost on fire; her hands stroked Senacal's penis as she licked his nipples and sucked his blood. Her touch was gentle, but he knew her mood could change to violence at any time. Yet, his manhood blossomed in her grip. Pleasant chanted. "The mighty Sennacherib comes to life in my grasp."

Senacal was shocked by his own sexual arousement. He saw himself making love to Pleasant on his motel bed.

With Nina's help, Pleasant straddled Senacal's hips and wrapped her legs around the tree. As Pleasant felt his manhood, she cried out into the still of the night. "With dew of heaven, fat of earth, rain of the rider of clouds." Slowly, she began gyrating her hips while sucking the blood from Senacal's arm. The women danced in place and chanted. "Progenitress of Heroes . . . widowed sister-in-law of nations, Mother of Warriors."

A strong perfume emanated from small colorful cones attached to a gold chain around Pleasant's neck. She pulled herself up and passionately kissed Senacal, jabbing her tongue in and out of his mouth in rhythm with the movement of her hips. He shot his tongue deep inside her throat. She groaned with delight and wrapped herself tighter around him. He wanted to rip his hands free and pull himself deep inside her. His helplessness only added to the eroticism of the moment.

The other women closed in around the tree. "Progenitress of Heroes . . . widowed sister-in-law of nations, Mother of Warriors."

Pleasant shouted in passion as she gasped for air. "Why have Gupan and Ugar come? What enemy has arisen against Baal or foe against the rider of clouds? Did I not crush El's darling, Sea? I crushed the crooked serpent, the mighty one of seven heads. I crushed the darling of the earth gods, even Mot, the calf of El . . ."

Her shouting only excited Senacal more. Anath's gyrations intensified, her body was covered with sweat and blood. She groaned loudly; then, with all her strength, she tightened her grip around Senacal and pulled him deep inside her. He clenched his fists and thrust his hips against her body. He held his breath as long as possible, then gasped as his manhood exploded inside her.

Senacal was cut from the tree. The wet earth revived him from his daze. Suddenly, he became aware of his nakedness, and his mind replayed the drama of the last half-hour. Near death at the hands of a lunatic mob of women, he had engaged in the most satisfying sexual experience of his life. He had tasted his own blood and had copulated publicly. Someone pulled a red woolen tunic over him. Its warmth felt good; he was still alive, and that's all that counted.

Nina pushed him toward the marble statue. The crowd of women were descending into the ground at the base of the statue. He looked down a flight of stone stairs into the cold earth. He wondered if the steps led down to hell. Nina prodded him on. The steps were slippery and the fumes from the lighted torches made him gasp for air. Below was a sepulcher guarded by a silver gate and lighted by a few candles resting on stone tablets. The women marched on through a passageway ahead. Senacal's attention was drawn to an object near the stairs that was partially out of view. It was a Boston Red Sox baseball cap.

Flashing red police lights lined the tiny airstrip in Morrisville, Vermont, as the plane carrying Lattimore, Schiff, and Hawkins arrived. The plane landed and stopped beside a small red building that resembled more a roadside vegetable stand than an airport terminal.

A Vermont trooper greeted the visiting trio and whisked them away to the Ski Top Motel, where they were greeted by two FBI agents and the Vermont State Police with the bad news. They were told that the Lamoille sheriff's department filed a report that Senacal had been in an automobile accident. He and his companion were unhurt but missing. The sheriff's department said that they were due at Saint Jude's Hospital moments after the accident had been reported but never showed up. The captain of the Eden Emergency Squad, Mary Kenite, had picked up the men.

Agent Hawkins and Lieutenant Schiff ordered the Vermont police to enter Mary Kenite's home.

When Lattimore asked about Adah and Jabal Howland, he was told that they were awaiting his arrival at the Eden Town Hall. The meeting at the Ski Top Motel lasted only moments. There was very little to discuss. None of the state or federal police agencies had any idea where Mary Kenite had taken Senacal and Twitchell. Only Frank Lattimore had a possible theory as to their whereabouts.

As a state trooper sped Lattimore, Schiff, and Hawkins up Route 100 to Eden, a voice sounded from a speaker on the dashboard.

"Suspect's house off Mine Road was empty."

Lattimore motioned to the driver to hand him the car radio. "Did you conduct the investigation?" Lattimore asked.

"Affirmative," came the militarylike reply.

"What did you see in the house? Was there anything unusual like old biblical statues or burning incense, things like that?"

"Yes, sir. The place looked like a horror house filled with spooky pictures of devils and statues of weird people. I'd say the lady is a real kook."

"I'd like you to go back in again and look for a picture or map or something that may refer to a hidden tunnel or hidden city. Look through everything. If you find anything please call back."

"Affirmative. Will do."

Lattimore handed the radio back to the driver.

Silence filled the police car for the next few miles until Lieutenant Schiff turned and looked at Lattimore. His speech was slow and deliberate. "I've got a serious problem here. I don't know what the fuck is going on with this case." Like a mask, a worried look fell across his face. "I'm in real trouble. My best detective is missing on an illegal investigation that could cost me my ass. And what am I going to tell my superiors? He's being held captive by a crazy woman in the City of Enoch. Get real. Will you please explain to me why we're on our way to speak to some guy called Jabal and his mother. And what is this City of Enoch all about?"

Lattimore explained to Schiff that Mary Kenite was a descendant of a man named Nathaniel Howland who had committed the sin of incest back in the eighteenth century. To avoid hell Nathaniel Howland moved to northern Vermont and decided to model his life after the biblical character Cain. The Book of Genesis recounts the story how Cain built his son, Enoch, a city. Thus, Howland, who wanted to follow the life of Cain in order to save his soul, did likewise when he arrived in Eden. Lattimore was sure that the City of Enoch was nothing more than an underground cave or quarry of sorts and that Senacal and Twitchell were probably held captive there. The old woman and her lumberjack son could help him find the hidden city. He then handed Schiff Lydia Howland's letter to read.

"Then who's this Baal character?" Schiff sighed.

Lattimore told Schiff that when Abraham brought the Jews into the promised land of Canaan, the inhabitants of Canaan worshiped Baal, god of life and fertility, and his sister, Anath, goddess of sex and war. The cult included licentious dancing and ritualistic meals. They often worshiped in 'high places' around trees and marble statues where sexual acts of fertility took place. The prophets of the Old Testament always preached against Baal and gods like him.

"You think Mary Kenite and her followers practice this ancient cult today?" Schiff asked.

"I'd say there was a connection. If Mary Kenite

thinks she's some kind of prophet, then anything's possible. We'll know when we find the City of Enoch."

Lattimore showed Schiff the map in Lydia Howland's book and said, "This ink symbol drawn by Lydia Howland is the cuneiform symbol for grain. I ask you, why did she put it here next to Hezekiah Farrington's gristmill? I think she marked the spot where a tunnel leads to the underground City of Enoch mentioned in her letter."

Schiff's wrinkled brow announced his disbelief. "Come on, Lattimore. You don't solve murder cases by reading old books with funny drawings in them. This is the real world."

Lattimore replied, "Mary and her executioners don't live in the real world."

Only one state-police car was in the Eden Town Hall parking lot beside the cinder-block building that served as Eden's political brain center. Inside, the trio from Saratoga Springs were first greeted by the stoic face of Hannah Smith, who sat at her desk in a small office to the right of the front door. She managed only a weak smile of recognition to Frank Lattimore. She appeared perturbed that the town hall was being used as a police headquarters.

A man with a red T-shirt sat handcuffed to a long table on a dais that was used by the town fathers to plan Eden's future. Jabal Howland's physique was of a man much younger. The old woman next to him with the wrinkled skin and patchy gray hair was his mother, Adah. Lattimore was drawn to her simple gold wedding ring; it was incised with the cuneiform symbol for grain.

"Watch him," warned one of the troopers who had brought Jabal Howland to the town hall. "It took three men to bring him here." The trooper pointed at Adah Howland. "She insisted on coming for our protection."

217

Jabal Howland glared at Lattimore as the ex-priest sat down next to Adah. Lattimore looked sympathetically into the old woman's eyes. "My name is Frank Lattimore and I'm a friend of Matt Senacal's. I'm afraid he's been captured by members of the Tribe of Cain and taken to the City of Enoch to be sacrificed. We found his wrecked car. Senacal told me to contact you if I needed help." He paused, then said, "And I do."

For a few seconds, Adah studied the face of the stranger that had come to Eden to end the curse of her husband. She saw a look of sincerity in his eyes. She reached over and touched her son's huge hands. Immediately, Jabal Howland's body relaxed and the anger in his eyes dissipated.

Lattimore turned to one of the troopers and said, "Remove his cuffs."

Nobody inside the town hall moved. Schiff and Hawkins just stared at each other and one of the troopers carefully unbuttoned the cover of his holster.

"Uncuff him, I said. If he were dangerous, he'd have killed Senacal the other night." Nobody moved. Lattimore's self-confidence had mushroomed with his deep commitment to the investigation. He took the trooper's keys and unlocked Jabal's handcuffs himself.

The son of Lamech sat placidly in his chair. He rubbed his wrists more as a symbol of freedom than a soothing of his irritated skin.

Lattimore showed Jabal Lydia Howland's map and pointed to Hezekiah Farrington's old gristmill. He asked, "Are you familiar with this area of Eden? Have you hunted or trapped here?"

Jabal reached for the book. His body remained taut, only his eyes moved. A few seconds passed. He turned to the police officer behind him; the officer flinched and moved back. Lattimore asked Schiff to remove the uniformed police from the room. Schiff obliged.

Jabal shook his head and pushed the book back.

"Please try to think; it's important," pleaded Lattimore. "I must know the area where Hezekiah Farrington's gristmill was located. We don't have much time." Jabal again nodded in ignorance. Lattimore felt his heightened spirits dissipate. Maybe a search party could find the old mill in the morning, but by then Senacal and Twitchell could be dead. He had to find the gristmill tonight.

Adah Howland's skeletal arm slowly reached out for the book. She studied the small map for a few quiet moments, then mumbled under her breath, "Sarah Farrington was my childhood friend. In the winter we would ice skate on the pond near the gristmill. The old waterwheel stood frozen in ice and there was always smoke curling up from the gristmill chimney."

A large wall map of Eden wrapped in plastic hung on the wall behind Adah. Each road and home were marked with colored pins. Lattimore whispered to Adah, "Maybe this map will help you find Sarah's gristmill." Lattimore pointed to the wall map.

The old lady stood up and walked over to the wall map. After a few long seconds, she placed a wrinkled finger next to a yellow pin. "The Harris Hotel stood here next to the Bean home." Her finger moved forward as her mind raced back in time. "Langston School was here." Finally her finger stopped near Belvidere Mountain. She turned her head slightly to catch Lattimore's eye.

"Here is the Farrington gristmill," said Adah.

"Have you ever seen the City of Enoch?" Lattimore asked softly.

Adah shook her head. "I was forbidden entrance."

"Did Lamech ever mention going to the gristmill for night meetings or anything?"

Adah again shook her head.

"You mentioned smoke circling up from the gristmill chimney. If the waterwheel was frozen in the winter, why would a fire be kept in the mill house?"

The old lady shrugged her shoulders.

It was just a minute's ride from the Eden Town Hall to gravel Road 21. The police cars carrying the search party parked in front of Peckman's General Store. Their roof lights flashed red circles of caution into the Vermont night. The search party started down a narrow gravel road past a few nervous citizens peeking out from behind trailer windows. Lattimore saw the huge silhouette of Belvidere Mountain straight ahead. He was confident Adah Howland was leading them in the right direction, but he was skeptical of the old woman's capacity to remember the location of the mill of her childhood.

The wet snow made the path slippery and dangerous. Jabal cradled his mother against him to protect her from falling. Periodically during the slow trip, Adah would stop and move her head around like a periscope to study the rugged terrain illuminated by the swirling police lights. The area was treeless, giving testimony to land that had once been farmed.

"Look for a witch's hand in the night," she instructed her followers. "All the farmers had apple trees around their homes."

Nearly a half-hour passed. Lattimore felt his hope of rescuing Senacal and Twitchell fade.

Adah Howland didn't share Lattimore's doubts. Her eyes were alert, her head moved back and forth across the narrow path in search of familiar sights.

Schiff tapped Lattimore on the shoulder and motioned for him to sound the order for retreat.

Suddenly, Adah grabbed Lattimore's flashlight. She shone a beam of light at a solitary tree with spidery limbs that bowed at the tips. Against the pale night, it looked like a witch's hand reaching up toward the moon.

"Look for millstones near the apple tree," Adah ordered as the search party flocked toward the lighted tree. Lattimore's heart skipped a beat; his hopes soared.

A police officer yelled, "Over here! There's a graveyard of millstones covered with moss."

Adah Howland touched the old tree with affection. It was a living remnant of her youth. "Look for heavy stones in a square," she said.

"Got it," Schiff yelled. He kicked some dirt and revealed a row of large stones joined by crumbling mortar.

Adah waved her hand in a circle and said, "Walk the foundation. Rebuild the house with your lights."

Slowly, the foundation wall of an old farmhouse was unearthed. Hawkins ordered the police officers to stand on the old foundation wall and hold up their flashlights so as to allow Adah to envision the dimensions of the home.

Adah's eyes swirled with recognition. "I'll take you to the gristmill, Mr. Lattimore, and may God deem your tale be true. The Tribe of Cain must be destroyed once and for all." She pointed toward a still pond. "This was the pond that fed the water to the mill. It was hard work back then, Mr. Lattimore. No trucks and big equipment. These rocks around the pond had to be dragged by sleds and put in place by hand." She affectionately patted one of the old stones. "I loved the winter and skating. For hours, Sarah and I would skate about this pond and laugh about silly things until we were beet red. Come! The mill is this way; we'll follow the path of the sluice."

A few rotten timbers buried beneath the dead brush were all that remained of the wooden sluice. Jabal walked ahead as a guide. He had grown to trust Lattimore with his mother. Adah cautioned her son to be careful. There would be a big hole covered with rotten timbers, where the wheel once stood. Jabal raised his arm and the search party stopped in place. The son of Lamech carefully searched the area in front of him.

"The mill stood to your right," Adah said to her son.

Jabal jumped on top of a millstone and examined the earth. Carefully, he circled the old mill, then looked at one of the state troopers and said, "Stand here next to me." The police officer obeyed after a nod from Hawkins. Jabal shouted to two other officers. "Stand over there!" He pointed to the other end of a large beam. Jabal squatted and grabbed an old beam that straddled the mill's foundation. The officer next to him did the same. Across from him, two officers also followed his example. The four men rocked the beam back and forth.

The earth around the beam loosened and exposed the old timbers that once supported the gristmill. "Lift!" Jabal ordered. The blood vessels in his neck swelled to the point of rupture. Lattimore was amazed at the old man's strength. Finally, they lifted the beam and tossed it to one side.

The search party circled around the mill grave.

"What do you seek?" Jabal asked as he prepared to drop into the mill grave. The mountain man's face was covered with dirt and sweat.

Lattimore shrugged his shoulders. "An entrance to an underground tunnel?"

Jabal jumped into the earth and thrashed about the mill floor. He pushed aside an old bellows that lay propped against the mill wall. His large arm reached up and aided Lattimore's descent into the ancient gristmill.

Lattimore was surprised at the warmth of the gristmill cellar. As he shone his flashlight around, he saw that the floor was an antique dealer's paradise—wooden gears and oak teeth, an old logging cart and log tongs, two neck yokes used to carry heavy pails of water, the ever-present discarded millstones, an assortment of shovels, axes, anvils, saws, and mauls. A large barrel filled with nail rods stood in one corner while a dozen or so maple sap buckets stood stacked to the ceiling in the other.

Cobwebs brushed against Lattimore's face as he moved around the cellar. He was afraid a snake or some burrowing creature might pop out from under a dusty artifact. He was glad Jabal Howland was his guide.

Slowly he swept the light from his flashlight across the foundation walls, studying each section for clues that might suggest a tunnel lay on the other side. His eye caught an inscription cut into the large sill beam that ran across the top of the foundation wall. Lattimore hopped from millstone to millstone across the floor for a closer look. The inscription read, "1880—Each heard the voice of the other who called his neighbor."

A smile broke out across Lattimore's face as he recognized the quotation. He examined the wall beneath the inscription. The cement binding the rocks was different in color than the rest of the foundation wall. Jabal Howland already had an old sledgehammer in his hands. Lattimore carefully stepped aside to allow Jabal room to swing.

The ex-priest wondered who carved the words into the beam. He recognized them as part of a six-line inscription discovered in Jerusalem in 1880 by two boys wading in the Pool of Siloam. Lattimore remembered reading the full quotation in classical Hebrew. "The boring through is completed. Now this is the story of the boring through. While workmen were still lifting pick to pick, each toward his neighbor, and while three cubits remained to be cut through, each heard the voice of the other who called his neighbor, since there was a crevice in the rock on the right side. And on the day of the boring-through the stonecutters struck, each to meet his fellow, pick to pick; and there flowed the waters to the pool for a thousand and two hundred cubits, and a hundred cubits was the height of the rock above the heads of the stonecutters."

Jabal's powerful swing easily crumbled the wall hiding the tunnel entrance. Lattimore felt pleased with himself. He was sure the road to the City of Enoch lay straight ahead. He just hoped Twitchell and Senacal hadn't become the latest victims of the Tribe of Cain.

Silently, Matt Senacal stood next to Nina Sadler in the tunnel outside the metal doors leading into the underground City of Enoch. He knew death awaited him on the other side, but it was the unknown manner of his execution that produced his greatest fear. Mary Kenite had promised it would be something special. She had told him in the van that his arrival in Eden had been viewed as a favorable sign from Baal and that homage had to be paid him for blessing her Curse of Lamech activities.

The sound of dripping water falling off the stone walls and ceiling echoed loudly in the empty tunnel. Senacal was sure Graham Twitchell lay dead on the other side of the metal door.

Nina broke the silent vigil. "When you enter the City of Enoch you will be called Athtar the Terrible."

"What?" queried Senacal.

"You will be Athtar the Terrible, temporary king of Saphon."

"I thought I was Sennacherib, son of Sargon the Second?"

"You are still a mighty warrior. Anath only mates with brave warriors, so the offspring will be brave and true."

Senacal's anger and frustration surfaced. "Screw Anath and all her goddamn offspring."

The doors to the City of Enoch opened and Nina shoved Senacal inside. From the center of the large bell-shaped room, a white marble ziggurat rose straight up like a silver staircase to heaven. At the top, three small trees shaded a sacred garden next to two golden chairs. Red and purple lights attached to the sides of the ziggurat delivered an eerie message of death down upon the underground city. A drum announced Senacal's arrival. Two figures, a male and female, appeared at the top of the ziggurat. Senacal recognized Mary Kenite. She was dressed in white and sat upon one of the golden chairs. The man was dressed in a rainbow cloak and held a ring and measuring reed in his hand. Senacal was sure it was Jubal Howland. The cuneiform symbol for grain was tattooed on his forehead. He was ugly, just as Agnes Connelly at the central Vermont Railroad had said. He sat down next to Mary Kenite.

A ram's horn sounded. Nina pushed Senacal up against the rock wall. A door from under the ziggurat opened and the dozen or so women who earlier had witnessed his mating with Pleasant emerged and paraded around the ziggurat holding torches high above their heads. The last woman in the parade led two masked figures in chains. One was a man, the other a woman, though it was difficult for Senacal to recognize them from where he stood. However, the man was too tall to be Twitchell. The prisoners were tied to separate wooden poles anchored to the stone floor. Two guards then gagged and placed a hood over Senacal's head, brought him over next to the other prisoners, and tied him to a wooden pole. He was sure he had been anchored to his death bed.

Suddenly, the red and purple lighting dimmed and a naked Pleasant Kenite appeared from behind the ziggurat. "Baal is dead," she shouted. "Who are the people of Dagon's son? Who are the multitudes of Athtar and Baal?"

Senacal recognized the voice as belonging to Pleasant. He made no sense out of her wailing.

Pleasant stopped and shouted to Jubal Howland and her mother atop the ziggurat. "El and Asherah, who sit high above me, your son, Baal, is dead. He was killed by Mot. My brother lies dead in the land of Mot."

The two figures at the top of the ziggurat stood up and servants dressed them in burlap cloaks. Then, the royal pair reached deep into a silver urn that stood between the golden chairs and scattered ashes over their bodies. The floodlights returned to full strength as Pleasant ascended the ziggurat. She stopped near the top and a guard handed her a small lamb. As she spoke, her voice echoed loudly. "I shall go down into the earth where the two rivers run deep and bury Baal, who has been slaughtered by Mot."

For a few seconds Pleasant looked tenderly at the small lamb that symbolized her brother, Baal. Then she stabbed the waiting lamb over and over again. Blood and sinew flew everywhere over the clean marble stairway as she reenacted the death of Baal, her spiritual brother. Her body dripped of lamb's blood. She descended the stairs holding the small ram like a mother a newborn and disappeared behind the ziggurat.

"Who will be king now? We need a king," shouted Mary Kenite with arms outstretched. "Baal is dead. We need a new king."

A loud chant rose from the torch-bearing crowd. "Let us make Athtar the Terrible our king."

Senacal's heart skipped a beat. Why didn't they kill him? he thought as two guards untied him. He hated being part of their horrible rituals and plays.

Nina Sadler pushed him up the bloody staircase. He felt sick at the sight of so much blood on the marble steps.

Up close, Jubal Howland was uglier than Senacal had imagined. The markings on his forehead looked like they had been made with a dull chisel. He was small and grinned at him with the charm of a shark about to attack.

Mary Kenite, true to her part in the pagan ceremony, bowed in reverence before her newly crowned king and placed a black tunic across Senacal's shoulders. She then commanded Nina to escort Senacal back down the ziggurat. The women below chanted repeatedly, "Hail Athtar the Terrible, King of Saphon."

After a few ceremonial trips around the ziggurat, Nina Sadler removed Senacal's tunic and tied him up in chains next to the door under the ziggurat from where the torch-bearing women had earlier exited. His reign as king had come to an abrupt end. He was sure Mary Kenite had other plans for him before her bloody ceremony was over.

Nearby the two hooded prisoners stood tied to their wooden poles with their heads bowed as if death had already possessed their souls.

Suddenly, Pleasant appeared from behind the door under the ziggurat with a sword in her hand. She passed Senacal but ignored him completely. Her mind had drifted into another world. A voice from a speaker anchored to the rocky ceiling filled the room. "I'm Mot. I killed Baal. I made him like a lamb in my mouth. Like a kid in my jaws he is crushed."

On cue, two guards walked over to the hooded male prisoner, untied him and escorted him some twenty feet to the front of the ziggurat. He was then chained to a metal hook that protruded up from the stone floor. The hood over his head was removed. Senacal gasped; it was Mike Derkowski.

A ball of fire burst from an opening in the stone floor next to Derkowski. He hardly flinched at the sight of the flames; he was numb with fear. He seemed resigned to the fate that Mary Kenite had cast him as Mot in her pagan ceremony. Pleasant approached him in swooping circles like a vulture over its wounded prey. She clutched her sword in both hands. From atop the ziggurat, Jubal Howland shouted, "Mot stands before me in disgrace for killing my son, Baal."

Suddenly, Senacal was startled by the approach of a female guard. His chains were unlocked and he was pushed forward and tied up to the wooden pole where Derkowski had just stood next to the female prisoner.

Pleasant's eyes glowed with revenge as she circled closer to Mike Derkowski. Atop, Mary Kenite held her sword with two lions' heads carved into an ivory handle high in the air. Pleasant stopped circling Derkowski. Silence fell over the underground city; all eyes watched Mary Kenite atop the ziggurat. She smiled and lowered her ivory handled sword. Instantly, Pleasant's sword swooped into the back of Mike Derkowski's neck. Senacal winced at the sight of Derkowski's head rolling toward him. It stopped inches from his feet. Derkowski's eyes lay on the stone floor. Two guards gathered up what was Mike Derkowski and dragged it away in a sack.

Senacal turned in disgust and recognized the gold cross that hung below the mask of the prisoner next to him.

"Leisa Dawkins?"

She said nothing but nodded her identity. "Is that you, Senacal?" came a wavering voice from beneath the hood of the prisoner next to him.

"Yes" was all he said.

She began crying, her body shaking from fright. "Mary Kenite is my aunt . . ." She couldn't finish what she wanted to say. Fear had taken control of her emotions.

It doesn't matter anyhow, thought Senacal. His own future looked bleak. Nina Sadler escorted him up to the exact spot where Mike Derkowski had been butchered. He was to be Mary's next victim. He just hoped his death would be swift like Derkowski's. He looked at Pleasant. It scared him to think he had made love to her in his motel room. She was warm and sensual then. Now she stood before him drenched in her victims' cold blood.

The original tunnel of Siloam was 1,777 feet long and twisted like a serpent around immovable rocks and ancient burial grounds. Frank Lattimore had every reason to believe the Eden tunnel was similar.

Upon discovering the tunnel, Robert Hawkins had left with some Vermont troopers to cordon off the roads leading from Belvidere Mountain in case Mary Kenite escaped from her underground city. Lieutenant Schiff had wanted to rush immediately into the tunnel, but a Vermont police sergeant had suggested he wait just a few minutes until some extra troopers arrived with assault rifles. Reluctantly, the lieutenant had agreed.

"What's at the other end?" queried Schiff as he pointed his flashlight into the dark tunnel.

"I believe the City of Enoch," Lattimore answered. "And I think we'll find all the heads of the murder victims there too." The yuppie ex-priest scratched his head and stared into the dark tunnel as he spoke. "What else is at the other end? I don't know."

"What are Twitchell's and Senacal's chances of survival?" Schiff asked.

"Again, I don't know. The elderly were greatly respected in biblical times, so maybe Twitchell might be spared from Mary's sacrificial altar. Yet, we're dealing with a schizo. In time, she would have to kill him. Remember, she's obsessed with fulfilling the Curse of Lamech. As regards Senacal, I think his name may be responsible either for his immediate death or for his continued life." Lattimore pointed toward the cave entrance. "The original tunnel of Siloam was built in preparation for an attack from Sennacherib of Assyria. Because Senacal's name is similar to that of the King of Assyria, it might save him. Who knows? His presence in Eden might be interpreted by Mary as a good omen. Then again it might be bad."

A host of flashlights appeared in the night. A half-dozen Vermont troopers had arrived to assist in the assault.

Jabal Howland laid a large hand on Frank Lattimore's shoulder. "I will lead. I will destroy Jubal."

"No," said Lattimore. "Stay with your mother. She needs your help in the night." Lattimore looked up at Adah Howland. Their eyes met for a brief second. Jabal Howland bowed his head in submission to Frank Lattimore's demand.

Seven police officers with an assortment of automatic weapons entered the tunnel behind Lattimore and Schiff. As Lattimore had suspected, the tunnel was serpentine, but hardly had he expected the dimensions to be so uniform and the walls and ceilings to be lined with white marble. Even the floor was tiled in blue slate. A strong breeze blew down the tunnel; cobwebs brushed against their faces.

Periodically, Lieutenant Schiff stopped and listened for noises ahead. At such times, Lattimore examined the walls of the tunnel for possible clues as to what lay at the other end. He noticed green moss growing in cracks in the wall. What he found most curious was a line of dried leaves and twigs along both walls. Each line appeared to be about the same height from the tunnel floor. He concluded the tunnel had served as an aqueduct of some kind, perhaps as an alternate source of waterpower for the Farrington gristmill.

They had traveled for about ten minutes when the sharp odor of burning oil filled the tunnel. Only the sounds of heavy breathing could be heard in the bowels of the earth.

"I'll go ahead alone," whispered Schiff. He told the Vermont troopers to stay ready.

"No! I'll go with you," Lattimore said. "I'll have a better idea of what to look for."

They made a strange couple. A hardened cop who grunted words in short gulps and an ex-priest in a herringbone sport coat. They proceeded slowly behind the dim light of Schiff's flashlight. Lattimore thought of how tranquil his life had been prior to meeting Senacal at Donna's divorce ceremony. Everything in his priestly life had been regulated by bells between lauds and vespers, sunrise to sunset. Even the people he had lived with had been cast from the same mold: white, Catholic, conservative, and submissive. His priesthood days seemed so long ago compared to his present adventure.

The pair had traveled alone about fifty yards when a light crept toward their feet. At the same time, a distant drum sounded. Schiff's burly arm pinned Lattimore against the tunnel wall. There was life ahead that would not look kindly upon their intrusion. Slowly, Lattimore lowered his eyes to the floor. The light fluttered like the wings of a butterfly. Schiff inched forward while pressed against the wall, his finger on the trigger of his revolver. Lattimore followed his lead. They walked into an underground grotto just as a ram's horn blared an ominous sound in the distance. Lieutenant Schiff pushed Lattimore back into the security of the tunnel's darkness.

They inched back into the lighted grotto. At the far end, a stairway led up through the stone ceiling. The tunnel continued its windy trail to the City of Enoch on the other side of the room. Lattimore's attention was drawn toward a sepulcher with a silver checkerboard gate. The walls of the sepulcher were lined with green velvet drapes. Silver cups and candlesticks were randomly placed about on a rug floor. Lattimore recognized the room immediately. It was the Cave of Macpelah. Lattimore reasoned Nathaniel Howland was buried below the lone cenotaph in the middle of the room. The details of the room were amazingly similar to the original gravesite of Abraham below the Mosque of Abraham in Hebron.

Schiff tapped him on the shoulder; Lattimore turned. The lieutenant held up a Boston Red Sox baseball cap. Lattimore gasped and held his breath. Senacal and Twitchell were here. The loud ram's horn sounded again from a short passageway leading from the grotto to the City of Enoch. Lieutenant Schiff called up the troopers who had been waiting in the gristmill tunnel.

The ram's horn sounded Leisa Hawkins' death knoll. She was called Pidray, the sister of Mot, in Mary Kenite's underground play, and like Mike Derkowski she was beheaded.

It didn't take a genius to figure out who was next on Mary's death list. In a way Senacal felt death would be a relief from the heinous underground world of Mary Kenite. His thoughts switched to his wife, Donna, and the many times he had mocked her deep religious convictions. Often he had professed to her his disbelief in the existence of heaven and hell. He wasn't so sure now as he stared at Pleasant Kenite standing in front of him drenched in human blood. He felt he was already in hell. Donna had told him God was always ready to forgive a sinner. Senacal lowered his head and prayed for the salvation of his immortal soul.

He felt someone unlocking the chains on his feet. A ball of fire burst from an opening in the stone floor as it had before Mike Derkowski's execution. As his hands were untied, he looked up at a tall bare-chested figure standing between Jubal Howland and Mary Kenite on top of the ziggurat. It was Tertius, Leisa Dawkins' son. He held a large sword with two lions' heads carved into an ivory hilt above his head. Senacal looked at Pleasant standing in Leisa Dawkins' blood. She pointed her bloody sword at him and said, "You Athtar, the king, must die. Baal has come back to reclaim his throne. You must die because you helped Mot kill my brother, Baal. You must fight Baal with your bare hands."

The crowd of women formed a semicircle around Senacal as they watched their god descend the marble steps. The crowd chanted, "They fight like animals. Athtar is strong, Baal is strong. They gore like lions. Athtar is strong, Baal is strong. They bite like serpents. Athtar is strong, Baal is strong. They kick like steeds. Athtar falls, Baal falls."

Senacal stepped back as Tertius walked off the last step of the ziggurat. Even if he had a sword, he knew he was no match in strength for the idiot son of Leisa Dawkins. Tertius flexed his body and whipped his sword back and forth over his head. He stared menacingly at Senacal. The muscles in his arms rippled like the ocean surf as he toyed with his sword. The women closed the circle around the warring gods. A large cymbal sounded the start of their battle.

Tertius sprang forward with a war cry on his lips that echoed off the rock walls of the City of Enoch. Senacal jumped and avoided the downward thrust of his attacker's sword. He fell against the ring of Baal worshipers. They pushed him forward and the circle of women tightened. There would be little room for escape next time. Pleasant fought her way through the crowd and implored her biblical brother on to victory. Baal readied for another attack. The crowd of women spat upon Senacal.

"Think, asshole, think," Senacal told himself. He knew this was his last chance. He felt his sweat running down his face. The ring of women had narrowed too much for him to dodge Tertius' next charge. He wanted to live. Just when he thought of grabbing one of the women and using her as a shield of some kind, he noticed the ball of fire shooting up from the stone floor. It was just a few yards behind the circle of women. In a second a plan took shape in his mind. He didn't have time to pray for its success.

Senacal fell to his knees and pleaded with Tertius for mercy. The prophecy had called for Athtar to gore, to bite, to kick, and to fight. He figured Tertius might get confused if he did the opposite of what he had been conditioned to expect.

"How can I now battle with Mot?" Tertius grunted; his face showed the struggle of his dilemma.

Pleasant yelled up to her mother. "Athtar has desisted. He will not fight Baal."

Senacal noticed Tertius' body relax as he lowered his sword to his side. He was distracted by the confusion around him.

Jubal Howland rose from his throne and raised his ring and measuring rod into the red lights. "His sovereignty will be guaranteed."

"No," Mary Kenite replied. "He must die to give homage to Baal." She drew her sword from its gold scabbard, looked down at Tertius, and said, "Kill him, my son!"

The huge man again raised his sword.

"Now," Senacal said aloud. He leaped to his feet and with all his strength thrust his shoulder into Tertius' stomach and drove him backwards until he fell unto the fire shooting up from the stone floor.

Suddenly, a gunshot sounded and Lieutenant Schiff's voice brought reality to the City of Enoch. "This is the police. Everybody freeze!"

Senacal felt more scared now than he had at any other time during his captivity. He didn't want to die with his freedom so close at hand. It reminded him of his last days in Vietnam when he didn't want to go anywhere or see anybody or walk the dirty streets of Saigon for fear of being killed so near the end of his tour. He remained perfectly still while confusion reigned about him.

Nina Sadler reacted violently to the intruders. She charged an approaching policeman, but was instantly killed by automatic fire. Tertius stood dazed and badly burnt. Some women ran, others raised their arms to surrender.

Senacal stared at Pleasant Kenite. She appeared to get more confused with each passing second. Her fantasy world was crumbling. She was like a cornered animal with no place to hide. Slowly, he reached for Tertius' sword, which lay on the ground nearby.

Pleasant noticed his movement and yelled, "Athtar! You have killed Baal. You must die too!"

There was little time to think. In one swift motion, Senacal thrust his sword deep into Pleasant Kenite's stomach. She moaned and froze as blood spilled down her legs. Her eyes bulged and she crumbled to the stone floor.

Senacal's thoughts turned to Graham Twitchell. He hoped the old man was alive. He looked up at the top of the ziggurat. Jubal Howland was engaged in a struggle with a police officer. Mary was nowhere to be seen. He looked around the City of Enoch. All the followers of Mary Kenite had either been killed or captured.

Suddenly, a gunshot sounded from atop the ziggurat. Senacal flinched. The body of a man dressed in a rainbow robe twisted end over end through the air. A large gold ring and a measuring rod remained clutched to his hands as he lay in a heap on the stone floor.

A familiar voice sounded. "Are you all right?"
Senacal turned.

Frank Lattimore affectionately grabbed Senacal by the shoulders. The men embraced and Senacal whispered into Lattimore's ear, "You're one hell of a cop, Virg. I don't know how the hell you ever found this place, but thank God you did."

"What the fuck was going on down here?" Lieutenant Schiff joined Senacal and Lattimore. His face showed the strain of the City of Enoch's deadly games.

"I'll tell you on an empty stomach," replied Senacal. "For now, though, I'd like you and Lattimore to find Mary Kenite. I'm going to look for Twitchell."

Senacal ran to a door under the ziggurat. Earlier he had seen Pleasant emerge from it. Inside, a small light cast a dim glow through a room that smelled like a barn.

"Twitchell, are you in here?" Senacal shouted as he felt for a wall switch. There was no answer. He repeated himself. "Twitchell, are you in here?"

He found a light switch and immediately a wall of human skulls greeted his eyes. Some of the skulls were only partially decomposed while other heads were reduced to mere bones. Above each skull was a number followed with the word "left." There was an empty space below the expression "56 left."

Senacal took a deep breath. He was sure that was the spot where his head was to hang. He took another deep breath and continued his search. He found sixty-seven, Ken Newell's infamous number. The young boy's murder seemed so long ago and in such a different world than the City of Enoch. Much had happened since that cold January morning when Lieutenant Schiff announced on the phone that an execution had been performed in Fort Ann, New York. Even Matt Senacal felt he had changed. He cared more about Graham Twitchell's safety than the pursuit of Mary Kenite.

"Twitchell, are you in here?" Senacal yelled again. His voice echoed for a few seconds inside the marble ziggurat. He feared the worst and searched the walls for Twitchell's remains.

"Over here, goddamn it! Where the hell have you been, and who's been banging those damn cymbals? I have a headache. This place could use a good enema."

Senacal found him with one foot chained to the wall and sitting on a mound of straw next to a pen of sheep. He wore a blue turban with a matching tunic. A pair of leather sandals were tied to his ankles. He appeared unhurt.

Twitchell yelled at his friend. "What the hell ya staring at? Get this damn leash off me and get me out of these damn silly clothes."

As both men laughed and embraced, Lieutenant Schiff shouted a message from the door. "Mary Kenite has escaped."

Mary had found the hidden shaft at the top of the ziggurat quite by accident. Upon her arrival from Wyoming, she had spent much time and money preparing for her ministry of human destruction by renovating the City of Enoch. It was during this time that she had found the hidden passageway that led from the City of Enoch to Nathaniel Howland's tomb beneath the Cave of Macpelah.

Slightly out of breath from her escape, she stopped and knelt before Nathaniel Howland's marble tomb. Beads of perspiration dotted her puffy cheeks as she struggled to speak. "Dear Father of the Tribe of Cain, I failed you. Like you, the devil spits his hot bile upon my naked soul. For He warned me about Sennacherib advancing on our Holy City. I heeded not His words." She rose and touched his grave-stone with the tip of her sword. "I vow to fulfill the Curse of Lamech elsewhere."

She put her sword back into its scabbard and pulled hard on a metal chain that was hooked to a pulley system in the rock ceiling above Nathaniel Howland's tomb. Slowly a marble slab slid open and the light from above poured into the passageway below. She removed a narrow metal ladder that had been fastened to the wall, and placed it into the opening above.

Cautiously she ascended the ladder. She popped her head through the opening. She was inside the Cave of Macpelah and its protective silver gate. In the distance she could hear gunshots coming from inside the City of Enoch. She listened for footsteps. Nothing. She was alone, but she knew it would not be for long. She hurried up the narrow ladder, slipped through the silver gate, and hid near the rock stairway that led to the "high place" of worship where Senacal had earlier been seduced by Pleasant Kenite.

Freedom was but a few steps away. She looked around to be sure her escape would go unnoticed, then she raced up the stairway to freedom. The cool night air rushed past her face. She stopped near the top and surveyed the "high place" of worship. Suddenly, the rustle of leaves sounded in the woods to her right. She turned and squinted to recognize the bent figure that approached across the clearing. Slowly, Mary Kenite reached for her sword. Half her body extended into the clearing from the hidden stairway.

A voice sounded in the night. "Why have you done these terrible things in my husband's name?"

"Adah Howland! Is that you?" yelled Mary at the approaching figure. She squeezed the hilt of her sword and readied herself to attack when the intruder drew closer.

Adah stopped within a few feet of Mary and said, "Lamech was a good and kind man, you are an evil woman. There was no need to begin the Curse of Lamech. He died by drowning."

The police would soon be upon her. Mary drew her sword and quickly ascended the last few stone steps into the clearing. "You are a fool to come here, old lady." Just as she readied to thrust her sword deep into the heart of Lamech's wife, Jabal Howland appeared from behind the marble statue of Anath. He grabbed Mary Kenite's wrist with his powerful hand. The forward movement of her sword came to an immediate halt. The pain in her arm was instant from the viselike grip of a man who had labored his whole life as a lumberjack. She gasped for air and helplessly surrendered her sword to Jabal.

For a few seconds Adah studied Mary's eyes, then slightly nodded her head.

In the space of a second Jabal forced Mary to her knees and, with the powerful swing of a woodsman's ax, struck her on the back of the neck with the sword. The trunk of her body dropped like a rock back down into the Cave of Macpelah as her head rolled forward on the wet earth.

Adah fell to her knees in exhaustion. Jabal ran to her side and gently encircled his powerful arms around his mother. She lovingly patted his hands as she spoke to him. "You have been a true and loyal son. Without your help tonight I would not have been able to avenge the death of your father. It was here, on these sacred grounds, that he vowed his love to me in marriage. He was a good and kind man." She looked up into the starry night. "It is over, my dear husband. The Curse of Lamech is over. You may rest in peace."

Senacal pulled over to the side of the road and walked through a cemetery gate with a single rose in his hand. Twitchell and Lattimore accompanied him.

"I want to be cremated, Senacal," Twitchell said. He fixed his baseball cap so the wind would not toss it about the treeless countryside. "Want my ashes scattered over Fort Ann."

"There's enough shit there already," said Senacal as he extended his hand to help the old man navigate around some bumpy ground.

Twitchell slapped his friend's hand. "Bullshit! I ain't that old yet."

The names on the tombstones had faded, like the memories of their hosts. Black mildew covered what few letters were legible. Senacal was determined to find the right grave. He pulled away the matted brown grass around each gravestone. The time period was right. Most of the dead were laid to rest in the late nineteenth century. He looked up at Belvidere Mountain in the distance and smiled. "I beat you, you bastard!"

"I've got it," shouted Lattimore from the bottom edge of the cemetery. There was no name or date on the gravestone. Just a faded inscription: "2 Kings 20: 20."

Senacal gently placed his rose on Lydia Howland's grave. He looked up at Lattimore. "Say something nice, Virg. You're good at things like this."

Lattimore nodded his head back and forth. "I'm not a priest anymore. Besides, just speak from your heart. It doesn't hurt."

"I found a Stanley," Twitchell shouted. He had wandered off by himself. "Nel was a Stanley. Wonder if this guy wouldn't mind Nel buried on top of him. She'll have no one if I get cremated."

Senacal cleared his throat and looked down at Lydia Howland's grave. "I'm not much of a speaker, especially from the heart. Lattimore here is trying to teach me." He reached inside his jacket for a cigarette. "I guess the first thing I should say is thanks. If you hadn't written that letter, I wouldn't be here now. I'd probably be stuffed and hanging over Mary Kenite's fireplace. I've met some wacky families before, but yours takes the cake." Senacal took a lighter from his pocket and held the flame to his cigarette.

"Well, I can't think of much more to say. When I get back to Saratoga, I'm asking for a transfer back to Long Island. I'm a city person, Lydia. I like the crowds and traffic jams and high crime rates. That's home to me. So, good-bye and thanks again for the letter. Keep an eye on me once in a while in case I screw up. An asshole like me can use all the help he can get."

ABOUT THE AUTHOR

Edward J. Frail is a native New Yorker who presently lives in Wilton, New York, with his wife, Carol, and his daughters Deborah and Diane.